SPACE TRUCKERS

BOOK ONE

Adventures of the Blue Eagle

Michael D'Ambrosio

Quantum Discovery

A LITERARY AGENCY

ISBN
978-1-960197-40-5 (Paperback)
978-1-960197-41-2 (eBook)
978-1-964982-09-0 (Hardcover)

TABLE OF CONTENTS

PROLOGUE

When mankind finally traveled beyond the stars, colonies and space stations were established. To maintain those locations, supplies were needed. As a result, shipping corporations evolved and bid for the contracts to deliver those goods. Over time, the corporations grew, and the shipping routes became competitive. With the evolution of the shipping industry came the greed of the corporations.

Space was still a lawless region with only private security firms to maintain order. One company, Sysco Galactic Services, excelled at the logistics of space transportation and controlled much of the shipping in the galaxy. Its competitor, Empire Shipping, was determined to overthrow Sysco and control all shipping in the galaxy.

This is the story of the adventures of the Blue Eagle, an obsolete freighter whose crew fought to keep their independence from corporate control.

CHAPTER I
EXES AND OHS

The Sysco Galactic Services Corporation's headquarters was based at Taurus, a massive, cylinder-shaped space station with thirteen circular modules mounted on a rotating axis. In addition to its docking and storage facilities, the various elevations hosted vital functions, including ship repairs, executive-level operations, logistics, medical, and even a prison section for the incarceration of criminals. Located in the center of the galaxy, the corporation managed over one hundred and twenty freighters. It also controlled seventy percent of the shipping in the galaxy, making it the leading shipper of the seven shipping companies. Led by Empire Shipping, Sysco's main rival, the six competitors pooled their resources together in an attempt to buy out Sysco and take over the magnificent station.

Gemini, the sultry CEO of Sysco, was as dangerous as she was beautiful. She assumed control of Sysco from her mentor, John Mallory, who died in a suspicious explosion at Taurus six months ago. Mallory had built Sysco into the shipping leader it now was from a small fleet and took Gemini on as a business partner a year earlier, due to her past expertise in handling Special Forces logistics. In doing so, he trained her to run the corporation and deal with the hostile competition that saw her gender as a weakness.

Female executives were rare in the shipping business and often the targets of envious and ambitious males. Her success through hardball tactics only increased the pressure she received from others, determined to force her out of Sysco. Several attacks recently occurred against her freighters and, although unsuccessful, they were ramping up in frequency. It was only a matter of time before losses were incurred and lives were lost. Once the first successful attack was accomplished, other rivals would surely escalate their attacks against her ships. In addition, her board members had already resigned due to threats against their lives, leaving Gemini to run the entire operation by herself.

Gemini entered her high-tech conference room, wearing a long, black dress and stiletto heels and carrying a small handbag. She sat at an oval glass table and tapped her fingers nervously, eyeing the intercom in front of her. A long-haired gentleman in a suit entered a few minutes later and tossed a packet containing a dozen white pills on the table. Gemini thanked him and he left. She removed one pill and slid the packet inside her handbag,

A tall, shapely brunette, Sara, entered the room and stood with arms folded. Lost in her thoughts, Gemini didn't acknowledge her. Sara remarked, "You look stressed, little sister. Relax."

After a brief pause, Gemini looked up and countered, "That's easy for you to say. Tell me you have something I can use."

Sara smiled confidently and walked around the table toward her. "A drink may be in order," she suggested, "if you get my drift."

Gemini's mood improved, and she responded with renewed enthusiasm. "I knew I could count on you, Sara. You always have my back." She went to the bar and poured two bourbons. Sara peered about the conference room, impressed with its luxurious finish. Gemini stared back at her, anxious to know what information she had, regarding her competitors.

"Empire Shipping is recruiting Scrat to disrupt your shipping lanes," revealed Sara. "They realized that their resources weren't enough to sustain human mercenary forces against your crews." Gemini approached her with a drink in each hand and set the glasses on the table. Sara sat down and took one.

"Scrat, huh?" Gemini mumbled and swirled the contents of her glass, gazing at her sister. Baffled by her sister's lax demeanor, Gemini ingested the pill, followed by a gulp of bourbon. She grimaced as the bitter taste overwhelmed her. A few seconds later, she grew confident as the effect of the pills took hold. She exhaled with a sigh of relief.

"I thought you were quitting that crap," remarked Sara, disappointed.

"Desperate times require desperate measures," Gemini responded coldly. "I'm trying to run a corporation here."

Sara tapped her glass against Gemini's in a mock toast. "To Empire's demise," she announced.

"To Empire's demise," Gemini echoed, and they sipped from their glasses. "Now what else do you have for me?"

Sara gazed into her glass, considering what she was about to divulge. "Empire blackmailed the other shippers into joining them," she revealed. "Empire plans to have total control of all shipping operations once they succeed in recruiting the Scrat."

"Do I have time to deal with this?" Gemini asked uneasily.

"I believe so. Be aware, though, a Scrat command ship is already in place. How it got there, I'm not sure."

Gemini sipped again from her drink and pondered. Sara knew her sister would come up with something conniving. She always did.

"Years ago, Mike and his partner left a path of destruction on the Scrat planet while taking out their military bases," Gemini related to Sara. "That was in the Nebula Galaxy, a very long way from here. I provided the intelligence and logistics for the job."

Sara suddenly became concerned. "Do the Scrat know you were involved?" she inquired.

"No, but..." Gemini paused, recalling that she fell in love with Mike Colby on that mission, and then continued, "Perhaps if I contact these Scrat, I can make them a better offer than Empire."

"They are traders of sorts," Sara added. "Maybe you can use that to your advantage."

"In fact," Gemini considered aloud, "I think I can make them an offer they won't refuse."

"What will it take to accomplish that?" questioned Sara, wondering what her sister had in mind.

Gemini remarked giddily, "All I have to do is have it delivered to them, and everything else will fall into place."

"But who would undertake such a dangerous task?"

Gemini grinned fiendishly and finished her drink. Her confidence grew to arrogance with the increasing effect of the pills. "I know just the person to handle this."

Sara's expression suddenly turned sour. "No, Gem, not Mike."

"Oh, yes," she replied, grinning deviously. "With his vanity, he will certainly take the assignment just to prove he's still the best."

"But what if they recognize him?" Sara asked, concerned for his well-being.

"So what?" Gemini replied arrogantly. "He'll figure it out. He always does."

Sara finished her drink and set the glass down. She wasn't at all happy with Gemini's plan. "Just because the two of you sucked at marriage, doesn't mean you should risk his life like this," she chided. "He's a good man."

Gemini glared at her and blurted, "He's an asshole! Do you know how much he hurt me by leaving?"

Sara was shocked by her reaction. "You were the one screwing around!" she reminded her. "Can you blame him?"

"One damn time!" shouted Gemini. "Besides, if he really loved me, he would have forgiven me."

Sara stood and remarked condescendingly, "If it were me, I'd have killed you." She stormed out of the room, upset with her sister's contempt for her ex-husband.

Gemini was surprised by Sara's concern for Mike. It didn't change her resentment against him for walking out on her a year ago, without even a chance to explain why it happened. She pressed the button on the intercom and summoned her security officer, Captain Jorgan Tieg.

Tieg was in his late twenties with shoulder-length blond hair and blue eyes. Gemini instructed him to contact her ex-husband Mike Colby, and then briefly discussed her plan to have him deliver terms of a treaty to the Scrat leadership. Tieg was miffed that he couldn't handle the task for her. Gemini patted him on the back and explained, "This is a very dangerous mission, and I can't afford to lose you."

"You underestimate me, ma'am," Tieg responded in disappointment and left the room.

Later that afternoon, a woman's voice sounded over the intercom, informing Gemini that her visitors for the afternoon meeting had arrived. Gemini promptly made another drink and frowned. "One of these days...," she muttered and chugged the drink. "Where are you when I need you, Michael?" she complained, disappointed over her divorce.

As Gemini waited at the head of the table, three men in suits entered the room. She gestured for them to sit. "Well, gentlemen, I hope this is important," she announced irritably. "I'm a busy woman."

The men sat motionless, staring at her with stone-cold expressions. She was used to intimidation tactics and knew a few of her own. Unfortunately, she relied on the pills for the courage to use those tactics. On the outside, she appeared tough as nails, but inside, she was fragile. One day, she feared, they would call her bluff, and she would crumble - but not today.

Antwan, a middle-aged, bald man with dark skin, stood and leaned on the table on his palms down. "I take it you've considered our offer," he remarked.

The second man, Grim, added, "This is our one and only offer. I suggest you think long and hard before you reply."

Gemini laughed and removed an electronic cigar called a perfora from her bag. Pressing a button on the side of the metallic stick, she inhaled and blew rings of smoke to amuse herself. The air filled with the scent of cherry as she stared them down. "Now why would I consider your lame offer?" she responded sarcastically. "After all, Sysco, which is my corporation in case you forgot, is the leader in this stinking industry."

Antwan grew impatient. He placed one foot up on the chair and leaned on his knee in a Captain Morgan pose. "Perhaps because your life is in danger, and you could easily be replaced by someone else - someone worthier of the position," he responded cynically. The men now grew edgy as they waited anxiously for her response. Gemini, annoyed by his disregard for her furniture, pointed to the chair for him to sit. She inhaled again from her perfora.

Jessup, bearded with long, scraggily hair, became impatient and slammed his fist onto the table. "This corporation was John Mallory's. You have no right to it!" he challenged her.

Still seated, Gemini leaned forward, on folded arms now. She responded mockingly. "How dare you come here with demands and accusations? You were the spoiled crack bitch who slept in dumpsters instead of learning the business like I did." She then pointed at Antwan and stated, "It's because of assholes like you that he left Empire and started his own business."

The others laughed at Jessup, realizing he had no grounds to speak. Embarrassed that his peers failed to support him, he stood with clenched fists, ready to assault her. Antwan glared at him and commanded with his eyes for Jessup to stifle himself. Jessup reluctantly obeyed.

"John knew better than to waste his time on a loser like you," Gemini added sarcastically. She hoped that by taking the offensive against a lesser partner like Jessup that Antwan and Grim would back off.

After a tense moment of silence with the two staring each other down, Antwan interceded. "One way or another, we will have Sysco. You, my dear Gemini, can either work with us or..." he gestured with his hand across his throat. "Well, you get the point."

"Shove it, Antwan," she retorted angrily, now showing her emotional side. "Go back to your ghetto satellite and stick to your simulator games. This is the real world where grown-ups play. Meeting over." Gemini pressed the intercom button and informed security that her guests were leaving the Executive Level and should be escorted to the main lobby. She stood and waited for them to leave.

The men glared at her, again as an intimidation tactic, as they passed on the way to the door. Jessup was last and remarked arrogantly, "When this is over, you'll be my whore. I'll do you like a dog, and I'll make sure there's an audience to see you humiliated."

Gemini touched his cheek affectionately and smiled. Before he could react, she kneed him in the groin, dropping him to his knees. Jessup cried and shuddered from the pain. She suddenly lost her self-control and kicked him repeatedly before jamming her heel into his eye socket. "Imagine this as skull sex, Jessup," she shouted, "and I'm using your eye for a vagina!"

The other two men paused at the door, stunned by the turn of events. Antwan requested and then demanded she stop her assault on Jessup. Gemini twisted her heel twice more into the man's skull and then removed it from his eye socket. Jessup's screams were heard in the corridor outside the conference room.

"Now who's the whore, done like a dog!" she exclaimed defiantly. "You're pathetic."

Five security guards rushed in, but Gemini gestured for them to stand down. She enjoyed humiliating Jessup and wanted more. Jessup moaned as he covered his ruptured eye with both hands. As Antwan and Grim attempted to remove Jessup from the room, Gemini kicked him once more in the groin and spat on him.

"Just as I thought," she mocked them. "Just a bunch of overaged punks with no balls! Now get the hell out of my station and don't ever come back!"

The men exited the room with Antwan staring back at her. "You're out of time," he warned. "Now you will pay."

Gemini approached him and pressed her nose against his. "Screw with me again, and I'll turn your life upside down. The shitter will look good to you when I'm done with you."

Antwan was worried by the confidence she exuded and needed to know what she was up to. Forcing a smile to hide his concern, he left the room. The security detail escorted them to the elevator.

When the door closed, Gemini dropped into her chair and cried. The effect of the pills faded as quickly as it started. She feared that over time, she wouldn't hold up to her competitors, even with pills to support her. Perhaps, she thought, Mike would finally forgive her and join her in running the corporation. *But he's a stubborn, self-righteous ass*, she reminded herself.

Her composure returned, and she wiped the tears from her cheeks. Glancing down at the blood-stained floor, she summoned housekeeping to clean and sanitize the area. She hated the monster she had become, but she blamed the men who left the room for making her that way. "If they'd just leave me alone," she told herself, "I could be the person I used to be. Maybe then Mike would take me back." Gemini went to the bar and poured another glass of bourbon. As she sipped, Captain Tieg entered, looking concerned.

"What is it?" she asked impatiently.

Captain Tieg was stunned by her attack on Jessup and the damage she inflicted. "We sent your message to Colby," he informed her, "but he hasn't responded."

"I'll handle it," she remarked curtly.

Tieg approached her and gestured pleadingly with his hands. "It is I who should deliver your terms to the Scrat General, ma'am," he revealed, disappointed. "I'm your security officer, and I'm responsible for what goes on both in and out of this station."

Gemini sat down at the table and finished her drink. She wasn't in the mood to explain herself, but Tieg deserved an answer. He was loyal and trustworthy, just not someone she wanted by her side in a street fight. He was all about rules and protocol, whereas she preferred down-and-dirty when necessary. She shoved the glass across the table, and Tieg dutifully poured her a drink, just another test of his dedication to her.

"I chose Colby so that I can gain credibility with the Scrat," Gemini explained. "If they accept the offer, I win. If they refuse it, they know they have to deal with him. I'm sure they'll remember what happened last time."

Tieg handed her the glass and sat across from her. "Will Colby know the risk?" he inquired uneasily, knowing the Scrat would kill him over their history.

"He doesn't have to," answered Gemini confidently. "He can get out of these situations better than anybody I know."

"I understand," Tieg answered disappointedly and left the room.

Gemini removed her shoe and eyed the bloodstains on the heel. With disgust, she threw it at the wall.

In the Stanton District on a poverty-stricken planet called Yord, a dilapidated shuttle glided between soot-covered buildings. Dense fog smothered the decrepit city, making its navigation dangerous. The buzzing of a failing floodlight from an abandoned apartment complex across the street echoed eerily. The shuttle paused near a six-story warehouse and rose above it before setting down on the rooftop.

Thirty year old Mike Colby, dressed in a long trench coat, boots, and boonie hat, exited the rusty shuttle and peered down the side of the building. Armed with a pulse pistol on his hip, he climbed down a rainspout to the fourth floor and stepped onto the ledge.

From an open window, he heard men argue about the fate of an heiress if the ransom wasn't paid. Mike crept to the window and peeked inside.

There were four mercenaries of various races in ragged uniforms, carrying archaic firearms.

A bald, muscular man, Virgil, urged his peers to move their hostage to a different location before they were targeted by corporate security teams. The other men were confident that Hellfire Fuels' CEO wouldn't risk the life of his only daughter and would surely pay the ransom.

Mike sidled across the ledge to the next window and peered inside. The vague outline of several file cabinets lined the wall of the storeroom. A woman's sobs caught his attention. She was tied to a chair in the corner with a rag stuffed in her mouth. Mike crept through the window and approached the woman. "Don't say anything, Zenith," he whispered. "I'm here to rescue you."

The young woman went into a rage, shaking her head back and forth, while moaning at him. Like a spoiled brat, she failed to understand the severity of the situation. Rarely are hostages set free after the ransom is paid, so she had no idea of the seriousness of her predicament.

"Stop it!" he ordered in a low tone. He couldn't understand why she would jeopardize the rescue like this. The men heard her moans and rushed to the door. Mike turned one of the file cabinets sideways and shoved it between the door and the wall, blocking the door from opening. The men tried to force their way in but with no success.

Mike took a remote device from his pocket and pressed one of the program keys on it. The shuttle sprang to life on the roof and descended the side of the warehouse with the hatch open. He waited anxiously for the shuttle to position itself outside the window. After several seconds, the shuttle appeared but was too low and far away. Frantically, Mike pressed the buttons but the shuttle still hovered too far for them to reach. "Son of a bitch!" he muttered to himself. He attempted to restart the program but with little success.

Virgil peered out the window and noticed the shuttle. He immediately alerted the others. Two of them used hand tools to disengage the hinges on the door while Virgil aimed his pistol out the window, ready to fire at

Mike. "Get that door open now!" he shouted at the others, growing more impatient. "I told you this was a bad idea."

Mike stood in front of Zenith and instructed her to keep quiet, while removing the rag from her mouth. She grunted and then head-butted him. "How does that feel, loser!" she shouted at him.

Mike staggered back two steps and became red-faced. He yanked Zenith to her feet and slapped her ass. "The next time, it'll be bare bottom, missy," he warned and shoved the rag back in her mouth.

Zenith considered his words, and her eyes widened as if she had perceived his threat as more of a treat. Mike lifted Zenith's squirming body over his shoulder and stepped out of the window onto the ledge. Gunshots immediately riddled the ledge by his feet, forcing him to leap right away. The damp surface made for an awkward push off the ledge. Mike slipped, and the two of them tumbled awkwardly through the hatchway of the shuttle with Mike face down on the floor and Zenith between him and the hatch.

Bullets peppered the top of the ship but only left dull indentations on the outer hull. Two of the mercenaries lifted a small safe to the window sill and shoved it out. The safe struck the rear of the shuttle with a loud crash, causing it to lurch. Another loud boom ensued as the safe smashed onto the sidewalk below.

The ship tilted, and Zenith rolled out the open hatch. Mike dove and caught her legs as she hung precariously out of the ship. Dragging her back inside, he closed the hatch and hurried to the controls.

The men watched in horror as Mike and Zenith escaped in the shuttle. Virgil appeared again at the window with a high-powered rifle and targeted the shuttle. Before the shuttle could disappear into the fog, a round from Virgil's rifle ripped a hole at the top of the shuttle and damaged the leveling device just over Mike's left shoulder. He jumped at the near miss and breathed a sigh of relief.

Once out of sight, Mike placed the shuttle on autopilot. Without the leveling device, the shuttle teetered repeatedly. "I hate this friggin' job," he uttered to himself. The transmitter beeped twice, and the monitor displayed an incoming message: Sysco Galactic—respond. He ignored it.

Mike helped Zenith to her feet. Her jeans were soaked with urine, and her eyes were teary. He removed the rag from her mouth and untied her. Zenith shuddered from her near fall from the shuttle and said nothing. Mike tossed her a set of scrubs from his locker. "Put these on," he ordered. "Your dad can't see you like this."

"Thank you," she muttered. "You saved my life."

Mike was surprised by her change of heart. He took his seat and piloted the shuttle away from the Stanton District. Zenith sat next to him, now wearing his scrubs. Looking tired, her hair hadn't been washed in days and her eyes were sullen. She confessed that she hadn't taken her kidnapping seriously, knowing her father would pay and that this was just a minor inconvenience in his life. Her near fall made her realize the peril she was really in. Twice more, the transmitter beeped, annoying Mike. It was Sysco Galactic again.

"Shouldn't you answer that?" Zenith inquired.

"No, it's my ex," he mumbled. "I'm not in the mood for her right now."

Mike stopped for shuttle repairs at a depot thirty miles from the Stanton District. The repair to the bullet hole was necessary for hull integrity before they could make the trip back to Hellfire Fuels on Sigma-3, a small industrial planet.

He and Zenith sat in a crude cafeteria and shared lunch while getting acquainted. Zenith questioned him about his solitary life as a mercenary and his coolness under pressure. Mike then probed into Zenith's poor attitude and violent nature. She revealed her frustration and disappointment in men who only sought her father's money and approval. They weren't dating her; they were dating him through her. Mike advised her to be patient and that her man will show one day. She eyed him, thinking that maybe he could be the one.

When they finished lunch, the two of them entered the service bay and inspected the shuttle's hull. The technician finished pressure-testing the shuttle and signed off on the repairs. Once inside, Mike and Zenith took their seats and prepared for their departure. Zenith gazed at Mike until she finally caught his attention. "What's wrong?" he asked uneasily.

"Are you still going to spank me bare-bottomed?" she asked coyly. "I wouldn't mind, you know."

Mike chuckled and politely declined her offer. Zenith then inquired if she could join him as his crew member. Again, Mike politely declined. Disappointed, Zenith rested her head against the side of the shuttle and slept the rest of the way to Sigma-3.

When they reached Hellfire Fuels' headquarters, Zenith's father, Dax, waited anxiously to greet them. He invited Mike to his suite for drinks and praised him for his perseverance with Zenith. Then to Mike's surprise, he offered his daughter's hand in marriage to him.

From the other room, Zenith shouted, "Stop it, Father! I'll handle my own business, thank you."

"Zee, shut your damn mouth before I shut it for you," shouted Dax. He rubbed his temples, a sign of frustration over his daughter's behavior. He turned his attention back to Mike. "You're just the kind of man she needs to keep her in line," Dax insisted. "She has a little bit of a problem with authority."

"I'm sorry, sir, but I couldn't do that," Mike explained apologetically. "I was already in one marriage with a woman just like your daughter."

"How long did that last?" Dax asked curiously.

"Oh, about two years. I caught her with another man because she had 'needs.'"

Dax laughed hysterically and then inquired, "Whatever happened to her?"

"I divorced her, and she went on to become the CEO of Sysco."

Dax's laughter ceased, and he grew serious. "You're talking about Gemini?" he asked, curious.

Mike sipped from his drink and responded sadly, "Yes, I am."

Dax assured him of an opening with his corporate security if he ever changed his mind. Mike briefly considered but realized that was a bad idea. Dax would likely be interested in corporate secrets in Sysco, and he wasn't about to become a spy for him.

They shook hands, and he departed. Dax sat at his desk and pondered Mike's divorce from Gemini until Zenith barged into the room. Dressed in a halter top and shorts, her hair was tied back in a ponytail, and she looked frantic. "Where is Mike? Did he leave?" she asked, concerned.

"I'm afraid so," replied Dax. "We'll see him again, I'm sure."

"We'd better, for your sake," she shouted and stormed off.

After a moment to consider his daughter's unexpected interest in Mike, he summoned his financial officer. Jim Sykes, an older man with thin, gray hair and wire-rimmed glasses, entered the room with a clipboard and notepad. Dax discussed the advantages of a merger with Sysco and how to make a palatable offer to Gemini.

Smiling, Sykes took several notes and assured him that they could obtain some leverage in a potential deal, if required. The meeting concluded, and Sykes departed. Dax leaned back, smiling as he contemplated a beautiful future with Gemini and the potential of their two corporations in a merger. Even better, a relationship between Mike and Zenith would remove a major distraction from his plans.

CHAPTER II

FOR WHAT IT'S WORTH

Mike's shuttle suffered several malfunctions as he navigated away from Hellfire Fuels. Frustrated, he took a course for Taurus, where he could make permanent repairs to his ship and, if lucky, pick up another job. His services were needed less and less over time as the sector became more civilized.

With the shuttle on autopilot, he dozed off for a short time until the transmitter again beeped, waking him. Sysco Galactic again requested he respond. Reluctantly, he accepted the call. It was Gemini's voice, so sweet and innocent. "Michael, you're hard to get ahold of these days."

"I'm busy, Gem. What's up?" he replied in a disinterested tone.

"I have something to offer you."

Mike checked his account on the overhead monitor to make sure he had received payment from his last job. To his satisfaction, the numbers incremented on the display. Then the number was halved as the cost of the repairs to his shuttle were deducted. Mike rubbed his eyes in frustration as he realized he was on the short end again with his finances. "We're not getting back together, Gem, so let's stop this right now," he remarked sourly.

"You're such a dick!" she blurted. "I'm past all that with you. Now are you interested or not?"

"Fine," he grumbled. "What do you have?"

"The Scrat have moved a command ship into the area, and I hear they are for hire."

The mention of the Scrat caught his attention. "What are they doing in this galaxy?" he inquired uneasily.

"I don't know, but I want a treaty with them before someone else does, namely Empire. They've already sent representatives with an offer. I need this, Michael."

"Forget it," he replied and terminated the call. Smoke spewed from one of the panels in the rear of the shuttle. Mike grimaced and then considered that maybe he should at least listen to the terms of her offer. With his shuttle badly in need of an overhaul, he was hurting for funds.

The transmitter beeped again. He placed his hand on his forehead and groaned. Against his better judgment, he answered the call. "What?"

"I'm serious, Michael," Gemini stated firmly. "One hundred thousand credits if you deliver my proposal to the Scrat leadership."

Mike leaned back in the seat with a pained expression. A paycheck like that would be more than enough for a new ship. "One hundred thou, huh?" he replied somberly. "You remember what we did to them three years ago. Don't you?"

"Things change and so do people," she responded coldly, sending him a subtle message. "I'll send you the terms immediately. You figure out how to deliver them."

"I'll think about it," he replied somberly, knowing this was a suicide mission and that no one else would take it. Besides, one thing he was sure of, he could never trust Gemini.

"No, you won't think about it. Yes or no," she demanded.

"You know they'll never go for it," he chastised her, "but, for a hundred thousand credits, I think I'll try." It was an opportunity for Mike to find out why and how they got a command ship into his galaxy. The Scrat were a violent and militaristic race, which was why he was ordered to destroy their military bases by the Space Federation when he was with Special Forces.

One of the panels in the rear of his ship let out a bang and shot sparks through the air. He glanced back and frowned. "There goes the remote navigation system," he mumbled to himself and punched the control panel. "Son of a bitch!"

"How soon can you meet with General Asher?" she pressed him.

"Asher, huh." He recalled the name from their prior mission against the Scrat. Mike reached back and nonchalantly turned off a circuit breaker from the smoking panel. Unhappy with his run of bad luck, he replied, "As soon as I see the credits in my account, I'll meet with him."

Mike immediately logged back into his account and watched the monitor for the credits to appear. He noticed Gemini didn't respond. "Something wrong, Gem?" he taunted.

"It's in process," she assured him. "You know I'm good for it."

"Are you?" he countered skeptically. Then his account indicated the deposit of ten thousand credits. He frowned and commented cynically, "A little short on cash this week? I only see a tenth of the fee."

"Of course not," she snapped at him. "You get the rest when the job is finished. It's insurance that you'll actually make the offer and not kill them."

"You know, after all we've been through," he complained, "I still can't trust you."

"Just get the job done," she ordered. "I'm tired of going down this road with you." The transmission ended with a distinct click. A document appeared on the monitor with Gemini's offer. Mike copied the terms to a small data disk in the console and removed it.

"What the hell am I thinking?" he uttered to himself. Then he considered that a job of this magnitude might get him new clients. He manipulated the long-range sensors until he found the location of the

Scrat command ship and then set a course for it. Exhausted from the last assignment, he slept soundly for the duration of the trip.

An alarm sounded when the alien ship targeted the shuttle. Mike awoke and promptly contacted the Scrat before they took action against him. Surprised that they granted him permission to dock, Mike slowed his approach to the ship and left the transmitter active on "receive." He knew the Scrat weren't here for trading purposes but more likely to incite havoc on the shipping industry as part of something bigger or to test their defenses. When his shuttle drew closer, the transport bay gates slid open vertically. Red lights flashed, and then the bay illuminated. Mike piloted the shuttle inside the cavernous bay and searched for the berth closest to the access hatch for a quick escape.

He was impressed by the command ship and the number of fighters that were docked inside. It appeared to be more of a ship transport for support equipment for a large colony than a command ship. Once the shuttle docked, the huge gates squealed and closed. A giant locking mechanism secured the gates, and several valves opened, filling the bay with oxygen. The glow of red lights changed to green. With the bay secure and habitable, the shuttle's engines shut down, and the bay became silent.

Mike opened a locker in the rear of the shuttle. Taped inside the door was a picture of him with his arm around Gemini on a beach. It was encased in a clear acrylic frame. A deep crack ran diagonally across the picture like a bolt of lightning that split them apart. Mike turned the picture around so he wouldn't see it. He donned a long trench coat over his tee-shirt and jeans. His snakeskin boots contrasted the jeans and black coat.

At the bottom of the locker was a wooden box of grenades. Half of the grenades in the box were silver for flash; the other half were black for incendiary. Mike picked out three of each and clipped the pull-rings of the black grenades to holes in his belt on the left side and the silver grenades on his right. The transmitter beeped, and a synthetic voice from an interpreting box broke the silence. "Enter now."

"Nice manners," quipped Mike. "How about 'hello' or 'welcome'?" He took the disk off the shelf next to the cabinet and waited patiently. The hatch on the shuttle hissed for several seconds and then opened. Mike appeared at the shuttle's open hatch, undaunted by his mission on the alien ship.

Another hatch at the end of the dock clanked and opened. Ten Scrat soldiers entered and approached him. They walked erect and had pointed ears, fangs, little (if any) body hair, and bulbous black eyes. "Still as ugly as ever," Mike muttered under his breath.

Armed with pulse rifles and leather uniforms, they surrounded Mike and targeted him with their weapons. He held his hands out innocently and turned around to show he had no obvious weapons. When he reached into his pocket to retrieve the disk, the Scrat cautiously backed away, wary of a trap.

Mike stepped away from the shuttle. "Greetings from Sysco Galactic, my friends," he announced sarcastically for his own amusement, assuming they didn't understand him. "This disk contains a proposal from my client offering the opportunity for a new and beautiful relationship between you ugly bastards and Sysco. I am here to present it to General Asher."

The soldiers laughed in their garbled dialect. One of the Scrat officers, Carnak, stood face-to-face with Mike. He adjusted a small electronic box on his neck and inquired, "Why would we want a treaty with you when we can take what we want?"

Mike raised his eyebrow and shrugged his shoulders. He responded quizzically, "Because you came here all the way from where?"

"Far from here, but we now have the ability to cross into any galaxy we choose," Carnak boasted. "Our military strength will be rivaled by none." The soldiers laughed again.

Mike pondered Carnak's remark and then inquired jokingly, "What about supplies, trade, resources, and... love?"

Carnak poked him in the chest and responded, "We need nothing from you. General Asher will decide if your life is worth sparing for dissection. Now follow me."

Mike was bewildered by how the Scrat had obtained technology to enter the galaxy in short fashion, and if they could possibly bring in additional forces. During his mission against the Scrat, it had taken over a year to travel to their galaxy. He also recalled that he had fallen in love with Gemini on that mission. As his handler, she rarely joined them in the field. Because of the duration of the journey, she accompanied them to provide intel and logistical support. Those were better times for both of them.

The soldiers led him from the transport bay through the gate and down the access corridor. The cleated heels of Mike's boots struck the floor with a metallic clang as he followed them. The soldiers were bothered by the sound and pointed their rifles at his boots.

One insisted on poking him with the barrel of his rifle. Mike grew annoyed and warned, "How about I shove that rifle up your crooked alien ass?"

"Silence!" shouted Carnak.

Mike continued down the corridor with them, taking note of every detail.

A small freighter, the *Blue Eagle*, traveled toward a depot on the fringe of the sector. On board, the crew of four lazed about the bridge, bored and tired. The captain, Tisch Mallory, was petite with short, black hair, wearing a blouse with jeans and boots. At twenty-eight, she was young for a captain, but when her father had died, Gemini offered her the opportunity to pilot her own ship out of sympathy for her loss.

Tisch suspected that Gemini was behind his death as part of an attempt to seize full control of Sysco and that she had given her the *Blue Eagle*, too old to be profitable, to discourage her from prying into the circumstances of his death. Tisch's determination enabled the *Blue Eagle* to remain profitable and a viable transport option for the corporation despite being antiquated.

Tisch had accepted Gemini's offer with the intention of getting even at a later time. With few trained personnel willing to take a chance on an unseasoned female captain, Tisch had to be creative in finding a crew. She discovered Wilmer first, perched on a barstool in one of Taurus's many pubs. His tattoo of an eagle on an arrow across his upper arm indicated that he had military experience and might prove helpful.

Wilmer, at thirty-two years old, was tall and rugged with a mustache and goatee. He was once Mike's partner until the team split apart. Soon after, his wife and daughter were seriously injured in a crash and, without the ability to secure a loan for their medical attention, they both died. Angry and distraught, he was content to drink his life away until Tisch found him. She convinced him to come aboard as her engineer and loadmaster. Reluctantly, he accepted.

Tisch then located Julian, her navigator, who had been imprisoned on Aurora for a controversial espionage charge. Julian, at thirty-one, was muscular and dark-skinned with a shaved head. Tisch bargained with the authorities for a rehabilitation assignment for him and paid a fee for his release. Julian was also helpful as a medical technician whenever injuries arose.

Geezer, the experienced pilot at fifty-two, was a longtime friend of her father's and a reliable mentor to her. Looking more like a Woodstock hippie, Geezer had long gray hair, a beard, and wore two tiny diamonds in his pierced ears. He was a second father to her and often inspired her to seek bigger goals.

Tisch sat in the captain's chair and watched the central monitor on the wall, where the display of stars always relaxed her. Julian programmed coordinates and fed them to Geezer. After a short period of silence, he complained, "You know Tisch, we really ought to get that onloader fixed. It's killing us."

"Talk to Wilmer," she replied with little interest. "He's the engineer."

Wilmer frowned and leaned back in his chair. "I'll get to it when I can. It's going to take some time to get all the parts and drawings together."

"Speaking of time," Julian interrupted, "when is our next leave?"

"We can't afford to take leave right now," complained Tisch. "The turrets cost a fortune, and that didn't include functioning auto-fire circuitry."

"So what good is that?" grumbled Geezer.

"Pirates are attacking freighters, and aliens have moved into this sector," she informed them. "We need protection."

"And who's going to fire those cannons?" quizzed Julian, expecting a futile answer.

Tisch stood proudly and announced, "I took a training course from the manufacturer, and I ranked in the top ten on their simulator."

The men chuckled at her. She dismissed their ignorance and turned her attention to the ship's log on the table in the middle of the bridge.

As Mike proceeded down the corridor with the Scrat escort, red lights from a heat-sensing device along the walls followed him. The lights were biosensors that collected information on his physiology as well as that of any other new life form that boarded the ship. Mike counted the steps from the transport bay to the end of the corridor, while taking note of the number of soldiers and their positions. Beads of sweat formed on his brow from the warm, humid atmosphere on the ship.

At the end of the corridor, another hatchway led to the main control room. Inside was a horseshoe-shaped control console, which faced toward him. Several monitors lined the top of the walls. Three alien technicians, wearing red uniforms, operated the controls. One was particularly focused on a small module with flashing green LEDs mounted on top of the console. Two large holographic images displayed over the console. There was a map of all the space stations in the sector on one image and a sizeable alien invasion force on the other. Data appeared on the monitor next to the module, indicating that calculations were underway for transporting the military force to their galaxy.

Beyond the control console sat General Asher. He was much larger than the other Scrat and issued orders from his mechanical chair on a raised platform. He had plumage on his head and a uniform that indicated he was decorated and high-ranking in his world.

Mike entered the control room and recognized him immediately. He recalled their previous encounter and thought about how he had left both

Carnak and Asher for dead. This proved to be a critical mistake as they were now in his part of the galaxy and not for peaceful purposes. As he approached Asher, two soldiers immediately cut him off. He held up the disk for all to see and waited for their response. The hatchway slid closed behind him.

General Asher stood and gestured with a wave of his clawed hand for his troops to stand down. The soldiers reluctantly backed off, their rifles still targeting Mike. General Asher adjusted the electronic interpreting device on his neck. "You have much nerve coming here, human," he remarked coldly.

Mike, in a salesman-like manner, moved about theatrically. "You must be General Asher, I presume." The General grunted at him and impatiently tapped his clawed fingers on the armrest. "I have come on orders from Gemini of Sysco Galactic Services," he announced, "to present to you a disk containing terms for a treaty."

Asher nodded to Carnak, who took the disk from Mike. Carnak hesitated and studied Mike for a moment. "We've met before," he remarked.

"Yeah, at your mother's," Mike responded sarcastically and then recalled the details of his mission against the Scrat. He and his partner, Wilmer, had gone into the Scrat Empire and destroyed all their military bases. Instead of leaving, they had sought out the Scrat leadership and eradicated most of them. Gemini coordinated their escape in thrilling fashion as they eluded the pursuing alien forces repeatedly.

Carnak punched Mike in the face, staggering him. "Not bad, lizard-face," Mike quipped as he rubbed his jaw. He got to his feet and instinctively struck Carnak in the jaw with a right hook. Carnak staggered back three steps, stunned by the punch. The other soldiers laughed at them. Carnak appeared dazed as he stepped toward Mike.

"Enough!" shouted General Asher.

Carnak snarled at Mike and handed the disk to the General. Asher eyed the disk curiously and tossed it on the console. Mike suspected that the alien officer had no intention of viewing the terms of the treaty. This was strictly entertainment for the aliens. He studied the console for anything of value he could use for collateral to guarantee his escape. The module with flashing green LEDs and the holographic images had his attention.

Then Carnak approached the General and whispered in his ear. Both stared at Mike for a long moment. General Asher laughed with a sinister gargle. Mike slid a hand under his coat and grabbed onto a silver flash grenade, ready to yank it from his belt.

"You will suffer more than you can imagine," General Asher announced. He pointed to one of the monitors on the wall.

The monitor displayed three gurneys with humans strapped down on them. Two had no eyes, and their torsos were gutted. Their organs were piled neatly in steel pans next to them. The third was still alive as the Scrat doctor dissected him.

Mike's fears had come true. The victims were representatives from Empire Shipping who came like him to offer the Scrat a deal. This was a suicide mission, just as he had expected. He kept his cool and quickly considered his escape.

General Asher stood and pointed at him. Before he could give the order to apprehend him, Mike already had a second silver flash grenade in his other hand. He yanked them from his belt and tossed one to his left at the console. Two of the Scrat technicians instinctively backed away, while the soldiers took aim at him. He tossed the other at General Asher. "Here's a little present from Mike Colby," he taunted and ducked down, covering his face with his coat.

Asher let out a loud groan and instinctively slapped the grenade toward his sentries. The flashes stunned them, and the brief blasts knocked them to the ground.

"Just like old times, eh!" Mike uttered boldly. He rushed to the console and yanked the remaining technician away from the module. The technician tumbled to the floor, giving Mike access to the module. General Asher screamed orders to his men, but the control room was now blanketed with thick smoke. They searched frantically for Mike.

As Mike removed the module from the console, one of the soldiers grabbed him from behind. Mike spun and kneed him in the gut, followed by a chop to the throat. The soldier staggered backward, allowing Mike the chance to disarm him. He tucked the module inside his coat pocket and rushed to the corridor with the soldier's pulse rifle in hand.

Mike took another flash grenade from his belt and tossed it toward the soldiers at the hatchway. The grenade exploded, creating more smoke in the control room. Random pulse fire struck the walls around him. He pressed the red control knob on the panel and the hatch slid open ever so slowly. Mike returned fire until he could squeeze through to the access corridor. He then retrieved one of the black incendiary grenades from his belt and fired it ahead.

Soldiers rushed into the corridor from a secondary corridor as the incendiary grenade exploded. Diving to the ground, Mike tossed another incendiary grenade down the access corridor toward the transport bay. Four soldiers appeared from the bay to block his exit but were eliminated by the blast. The hatch from the control room was now fully open, and pulse fire riddled the floor and walls around him. The fire-suppression system activated and then closed the hatch once more, isolating the control room.

Mike scrambled to his feet and hurried past the corpses toward the transport bay. The flashing sensors along the wall tracked his movement, distracting him immensely. He fired energy pulses from the pulse rifle at the tracks on both walls until several of the lights were extinguished.

The soldiers overrode the fire-suppression system and opened the hatch. When they exited the control room, they fired blindly through the smoke at Mike. The energy pulses peppered the corridor walls, nearly striking him several times.

Mike hurled the last incendiary grenade down the corridor in desperation. He actuated the hatch to the transport bay just as the grenade detonated. The blast knocked him forward into the bay. His head spun from the force of the blast, funneled through the hatchway.

Four more soldiers appeared in the corridor and fired at him. One pulse struck Mike in the thigh, forcing him to hobble to the shuttle. The soldiers pursued, firing repeatedly. Another pulse struck him in the shoulder as he closed the hatch from inside the shuttle. Hastily, he started the shuttle's engines and navigated away from the dock.

The sensors for the outer gates automatically initiated the opening sequence for departure. A Klaxon sounded, warning that the massive gates would soon open and that the bay would be void of oxygen. A sucking sound startled the soldiers as a vacuum formed inside the bay. They quickly retreated and secured the inner hatch.

Mike waited nervously for the outer gates to open until he heard the clanking sound of the locking mechanism echo through the bay. He inched the shuttle closer to the opening gates, fretting that the bay would soon be secured once more and trap him.

Inside the control room, General Asher screamed for someone to override the outer gates and close them. He cursed his men in their Scrat dialect as he stepped across the control room floor over the wounded and dead soldiers.

Once the gates had opened slightly, Mike's shuttle sped toward the widening gap. With barely enough room to clear, he piloted the shuttle out of the bay, scraping its top and bottom hulls against the gates, and then escaped. The bay gates ceased opening and closed once more.

Free of the command ship, Mike forced a laugh as he programmed the shuttle for maximum speed. With the ship on autopilot, he retrieved a first-aid kit from the locker and crudely bandaged his thigh. Sweat beaded on his forehead as he retrieved a syringe and a clotting agent from the kit. "I hate this part," he groaned and stuck the syringe into his leg.

Suddenly, the lights flickered, and another panel, the overdrive compensator, smoked and its indicator lights went blank. Within seconds, the ship's speed decreased. "You've got to be kidding!" he shouted angrily and kicked the panel in a rage.

Mike attempted to contact Gemini via transmitter. After four tries, Gemini responded. "Well, Michael?"

Mike wiped sweat from his brow again and responded frantically, "I need backup, ASAP! They weren't interested in your damned treaty."

"Negative, Michael. I can't risk losing this opportunity."

"They aren't interested in a treaty, you fool!" Mike screamed in frustration. "They're here to conquer us!"

Gemini's sarcastic laugh grated his nerves as she taunted, "You're so dramatic, Michael."

"I want the balance of those credits, Gemini!" Mike yelled as blood seeped from his shoulder, pooling on the floor at his feet. "I earned them!"

"We'll discuss it when I see you again," she remarked playfully. "Goodbye, Michael."

An alarm sounded, meaning ships were within short-range sensor proximity. Mike checked the monitor, which displayed seven small V-shaped objects indicating Scrat fighters. The fighters targeted his shuttle and launched proximity pulse torpedoes at him. They appeared intent on crippling his ship rather than destroying it. The Scrat wanted the module back no matter what.

Mike sent an open transmission to all channels and called out, "Mayday! Mayday! This is the *Rusty Bucket*. I have alien fighters in pursuit! Requesting help ASAP!" He grew faint from blood loss as blood dripped from under his coat sleeve. He removed the coat and tossed it behind him. The shoulder wound was worse than he had thought.

On board the *Blue Eagle*, the crew heard Mike's plea for help. They grew interested in an alien attack in this part of the sector and huddled around the central monitor.

"What do you think?" Geezer asked Tisch.

"It's a good opportunity to try out the new turrets."

"It's a good opportunity to get killed," Julian complained. "Let's get the hell out of here before we get involved."

Gemini's voice came across the radio and startled them. "No one is to engage those fighters. That is an order."

Mike's voice responded over the open channel, "How could you do this, Gemini?"

"I can't risk jeopardizing this opportunity," she replied arrogantly, forgetting that this was an open channel. "I need their services."

Tisch had a devious look about her and ordered Wilmer, "Respond to that SOS. Tell him we're on the way."

"Sure thing," he replied enthusiastically. "It's been a while since we had some fun around here."

"Julian, get me that ship's coordinates now!" Tisch ordered. Julian reluctantly obeyed. Bravery wasn't one of his stronger traits, but self-preservation was.

"Geezer, get us there pronto. Understand?" Tisch continued.

"Yes, ma'am," Geezer replied anxiously. He set a course with the coordinates from Julian for Mike's shuttle.

Wilmer made contact with Mike and announced, "This is the *Blue Eagle*. We're on the way."

"Thanks, *Blue Eagle*. Make it fast, though. These Scrat are a little pissed off right now."

Gemini interrupted their transmission and ordered, "*Blue Eagle*, stand down. This does not concern you."

"Kiss my ass, Gemini," barked Mike over the radio. "We're going to have a long discussion about this when I get back."

Wilmer looked surprised by the voice and inquired, "Is that you, Colby?"

"Sure is," Mike replied and, after a brief pause, inquired, "Is that you, Salazar?"

Tisch, Geezer, and Julian became interested in Wilmer's friend and how they knew each other. Wilmer glanced at them, aware that their eyes were on him.

"Yeah, it's me," he replied. "What the hell did you do now?"

"Long story," Mike answered. "Get me out of here, and I'll be happy to tell you."

Gemini ordered them again over the open channel, "*Blue Eagle*, if you don't stand down, you will be charged with insubordination and treason."

Tisch nudged in front of Wilmer and replied, "Sorry, Gemini, you're breaking up." She crumpled a page from her personal logbook over the microphone and terminated the transmission.

"Are you sure that was a good idea?" Wilmer questioned her.

"Of course it was," replied Tisch boldly. "Screw Gemini!"

"You know this will have consequences," he countered unhappily.

"Yeah, but he does have a cute voice," she kidded.

"A cute voice!" uttered Julian. "No wonder Gemini made you captain. It's our punishment, not yours."

"Stuff it, Julian," chided Tisch. "You sound like a whiny bitch."

"I'll try to isolate his channel and bypass Gemini," Wilmer announced. "This guy is an old friend of mine."

Tisch was pleased with the way events were unfolding. She had a chance to stick it to Gemini while possibly meeting a new ally. "I'm going up to the turrets in case our alien friends get too close," she informed the crew. She hurried off the bridge and closed the hatch behind her.

"We are so screwed," complained Julian.

"Have a little faith," Geezer suggested. "She's finally showing some life."

"Faith and I have nothing in common," replied Julian sarcastically. "I liked it better when she was in her stupor." Geezer and Wilmer glanced at each other and shrugged their shoulders. Her morbid attitude always annoyed the crew, and now Julian revealed that he had actually enjoyed her suffering.

Julian saw their reaction and grew incensed. He charged out of his seat at the navigation panel and pointed at them like a madman. "Did you not hear what Gemini said?" he blurted. "I don't want to go back to prison. Been there, and it's not nice."

"Again, Julian, I suggest you have a little faith in Tisch," repeated Geezer.

"That bitch couldn't make a decision on what to eat for lunch," he responded, losing his mind.

Wilmer stood up and got in his face. "That is your captain you're speaking about, who, by the way, is the bitch that got your sorry ass out of prison and gave you a job."

"But you heard Gemini!"

"Screw Gemini!" shouted Wilmer.

Julian backed down and returned to his seat. With no choice in the matter, he could only hope for the best. "That's all anyone ever says on this ship," he complained. "'Screw Gemini.' She must be one hell of a lay if you all keep talking about her like that."

Geezer became annoyed and responded, "Do us all a favor, Julian, and shut the hell up." Julian sulked as he monitored Mike's coordinates.

The shuttle rocked violently as the Scrat fighters hammered its aft end with cannon fire. Smoke filled the cabin, and sparks flew from the navigation system. Mike checked the monitor and saw the *Blue Eagle* close on him. Not having time to address his shoulder wound, he weakened from blood loss. He became despondent when he realized the *Blue Eagle* was only a small freighter. This was hopeless, he feared.

A fire erupted under the control panel, and the shuttle lost power. Mike donned an oxygen mask and uttered to himself, "If get out of this, I'm going to kill you, Gemini."

Mike removed a fire extinguisher from a rack and doused the fire. The ship rocked again and he was thrown to the floor. Feeling the heat of the flames, he retreated to the hatch. Two of the fighters fired grappling hooks into the shuttle's hull and decreased their speed for towing. One of the barbs narrowly missed Mike's head as it pierced the hull and embedded in the opposite wall.

"Holy shit!" Mike shouted as he stared at the barb. Loose items, including the picture of Mike and Gemini, were sucked to the small gaps in the hull surrounding the grappling hook cables. Ironically, the picture shattered and its pieces disappeared through the holes. Mike's coat flew across the cabin and briefly blocked one hole, while other clothing items from the locker blocked the other. The shuttle drifted aimlessly with the loose tag lines trailing behind.

The *Blue Eagle* drew close to Mike's shuttle and then veered between the shuttle and the incoming fighters. In the upper turret, Tisch activated the twin cannons and targeted the fighters. Two fighters came close to the freighter in an attempt to drive it away. Tisch promptly destroyed both with short bursts of energy. The other fighters turned on the freighter, but Tisch was ready for them as well. Despite the several rounds of energy pulses from the fighters that struck the freighter's hull, Tisch targeted them and fired repeatedly until the last fighter was destroyed. Content with her success, she left the turret.

On the bridge, Geezer and Wilmer hugged each other while Julian sulked. Wilmer got in Julian's face and taunted him over Tisch's success. Tisch entered, beaming with pride. "I told you I was more than competent on those turrets," she declared.

Wilmer and Geezer high-fived her excitedly. Geezer hugged her and remarked, "Your father would be proud of you."

Tisch noticed Julian's disappointed demeanor. She approached and stared at him, awaiting a response. When none came, she spun him around in his chair toward her. "What's wrong, Julian? Are you afraid I ruined your meal ticket?"

Julian, red-faced and upset, replied, "How are you going to handle Gemini after this?"

Tisch, Wilmer, and Geezer shouted in unison, "Screw Gemini!"

"And when the screwing's over, we'll all be in prison," he grumbled feebly.

"Have a little faith in me, Julian," Tisch suggested. "I had faith in you when I got your ass out of prison."

Julian punched the panel with his fist and answered tersely, "I don't believe in faith. It only destroys any hope you have for a better life."

Wilmer interceded. "I'll bet that one day, you will change that perception."

Julian rolled his eyes at Wilmer in disbelief. In his mind, that would never happen. Faith always betrayed him, and he had learned his lesson.

"All right, boys," announced Tisch, "let's get our new friend on board. He probably needs a little TLC after that ride."

Geezer maneuvered the ship over the crippled shuttle. Wilmer operated the bay doors and manipulated the booms from the ship's cargo bay. The viselike claws at the end of the booms locked onto the shuttle and retrieved it. Once it was secured inside the maintenance section of the cargo bay through magnetic bands along the wall, Wilmer closed the bay doors. "We got him," he announced to Tisch and the crew.

CHAPTER III

A HEALTHY ADDITION

Tisch, Wilmer, and Julian departed the bridge, leaving Geezer alone to pilot the ship. Tisch was anxious to meet their new guest, and the men noticed the extra spring in her step. Unfortunately, Wilmer sensed trouble in the coming encounter. Mike's history with Gemini was bound to be a problem.

"Look, Tisch, Mike isn't the kind of guy you want to get mixed up with," he warned. "I knew him for a long time."

Tisch placed her hands on his arms affectionately and replied, "I already know we're going to get along just fine. So relax." Wilmer glanced at Julian nervously and shook his head.

"Maybe Wilmer's right," added Julian. "Perhaps this man is a lowly dog with no morals."

"No morals," Tisch taunted. "That's funny coming from you, Julian." Julian paused to consider her remark and then nodded in agreement. He continued after them, proud of his perceived reputation.

Tisch hesitated at the hatch to the cargo bay. "Let's put it a different way," she clarified. "If one of you idiots ruins this for me, I'll make your life a living hell. Got it?" Wilmer and Julian reluctantly acknowledged her warning and followed her into the cargo bay. They approached the battered shuttle in the maintenance section and waited anxiously for Mike to emerge. The grappling hooks protruding through the hull and hatch gave them an uneasy feeling.

Tisch ordered, "Get him out of there, now!"

Wilmer rushed to the shuttle and operated the external hatch release. The shuttle emitted a loud hissing sound. The hatch opened partway with the grappling hook blocking its path. Smoke billowed from inside the ship, lending an eerie atmosphere to the shuttle's interior. He strained to see through the smoke and spotted Mike on the floor.

"Give me a hand!" Wilmer shouted. "He's down!"

Julian followed him inside as Tisch waited uneasily, fearing for Mike's fate. The men emerged from the shuttle with their arms around Mike's waist for support. Gently, they set him down on the cargo bay floor. Tisch promptly removed his oxygen mask while Wilmer checked his vital signs. Julian used a pocket knife to cut away the clothing and rags wrapped around his wounds.

"He's breathing!" exclaimed Wilmer.

"The wounds aren't fatal," Julian announced nonchalantly. "I think he'll live."

Mike came to and peered at the shuttle in dismay. "Damn, I hope my insurance covers this," he joked weakly.

Tisch studied his muscular body and short haircut. She glanced back at Wilmer and Julian with a devious smile. "Oh, yeah," she whispered. "He'll do just fine."

"No, Tisch," blurted Wilmer. "You don't understand."

"Welcome aboard, Mr. Colby," Tisch greeted him.

Mike looked unsteady and pale. "Thanks for..." Before he could finish, he passed out.

"Get him to the infirmary now!" Tisch shouted.

The men lifted Mike to his feet and ushered him from the cargo bay. Tisch pressed them from behind until they got Mike onto a gurney inside the infirmary.

Julian immediately took control and ordered Tisch to leave. "I won't work on him with you bitching over my shoulder."

"I won't say anything," she promised. "Just help him, please."

Julian pointed toward the door and refused to do anything until she left. Wilmer put his arm around her waist and ushered her into the corridor. "I promise you, Tisch. We'll take care of him. Now go help Geezer out and let us do our job. There may be more of those fighters coming after us." Realizing he was right, Tisch reluctantly returned to the bridge.

Wilmer closed and locked the hatch. Julian cut away the remainder of Mike's clothing and the crude bandages on his wounds. Wilmer returned and assisted in cleaning the wounds. Julian stared at him suspiciously until Wilmer responded, "What's the problem?"

"What do you know about this guy that we don't?" Julian asked somberly.

"Mike is Gemini's ex-husband."

Julian was stunned. "Oh, shit! You've got to be kidding!"

"I wish I were. Can you imagine what will happen between Tisch and Gemini if she gets involved with Mike?"

Julian suddenly looked ill. "Gemini will have such a vendetta against us," he replied dismally. "Life will be hell."

"And that's the best-case scenario," added Wilmer. "Don't say anything about it to Tisch until we figure this out."

Julian gestured with his hands, clearly wanting no part of it. "I ain't saying nothing," he stated firmly. "He's your friend."

Wilmer sighed, realizing this was going to be tough. The men resumed treating Mike's wounds.

Tisch sat silently in the captain's chair, lost in her thoughts. Geezer glanced over at her several times and finally asked, "Why are you so concerned with this guy? You don't even know him."

"He stood up to Gemini. That takes brass ones," she replied.

"Or he's really stupid," kidded Geezer.

"He had no respect or fear of her," she continued.

"Maybe they're relatives," he suggested. Tisch wondered if there was some connection between them.

The transmitter beeped and interrupted her thoughts. Geezer pressed 'receive' on the transmitter and answered the call. He cringed when he heard Gemini's voice. "Listen, you old cooter! Put that dumbass captain of yours on now or I'll have you imprisoned for what's left of your wretched life!" she shouted.

Geezer turned to Tisch for direction. She responded from her station, "This is Captain Mallory. What ails you now, Gemini?"

"I gave you orders not to interfere. You deliberately disobeyed me."

"So now what?" she replied sarcastically. "We rescued the guy."

"How is he?" Gemini asked in a more civil tone.

"My men are working on him. He's unresponsive thus far."

"Keep me informed of his condition," she requested. "Oh, and Tisch, don't ever defy me again," she warned. "The next time, I might not be so understanding."

Tisch was about to explode on her, but Geezer quickly ended the transmission. "There's something weird about her interest in your new friend," he commented.

"Yeah, he must have really pissed her off. I like that." Geezer rolled his eyes at her, and she acknowledged him with a smile.

Wilmer and Julian sat across from the gurney, watching over Mike, and fretted the consequences of Mike's involvement with Tisch. The two men argued over who was going to take responsibility for keeping them apart. Finally, Mike stirred and awoke.

"What's all the racket?" he asked irritably. "You two sound like a couple of magpies."

"How are you feeling?" asked Wilmer.

Mike sat up, rubbing his eyes and forehead. "Like hell." He attempted to sit up, but Wilmer and Julian grabbed his arms and eased him back down onto the gurney. Frustrated, Mike requested to speak with the captain of the ship.

With a condescending stare, Julian turned to Wilmer for a response. Wilmer fidgeted and then replied, "Soon, Mike. We're approaching our next destination, and arrangements have to be made."

Mike recalled stepping out of his battered shuttle and meeting a pretty brunette. He sat up again and, despite their objections, slid his legs off the gurney.

"Easy, Mike," cautioned Wilmer. "We had to do a lot to get you back."

"How bad was I?"

Julian stood in front of him, hoping to persuade him to lie back down by intimidation. "We had to give you an infusion of blood, and, as my luck would have it, I was the only one with a matching blood type." Mike shook Julian's hand and thanked him.

The two crewmen were anxious to know what had happened to Mike that the Scrat were so eager to capture him. Mike joked about ruining Gemini's blind date with the Scrat General.

"So what did you do?" inquired Julian, unable to restrain his curiosity.

"I knew not to trust those scaly-ass bastards. When they turned on me, I showed them a little Colby live-action."

Wilmer was amazed at how Mike managed to escape death, just like he had so many times with Special Forces. Julian, meanwhile, feared the consequences of Mike's actions and how it would affect them, due to their involvement in his rescue.

The hatch door opened slowly, and Tisch peered in. She was elated to see Mike looking well. As she closed the hatch behind her, Mike immediately took notice of her.

"Welcome aboard the *Blue Eagle*, my friend," Tisch greeted him. "I was afraid your rescue was for naught."

Mike glanced at Wilmer and asked, "How long have I been here?"

"Oh, about five days."

Mike was surprised and recalled being injured on board the shuttle. "I didn't realize I was hurt that bad."

Tisch stepped toward him, her hands folded together in front of her. "You're in the best of hands here," she assured him.

Mike grew wobbly and again Wilmer grabbed his arm to support him. Julian took a syringe and filled it with contents from a vial. Mike became uneasy when he saw the syringe and asked, "What's that for?"

Julian held it upright and tested for air bubbles with a short squirt. "It's a sedative to make you sleep. You aren't strong enough to be up and about." He then injected Mike and nudged him back on the gurney.

Tisch placed her hand on his arm. "Relax, Mr. Colby. We'll talk when you're stronger."

"I'd really like to thank..." he started to say and then passed out. When she turned around, Julian and Wilmer glared at her.

"Please, Tisch," urged Wilmer. "Don't do this."

Tisch poked a finger in Wilmer's chest and warned, "When you are the captain, you can tell me what to do." She opened the hatch and looked back. "Thanks for taking care of him," she added and then left them.

Julian covered his eyes and moaned, "This isn't going to be easy."

"I'll think of something," Wilmer muttered unhappily.

"Get him involved in working in another part of the ship," pleaded Julian. "Just keep them apart!" The two of them left the room, concerned about their pending challenge.

Impatiently waiting another two days for Mike to recover, Tisch walked down to the cargo bay and stepped inside his battered shuttle. She was amazed at the damage it sustained and was saddened by the streaks of blood on the controls and the floor. The thought of dying alone always frightened her, and to imagine what Mike felt, being trapped and his shuttle nearly destroyed, was hard to fathom.

Curiosity got the better of her and she investigated the recordings on the shuttle's computer. To her surprise, the conversation between Mike and Gemini, prior to Mike's boarding the alien vessel, was there. It was then that she realized Mike and Gemini were acquaintances prior to his disastrous mission. Curiosity drove her to search further into the database, where she found a recording from an earlier conversation between Mike and Gemini. She was appalled at how cold Gemini could be toward someone—toward anyone. Mike peered inside the shuttle and was pleased to see Tisch seated at the controls. He crept up behind her and slid into the co-pilot's seat.

"Holy shit!" she blurted and placed her hand over her heart. She was embarrassed that he had caught her intruding on his ship's recordings.

"Well, hello to you, too, Captain," Mike responded coolly. "You're welcome to anything on my pile of junk."

Tisch turned off the shuttle's computer system and inquired playfully, "Will you be conscious long enough to have a conversation with me this time, Mr. Colby?"

"Please, call me Mike. Colby's too formal." Mike assured her that he was feeling much better. He kept the conversation about her, querying Tisch about her life and experiences on the *Blue Eagle*.

Whenever Tisch attempted to question him, he expertly deflected the conversation back to her. She admired him for that. In her life, most men she knew had a difficult time actually listening to a woman. That always irritated her to no end. Mike gave her the opportunity to open up about how she felt when her father died and what drove her to accept the position of captain on an obsolete-class freighter. Tisch revealed that she was determined to make Gemini pay for her father's death. She took the freighter to prove herself. Revenge would come later.

At the end of their conversation, Mike offered to stay on to help with repairs and the day-to-day operation of the ship in appreciation for Tisch taking such a risk in rescuing him. She was more than happy to accept his offer. He also realized that his past relationship with Gemini could be a problem between him and Tisch. Silence on the matter for now was the best course of action.

When they stepped out of the shuttle, Mike took her hands and pressed her gently against the side of the ship. Tisch was caught off guard and embarrassed. She wasn't ready to behave romantically with him yet. Before she could respond, Mike asked, "What is it that you dream about? I mean where do you want your future to take you?"

Tisch was relieved that this wasn't an advance toward her but, in a way, it disappointed her. Deep down, she wanted the thrill of a passionate kiss with a handsome man she barely knew. She smiled coyly, feeling her confidence grow with him, and responded, "I want my ship and crew to be free of Gemini's control. I want to conduct my own business as I see fit."

"I'll do what I can to make that come true," Mike assured her. "I have an influence on people that could help."

"You would do that for me?" Tisch asked, unsure of how she should react.

"Of course," he answered with a gleam in his eye.

They gazed at each other until the silence became uncomfortable. Then Mike inquired, "How is it that you rescued me in an old freighter with those Scrat fighters swarming all over the place?"

Tisch was reluctant to reveal that she was on the cannons and defeated the alien craft. "It was more of a surprise thing," she explained modestly.

"My ship is equipped with two turrets, each with a pair of cannons. No one expects a freighter like mine to have those."

"I see," said Mike as he remembered giving up all hope when he had seen that a freighter was coming to his rescue.

With the conversation seemingly done, Mike backed away from her. Tisch sensed that they weren't alone and looked up at the operator's cab for the onloader system. Julian and Wilmer were watching nervously. She was aware of their thoughts and tried to hide her displeasure with them.

Mike noticed as well and quipped, "The boys are a little concerned for your well-being."

"They'll get over it," she remarked giddily. "However, I could use your help with some maintenance items on board the ship."

"Whatever you need, I'm yours," he teased. Tisch blushed as she thought of some personal things that needed tending to. Mike stepped aside and gestured for her to lead the way.

As they followed a long corridor past several hatches to the stairs, Tisch explained the issues with the onloader, their biggest headache, and how it affected their operation. Then there was the issue of the auto-firing system for the turrets. They had been removed from a scrapped cruiser and hadn't worked in years prior to her purchase. Mike questioned her on why Wilmer hadn't taken care of it. He knew Wilmer was sharp when it came to engineering, but Tisch indicated that his motivation wasn't always there.

Mike ogled her ass as she ascended the stairs ahead of him. She knew but said nothing. When they reached the bridge, Geezer was standing before Julian and Wilmer, having just chastised them for their intrusive behavior toward Mike and Tisch.

"Did I miss something?" Tisch asked, looking to embarrass them.

Wilmer and Julian were antsy and hoped Geezer would keep quiet about the lecture. Tisch noticed their unease and folded her arms. The men knew that that was a sign of impatience; a response was required.

"Just reminding the boys about their manners, Captain," explained Geezer as he took his seat at the controls.

Tisch stepped in front of the two men with a cold stare. "Wilmer, Mike is going to help you fix some things around the ship."

"But I can handle it by myself."

"It's settled," she informed him. "You'll give him whatever he needs."

"I have to do an inventory of the medical supplies," Julian interjected and hurried to the hatch.

"Stop right there, Julian," she ordered. "Since you have such a keen interest in what's going on around here, you'll do the honors and cook us a nice dinner to welcome our new crewman."

Julian's jaw dropped in horror. Tisch relished the moment and added, "I knew you'd be happy to help out, given you're such a sharing person." Julian was about to respond but thought better of it. He frowned and left the bridge, slamming the hatch behind him.

Mike placed his hands on his hips and admired Tisch's take charge attitude. "We'll arrive at our next stop in two days," Tisch explained. "We have to be out of Gamma-5 promptly to get to the following stop on time. It's a tight window, and I need that onloader functioning. I'm counting on you and Wilmer to make that happen."

Mike glanced at Wilmer and assured her that they'd repair it. He turned to Wilmer and pointed to the hatch. "Let's go, buddy. You're going to teach me all about this onloader thing." Wilmer reluctantly led him off the bridge through the hatch. Mike glanced back at Tisch and winked as he closed the hatch behind him.

Geezer chuckled and remarked, "Nice show."

Tisch strutted toward him and replied, "Perhaps Mike's presence will motivate the other two."

"You might just be right." They laughed, both aware that she was manipulating the men. Tisch sat in her captain's chair and updated her ship's log.

Inside the operator's cab, Wilmer stepped aside, allowing Mike to study the controls. He explained to Mike the issues that plagued the system, despite his many attempts to fix it. Then there was an uncomfortable moment of silence between them.

"What's going on?" Mike asked somberly.

"Look, Mike," Wilmer started, feeling embarrassed. "We're here for the long haul with Tisch."

"Okay," he responded, somewhat baffled.

"We don't want you to start something with her and then bail."

Mike became defensive. "Now why would I do that?"

"Gemini. Your divorce," replied Wilmer. "Tisch is already a handful. Please don't make it worse for us."

Mike became annoyed with him. "I'm disappointed in you, Wilmer," he chided.

Wilmer shook his head in frustration, unsure if he had done the right thing. Mike patted him on the shoulder and explained, "I'm not looking to ruin your life. For what it's worth, I missed you, buddy."

Wilmer, now feeling guilty, man-hugged him. "I missed you too, man. I still can't believe you're here." They stared at each other, taking in the moment. Then Mike suggested, "Why don't we fix this thing for Tisch and see where things go?"

Relieved, Wilmer pulled out several schematics for the control circuitry and laid them out on a table for Mike. He then stared at Mike for a long moment before Mike noticed and faced him.

"All right, Wilmer, go ahead and ask."

Wilmer hesitated as he feared opening old wounds. Finally, he inquired, "What's going on with you and Gemini?"

Mike burst into laughter. "Is that what's really bothering you?" he asked.

Wilmer was embarrassed by Mike's reaction. "Well, yeah."

Mike shook his head in disbelief. "I just finished a job, and my shuttle took a beating. I needed money."

"So you went to her for work?" Wilmer asked curiously.

"Hell, no!" he replied, offended that his friend would think that. "She contacted me with her cockamamie story about the Scrat and a treaty for a pile of credits—a hundred thousand, to be exact."

"A hundred thou, huh?" quipped Wilmer with a sly grin. "She doesn't have that many credits to give for a treaty."

"Don't you think I know that?" he countered. "It's a marker for a new shuttle."

"What happened then?"

Mike paused to recall the details. "Remember our mission to destroy the Scrat military bases?"

"How could I forget?" answered Wilmer giddily. "That was epic!"

"Remember the Scrat officer who slugged it out with me until I got him with an uppercut and knocked him out?"

"Oh, yeah," replied Wilmer, now amused. "Carnak was his name, I believe."

"Sure is. When I boarded the ship, he was there. Even worse, General Asher was there, too. They both recognized me."

"Dude, you're as good as screwed," kidded Wilmer. "So what is a Scrat command ship doing in this part of the galaxy?"

"Why do you think they're here?" Mike countered.

"I'm sure it's not for a social call," Wilmer replied cynically. "What do you know so far?"

"I stole a module from them," Mike confessed. "When I saw a hologram of all the stations in the sector, it caught my attention right away. On a second hologram next to it was a Scrat armada. That was no coincidence."

"And you stole this gizmo from them," chided Wilmer.

"Damn right. As soon as I removed it, the images disappeared. They're related." Changing the topic, Mike took a marker and circled four points on the schematic. He pointed to one of them and suggested, "We start with this one."

Wilmer studied the points on the drawing and commented, "It's not a limit switch. I'm sure of that."

Mike frowned at him. "It's a limit switch," he insisted. "I'm telling you."

"How did Empire know they were in the sector?" inquired Wilmer. "And how did Gemini find out?"

"I don't know, but I intend to find out," Mike replied in a concerned tone. He requested to Wilmer that he not mention any of this to Tisch yet. He would discuss it with her at a later time.

"How about we start tomorrow?" suggested Wilmer. "I'm not in the mood to play with this thing now."

Mike placed his hands on his hips and stared at him disappointedly. "Tisch needs this fixed before we get to Gamma-5," he reminded Wilmer.

"Then you fix it," Wilmer grumbled irritably. "I've got other stuff to do."

Mike placed his hand on Wilmer's shoulder and stopped him. Wilmer turned to him. "I'll fix this onloader by myself," Mike volunteered. "If I give you the module, can you figure out how it works?"

Wilmer laughed at him. "You're kidding, right?"

"No," Mike replied humbly. "I mean it. This thing's important, and I'm sure they're going to come after it again."

Wilmer relented. "Fine. I'll look at it."

"That's my partner," Mike said confidently and slapped him on the back.

Wilmer patted his arm and left the operator's cab. Mike sighed over his impending task and folded the schematics. It was time to do some hands-on work now.

Julian cooked up a fine dinner of steak, potatoes, and corn. It was an expensive meal, saved for special occasions. Along with it, he filled their glasses with wine from a decanter. With a frown across his face, he still feared what was to come from Mike's presence on the ship. Tisch's volatile emotions over Gemini were already a source of tension among the crew.

Wilmer, Tisch, and Geezer entered the galley and approached the tables. "Did anyone inform Mike that it's time for dinner?" Tisch inquired. Their blank expressions answered her question.

As if on cue, Mike entered the galley, clean and shaved, wearing a new set of work coveralls. Tisch felt her heart skip a beat when she saw him.

"Sorry if I'm late," Mike announced apologetically.

"Just in time," responded Julian, displaying his lack of enthusiasm.

"You clean up nice," Tisch teased.

Mike blushed and stood by the table furthest from her. Annoyed by his humble attitude, she scolded him, "Oh, no, Mr. Colby. You're my guest on my ship. You sit at my table." Despite the grimaces on the faces of the crew, Mike was pleased.

With everyone seated, Tisch made a toast. "To our new friend and crewman, Mr. Mike Colby."

Julian and Wilmer were horrified that she had already designated him as one of their crew. Geezer enjoyed their reactions. Reluctantly, they raised their glasses and replied in unison, "To Colby."

Mike was amused by the gesture and played along. "Thanks, everyone. I really appreciate all you've done for me."

Tisch followed his response with her own comment. "Mike has agreed to stay on as one of the crew. You boys have a new friend."

Wilmer covered his eyes, frustrated by the daunting challenge ahead of them. Mike noticed and took advantage of his opportunity. "Wilmer and I went over the schematics for the onloader. We've already investigated the positioning of the limit switches on the assembly. I'm optimistic we'll have this solved in no time."

"That's great!" exclaimed Tisch. "I knew I could count on you boys."

There was an odd silence for several moments until Julian inquired, "What was it like on the Scrat ship?" Tisch interrupted and suggested that they begin eating while Mike related his story.

Mike told them about the Empire reps on the gurney and General Asher's remarks about conquest. He described the incredibly humid atmosphere on the ship and the intimidating biosensors traversing the wall from the transport bay to the control room.

When dinner was finished, Tisch escorted Mike from the galley, her arm hooked in his. They traded stories about each of their adventures in space until they had reached his cabin. Mike turned to Tisch and pressed her against the wall. His lips were so close to hers; he was dying to kiss her. She was about to respond, but then panicked. She turned away and gently pushed him back. "I'm sorry, Mike. It's too soon to go down this road."

Mike was surprised by her reaction. He knew she wanted to kiss him but could tell something else got in the way. "I'm sorry, Tisch. I didn't mean..."

"No," she interrupted him. "It's my problem, not yours."

Mike brushed her bangs from her eyes and stroked her cheek with his hand. She felt as though he put a spell on her; she wanted to hold him so tight. "Perhaps another time," he suggested.

"Thank you," she responded and returned to the bridge. She grew upset at her missed opportunity and tormented herself over it.

CHAPTER IV

TROUBLES

Tisch stepped onto the bridge and stood by the control console next to Geezer. She wanted to speak with him about what had just happened between her and Mike, but was at a loss for words. Geezer initially ignored her and studied the schedules of flights arriving and departing on Gamma-5. "If we can shave an hour off our arrival time, we can get right in," he finally responded. "If not, we could have a three-day delay."

"Can we do it?" she asked.

"Our engines are only maxing at eighty-five percent for some reason," Geezer explained. "Wilmer was supposed to check it out during our last stop on Taurus."

"I'll talk to Mike," Tisch suggested. "Maybe he can help."

"He seems like a good guy," Geezer commented. "What gives with the two of you?"

"I'm concerned about his prior relationship with Gemini," she confessed. "It worries me what we're getting into with him, with Gemini, the aliens, and who knows what else."

"Maybe Wilmer and Julian can find out more about him," suggested Geezer. "They seem keenly interested in him. Perhaps a budding bromance."

They giggled over the idea but the conversation was interrupted by a Klaxon from the control console. Geezer urgently pressed several switches, changing screens and switching from short-range to long-range sensors.

"What is it, Geezer?" Tisch asked with a sense of urgency.

Geezer grimaced as he expanded the sensors' range. "Scrat fighters. Two closing. Four further out."

"I got this," replied Tisch confidently. "Get Wilmer and Julian up here to help."

"Will do."

Tisch hurried off the bridge. Geezer paged Wilmer and Julian on the intercom to report to the bridge immediately.

In the maintenance section of the cargo bay, Mike worked diligently on the cargo onloader. Standing at a large toolbox, he pulled schematics from his pocket and studied them briefly. Rock music blared from inside his crippled shuttle, preventing him from hearing the intercom. He eyed a terminal box near the ceiling. Searching the bay, he noticed a man-lift parked in a caged area. The cage was secured by a chain and hasp with no lock. Several other pieces of equipment were stowed inside the cage to keep them clear of the onloader's feeder platform.

Mike unlatched the hasp and slid the cage door open. A leather pouch on the side of the man-lift held the operating procedures for the lift. He took them out and climbed inside the bucket. "It can't be that hard to operate one of these," he muttered to himself and began to read.

Tisch donned the high-tech helmet that aided her in targeting the fast-moving fighters. She strapped herself in and powered up the system. Without the automatic targeting system, the cannons were manually operated from the turrets. The system provided the coordinates, but it was up to her to use those coordinates to accurately target the fighters.

Wilmer arrived on the bridge and immediately sensed trouble. He placed his headset on and took his seat at the engineering station. Julian leaned over Geezer's shoulder and pointed out several moving targets. "What the hell are those?" he shouted.

"Not now, Julian," he replied sternly. "Get to your station." The transmitter beeped and interrupted them with an incoming message.

"Great. Here it comes," Julian remarked sarcastically.

"Oh, crap," uttered Geezer as he pressed the "receive" button.

"I want Colby and the module," Carnak's gruff voice demanded. "If you don't surrender them to us, we will destroy your ship."

"Do that and your module thingy goes with us," challenged Geezer.

"Then we'll board you and dispense of all of you." The transmitter beeped and went silent.

"This is going to get ugly," Geezer groaned.

"What the hell is he talking about? A module?" blurted Julian.

"We'd better let Tisch and Mike know," Wilmer replied nervously.

Geezer pointed to the intercom light. It was illuminated. "Tisch already does."

"I knew that guy was trouble," complained Julian.

"Why are they coming at us from behind?" asked Wilmer.

"They're onto our turrets," Geezer replied.

"Meaning what?"

Geezer turned to him with a somber expression. "Meaning, they know we only use one turret. They're splitting up." He activated the rear force field and announced, "Rear shields up."

"We can head to Taurus and pass on Gamma-5," suggested Julian. "I'll call for backup from Captain Tieg."

Geezer frowned and changed their heading. "We won't make it in time."

"I'll make the call anyway."

Geezer searched for any location with shelter. Suddenly, he found one station within reach. "Julian, forget the call. I need one hundred percent out of those engines!"

"Don't look at me," he remarked cynically. "I'm not the engineer."

"Wilmer, figure it out or we're dead!" ordered Geezer. He switched back and forth from short-range to long-range sensors. When he swapped to the long-range sensors, his face grew taut. "Holy shit!" he blurted.

"What now?" asked Julian nervously.

"Ten fighters, dead ahead!"

Wilmer was horrified and stormed off the bridge. Geezer monitored the position of the approaching Scrat fighters. "The first two fighters split wide," he informed Tisch. "The next four also split, two high and two low."

"That's unusual," she responded. "Keep me under them, and I'll handle it."

"There are ten more coming at us from ahead!"

Tisch realized they were overmatched. "Can we outrun them?"

"Negative. Not without full power."

"Then we'll go down fighting," she declared somberly. "Notify the others."

"Will do."

Wilmer burst into the cargo bay and startled Mike. He shouted over the music, "Can you man the underside turret?"

Mike suspected a joke and replied smartly, "Maybe when you give me a hand with this onloader." He turned down the music to converse with Wilmer.

"We've got a butt load of Scrat fighters chasing after us, and we can't outrun them!"

"Maybe if you fixed the engine problem, we'd have full power," Mike chided.

"I'll fix it. I promise!" he blurted. "Now please, take the underside turret. Tisch can't handle them alone." Mike realized the seriousness of their situation and hurried out of the bay.

Wilmer understood that their lives depended on those engines working properly, and it was his fault that their speed was degraded. He paced the floor nervously and then followed Mike. They reached the stairs that led to both turrets. Wilmer directed Mike to the underside turret. "Why that one?" Mike questioned.

"Because Tisch likes to be on top."

Mike burst into laughter as Wilmer just realized how that sounded. "Just get in the damn turret," Wilmer barked at him. Mike smiled and descended the ladder. It always irked Wilmer that Mike was calm under fire, making him feel like a coward.

Once inside the turret, Mike studied the controls. The turret was similar in many ways to weaponry he had used on smaller assault ships when he was with Special Forces.

Wilmer shouted down to him, "You okay with this?"

As Mike donned the helmet, he became annoyed with Wilmer. "Beat it! I got this."

Geezer's voice came across the intercom. "All right, boys and girl, fasten your seatbelts. We're in for a rough ride, and it don't look good."

Mike powered up the turret and studied the images on the sensor screen. The ten fighters ahead of them appeared. Tisch noticed the additional fighters on her screen as well. "Geezer, any suggestions?"

"Pray," he replied solemnly over her intercom.

Mike eyed the formations and had an idea. "Geezer, this is Mike. Take us straight at those fighters."

"But, Mike, that's a lot of fighters."

Tisch interrupted. "You know how to operate one of these turrets?"

Mike answered confidently, "There isn't much I can't handle."

"Back it up, big boy," she challenged. This time, she was glad to have someone to assist her with the cannons.

Wilmer burst through the airtight door to the engine compartment. He browsed over all the indications on the panel, looking for anything abnormal. The nitrogen pressure was low by fifteen percent. The coolant flow around the engines was low by ten percent. The reactivity level of the fuel was at seventy-two percent.

"Damn, I don't see anything that is normal?" he complained to himself. At the remote engineering station, he promptly brought up schematics and maintenance documents for the engine control system. "Engineers diagnose! They don't fix," he grumbled to himself. As he scrolled through the documents, he added cynically, "That's what maintenance techs are for!"

The *Blue Eagle* raced straight toward the oncoming formation of ten fighters. Behind the *Blue Eagle*, one fighter flew to the left and another to the right. Two more were high and two low. They closed in on the freighter.

"Geezer!" shouted Mike. "Slow down and head directly at one of those fighters - any one of them."

"Are you crazy!" he replied.

"When the fighters behind us lock onto the ship, split between the forward fighters."

Tisch understood what Mike was thinking. "Do as he says," she ordered.

"Oh, man," Geezer complained. "I don't know about this."

"You're one of the best pilots I know, Geezer. I believe in you," Tisch reassured him.

"It's a twalk in the park," Mike added. "Just focus on the fighters' positions." Geezer felt reassured by Mike's calmness and obeyed. Mike targeted the two end fighters and, with two quick bursts, destroyed them.

Tisch's confidence improved vastly when she realized Mike could handle the turret. She selected the two fighters at the other end of the formation and fired two short bursts. One exploded, and the other was crippled. It spun away wildly.

Mike joked, "It's a good thing we aren't hunting duck!"

"Oh, so that's how it's gonna be," she countered, enjoying the challenge.

"Will you two concentrate!" shouted Geezer over the intercom, still nervous.

Tisch targeted the next three fighters and fired one long burst in a sweeping pattern. All three fighters exploded. She beamed proudly, feeling redeemed.

"Not bad," commented Mike. "Let's see what else you got under the hood."

"Don't you worry about what's under my hood," she responded playfully and fired another long burst. Two more fighters exploded. The remaining forward fighter continued at them.

"I think this guy's got a death wish," Geezer mumbled. "What should I...?"

"Veer left, now!" shouted Mike.

Geezer promptly guided the *Blue Eagle* to the left. The fighter behind him fired two short bursts and missed. The pulses struck the approaching fighter and destroyed it in a brief fireball.

"Mike, you are one lucky son of a bitch," Geezer uttered, feeling better about their predicament.

Tisch was impressed with his confidence under pressure. "There are still six fighters out there," she reminded them.

Mike targeted two fighters on the port side and traded fire with them. The freighter rumbled as cannon fire struck its hull from above. "You all right, Tisch?" Mike asked with a note of concern in his voice.

Tisch searched frantically for the source of the cannon fire. "Pity the asshole that hit my ship," she announced angrily.

The ship rocked violently as Geezer attempted to shift the shields from the rear to the front. The trailing fighters still peppered the freighter with cannon fire. After several attempts, Mike finally struck one of the forward fighters and destroyed it. Tisch located the one above her and ordered Geezer to veer right. As soon as the ship changed position, Tisch fired and destroyed the fighter. The remaining four fighters approached from ahead. Firing repeatedly, the aliens' cannon fire struck the ship's force shield several times.

Mike and Tisch both targeted the fighters, but then the red power light blinked. They attempted to fire but with no success. "Something you want to tell me about this system, Tisch?" Mike asked uneasily over the intercom.

"Thermal overload protection for the turrets' power distribution system," she replied sheepishly.

"You're kidding, right?"

"Nope," she replied dryly. "The shields draw their power from the same source."

"Wait until I talk to Wilmer about this," he groaned.

"This one's on me," confessed Tisch. "I supervised the technicians who installed it." Mike shook his head in disbelief as if he couldn't believe their luck.

Down in the engine bay, Wilmer was immersed inside the control panel for the engines. He tossed an old solenoid valve onto the floor, followed by a cracked pressure modulator. When he backed out, he tossed a screwdriver, pliers, and wrench onto the table. Sweat poured off his brow as he rushed to the indication panel. The nitrogen pressure slowly increased. Once it stabilized, the coolant flow increased, and the engine temperature dropped. As it approached its normal range, the reactivity level increased.

On the bridge, Geezer glanced repeatedly at his indications, hoping for some revelation that would save them. Then he noticed their speed increased to ninety-two percent. His eyes widened with surprise. "Anyone screwing with the engines?" he shouted over the intercom.

"It'd better be Wilmer," replied Mike. "I told him to fix it or else."

"The Scrat are making another run at us!" shouted Tisch.

"I'm switching the force field to rear shields," Geezer announced and watched anxiously as the engines increased to ninety-seven percent. The Scrat fighters no longer gained on them but still pursued. Cannon fire ricocheted off the rear shield of the freighter.

Looking upward in the engine room, Wilmer blurted, "Please, God, get us out of this, and I'll be a better man." The indicator moved forward again and peaked at one-hundred percent power. He jumped up and down, dancing with joy. "I swear, I'll be a better man!" he exclaimed to finish his prayer.

"Geezer, when I tell you, shut down the shields," ordered Mike.

"You're out of your mind!" he responded in disbelief.

"Tisch, you target the two on the left," Mike instructed. "I'll take the two on the right."

"We have full power!" shouted Geezer. "Let's cut and run!"

"No, we got this," Tisch replied. "Listen to Mike, Geezer."

"I'm not liking this part of the plan," he complained and reluctantly turned off the shield. The power button for the turret operation changed to solid red.

Mike and Tisch immediately fired several short bursts and destroyed three of the remaining Scrat fighters, but not before the Scrat fighters got off bursts of their own. One of the bursts struck the topside turret and nearly shattered it. The impact rattled Tisch. The fourth and last remaining fighter fled the battle.

The transmitter beeped again. Geezer and Julian glanced at each other uneasily. Geezer pressed the "receive" button.

"We'll be back," warned Carnak. "You won't be so lucky next time." The transmitter beeped as the transmission ended.

"Screw you, asshole!" Geezer shouted at the intercom. He switched to "local" and hollered excitedly, "You lucky bastard, Mike!"

"Thanks, Geezer," Mike responded. "Hey, Tisch, are you okay?"

Hearing no response, Mike unstrapped from his turret and rushed up the two flights of ladders to the topside turret. Tisch leaned forward with her head tilted against the damaged turret. She was dazed from the impact. Mike unstrapped her and gently lowered her down to the deck. He removed her helmet and sat her upright. Geezer and Wilmer appeared from opposite ends of the corridor, both looking concerned.

"Get her to the infirmary!" ordered Geezer. "I'll get Julian." Geezer then hurried away.

Wilmer tried to help, but Mike had already lifted Tisch in his arms and instructed Wilmer to lead the way and open hatches for them. They entered the infirmary and Mike set Tisch on a gurney.

"I'm okay," she uttered weakly. "A cold beer would help."

"You gave us quite a scare," complained Wilmer. "I was afraid I'd be working for Julian, or even worse, Mike." Mike groaned at the joke.

"Thanks, everyone," she responded appreciatively, glancing at Mike with a brief smile.

Mike added, "Now that you fixed the engines, Wilmer, what say we try the onloader next?"

"Don't push it," he responded sarcastically. "I don't work well under pressure."

Tisch giggled at them and remarked, "You two are the perfect team. Nice work, Wilmer." Wilmer nodded in appreciation.

Geezer and Julian rushed through the hatchway. Julian frowned, seeing that Tisch was okay. He chided Geezer, "I thought she was dying?" Geezer, embarrassed by his overzealousness, left them and returned to the bridge.

"I should probably check you out anyway," Julian commented, "in case of a concussion or something." He glared at Mike and Wilmer, an indication for them to leave.

"Oh, Mike," called Tisch as the men approached the hatchway. "We need to have a little discussion about a certain module when I'm finished here."

Mike and Wilmer glanced at each other uneasily, knowing that the Scrat would try for the module again. "Sure thing, Tisch," Mike replied and then left the bay.

Julian pointed a flashlight in each of her eyes and put her through the optic exercises to confirm that she was okay. "Guys like Mike don't last very long," he mentioned nonchalantly. "They're gypsies with no home to lay roots in."

Tisch lost her humor. "You don't want me to get involved with him, do you?"

"Nope. It's bad for business."

"I certainly hope that was a joke," she commented. Julian stared at her with a grim expression, a sign that it wasn't. He stowed his flashlight and checked her blood pressure.

Tisch considered his words and suddenly felt alone again. Just when she had started to feel alive again, Julian brought her back to the realization that Mike would probably move on, perhaps another mission, another job, or another woman. She knew that she had to prepare for it, like it or not.

Mike and Wilmer sat in the galley, each with a mug of beer. Mike leaned back in his chair with an arrogant look on his face. "I know what this is about," he replied irately. "You think I should've given Gemini another chance."

"I didn't say that," replied Wilmer defensively. He knew there was no avoiding the topic now.

Tisch stood in the hatchway and overheard them. She peered in and asked, "Something I should know about, Mike?"

Mike glared at Wilmer and then stood up. "It's nothing worth discussing."

Tisch walked across the galley to the cooler and took out two beers. Recalling Julian's words, she approached the table with an uneasy look about her. Mike knew she had heard enough of their conversation and that he'd have to explain his past to her eventually, just not today. If he was a short-timer on the ship, he couldn't reveal details that would endanger Tisch and the crew. Wilmer excused himself and left the galley. Tisch sat across from Mike, staring at him intently.

"I'm sorry if I said anything to upset you," Mike began. "I can..."

"What did you take from the Scrat?" she interrupted.

"It was just a part of their main console," he reluctantly replied.

"They're sending a lot of fighters after you... after us for this *part*," she reminded him. "And Gemini obviously has something to do with it. I want answers."

Feeling cornered, Mike related how he became involved in taking Gemini's terms to the Scrat and what was supposed to happen. Tisch was even more irate when she realized that Gemini was likely responsible for bringing the Scrat to their sector. She questioned Mike about how the Scrat had made their appearance in this galaxy. Then she pressed for more information about his relationship with Gemini.

Mike explained that, in his line of work, he couldn't always reveal the identities of people in his life for their own safety. "Gemini couldn't have done this," he admitted reluctantly. "She knows what the Scrat are. Someone else started this, and she's trying to capitalize on it."

Tisch rolled her eyes in disbelief. "Who is Carnak?" she inquired sternly. Wilmer peered in from the corridor. Mike gestured for him to join them. Tisch glared at him for eavesdropping.

"I couldn't help myself, Tisch," Wilmer uttered humbly. "I was part of what Mike's about to tell you." Tisch stood up and chugged her beer. She finished with a belch and allowed them to continue.

"We went on a mission to the Nebula Galaxy several years ago to destroy a Scrat weapons plant and some bases," explained Mike.

"Our journey took over a year," Wilmer interjected, "so you could imagine they didn't get here overnight either."

"I had to find out what the Scrat were really up to. That's why I took the job from Gemini," Mike informed her. "They aren't here for any treaty or partnerships with shipping companies—just to conquer and destroy."

Tisch opened the second beer and chugged half of it. "Really, Mike, I don't know what to think. You've put us right in the middle of what could be a galactic war, and we have no backup. Gemini is too stupid to realize that, or she wouldn't be involved in this at all."

"We'll figure out what the module does, and we'll use it against them," Mike assured her. "Wilmer's helping me."

"Tell that to Carnak," she shouted angrily. "He's determined to get to you through us!"

"We'll handle it, Tisch," Mike promised. "I know Wilmer can figure it out."

"That's real encouraging," blurted Tisch as she finished her beer. "I think I'm gonna be sick," she muttered and then fired the empty bottles into the disposal. She looked back at them with a piercing stare and then left the galley.

"I guess that went well," uttered Wilmer. "She doesn't have much confidence in me."

"I'm sure you and Julian will be very happy now," Mike responded angrily. "Thanks, friend." He got up and left the galley. Wilmer finished his beer and sighed. This wasn't how he had expected things to go.

Tisch returned to the bridge and took her seat. Geezer turned his attention to her. "Did you find the answers you were looking for?"

Tisch tapped her fingers on the table and replied curtly, "Some."

"Well, for what it's worth," Geezer began, "with the engines at one-hundred percent power, we can make Gamma-5 in good time." Tisch wasn't impressed. She looked down at the floor and frowned. Geezer was about to speak when Mike entered the bridge.

"Can I talk to you, Tisch?" he asked humbly.

Tisch gestured with her finger for him to approach. He slid a chair over and sat down next to her. "Look, you saved my life, and I'm indebted to you."

"I thought we established that already," she sniped at him.

"I didn't plan to drag you into this mess with the Scrat. I'm sorry."

"That doesn't help my ship from getting pounded by Scrat fighters."

Mike was embarrassed that he couldn't change the situation with the Scrat. He wrung his hands nervously; reluctant to say what needed to be said. "Is that it?" inquired Tisch coldly.

Mike looked at her with saddened eyes. "When we get to Gamma-5, I'll leave," he announced and then he left the bridge.

Tisch was even more confused as to what to do or say. She wanted him to stay, but she couldn't risk the collateral fallout, not just from the Scrat but from Gemini herself. Geezer approached her from behind and massaged her shoulders. Tisch touched his hands and asked, "Am I doing the right thing?"

"Only you can make that determination," he answered and returned to his seat at the control console. "Just be sure you're ready for the consequences of that decision."

Tisch bit her lip, frustrated by the outcome of things. "How's our time, Geezer?" she asked.

"We're going to slide right into that early slot."

"Finally, some good news," she remarked. "Can we squeeze in a stop on Galleon-IV afterward? That would save us a stop later and give us a big jump on the schedule."

Geezer hesitated briefly, arousing her suspicion. "We'll be delayed leaving Gamma-5 just long enough to miss an early window there."

"I'd better do some calculations," she replied and sat down in her captain's chair. "There's got to be a way to get us in there earlier."

CHAPTER V

A BATTLE OF WILLS

Mike resumed maintenance of the onloader in the cargo bay. He methodically tested the switch contacts on several limit switches and made adjustments. For four hours, he worked out of the man-lift bucket, moving from terminal box to terminal box and back to the limit switches on different stages of the system. Mike enjoyed belonging somewhere once again and having friends. Unfortunately, it appeared to be short-lived. He looked up at the operator's cab and noticed Tisch. When she left abruptly with no sign of emotion, he wondered if there was any chance to repair their friendship. As he adjusted the last limit switch, Wilmer arrived. "Hey, how about a dinner break?" he called up to Mike.

"Is the pariah slash guest of honor still invited?" Mike quipped.

"Apparently so."

Mike lowered the man-lift and climbed out. "You saved our asses when you restored full power to the engines, Wilmer."

"Yeah, I guess I did."

"It brought back memories," Mike said proudly. "You were always there to bail me out."

"I remember." The two men left the cargo bay and made their way to the galley. "So, you're really leaving us at Gamma-5?" Wilmer inquired disappointedly.

"Yeah, it's better for all of us."

They entered the galley and sat down at one of the tables. "I really wanted to be part of this crew," confessed Mike. "I've been on my own a for long time."

"It would have been cool. It's just that, well… you, Tish, and Gemini— that's an explosive triangle of emotion."

"I really don't want to tell Tisch yet about what my relationship with Gemini was. I'm concerned it will lead to attempts on her life as well as Gemini's if the wrong people tie me to either of them romantically."

Outside the galley, Julian stopped and eavesdropped on their conversation. Wilmer folded his arms and glared at Mike. "So Tisch hasn't already endangered herself on your behalf?"

"I see your point. But no matter what I do, Gemini will always be an issue," he explained.

"Maybe there's a way," suggested Wilmer. "We just haven't thought of it."

Julian entered the galley and took three beers from the refrigerator. He joined them at the table, handing a beer to each of them. "I hope you don't mind if I join the discussion," Julian requested. "I've given a lot of thought to our problem."

"You don't say much, Julian," Mike commented. "Let's hear it."

Julian sipped from his beer and calculated his response. "In simple terms," he started, "I don't want to see you and Tisch start something you can't finish."

"That's an interesting way of putting it," Mike responded.

"She's got a lot of emotional issues that already impair her ability to handle social matters in her life."

Mike and Wilmer chuckled briefly. They held their beers up and tapped for a mock toast. "Touché," Mike remarked. The three of them drank from the bottles.

"If you leave her, it would be a living hell for us to the point where we might actually leave the ship. If you stay... well, it can't be any worse."

Mike stared at his beer bottle and surmised, "You know, I can't promise that things will work out. No one knows that."

"And I think we failed to consider that," replied Wilmer. "I'm sorry."

"I can promise that I won't do anything to intentionally disrupt your lives here," Mike assured them.

"Perhaps you should have one more discussion with Tisch before we leave Gamma-5," suggested Julian.

"Perhaps I will," Mike responded.

As soon as the *Blue Eagle* docked on Gamma-5, Wilmer and Julian hustled down to the dock and inspected several containers of cargo for loading. Geezer met with the dispatcher to confirm their cargo delivery and receipt of a new load. Tisch, meanwhile, coordinated the time of arrival for their next stop. She wasn't thrilled with the results and left the bridge.

When the cargo bay doors opened, bright light from the dock flooded the cargo bay and caught Mike's attention. Using a manual hydraulic lift took a long time to lower or raise and then insert a container into the cargo hold. Wilmer and Julian dreaded this part of the operation, but they also knew how critical it was to meet their times on both arrival and departure.

Mike sensed the importance of the onloader and rode the man-lift bucket up to another terminal box. After attaching a device with an indicating light and a timer, he operated the onloader from a remote pendant. Satisfied with the operation of the switch, he was ready for a test. He positioned the man-lift out of the way of the equipment and operated the onloader through several cycles. Looking up, he noticed Tisch in the operator's cab once more. He lowered himself to the ground and left the bay.

Tisch leaned forward, wondering where he went. She hoped that the onloader would be functional, but knew it was a complex piece of equipment. Then Mike burst through the door and startled her. "Did you miss me?" he asked playfully.

Tisch was relieved that he had broken the tension between them first. "No," she responded. "Just wanted to see if you really could fix this piece of junk."

Tisch pointed down through the window to the dock below. Wilmer and Julian tediously operated the lift by cycling a hand bar up and down continuously. They watched the men unload one container. Sweat streamed down their foreheads as they labored. "See how long it takes to move one container," Tisch remarked.

When they finally finished with the offloads, a conveyor delivered four new containers to them. "Well, what do you think?" Tisch asked.

Mike didn't respond but merely operated the controls. He switched control from 'manual' to 'auto' in the operator's cab. The boom overhead retrieved a large magnet from its storage location and then lowered it over the container. Tisch watched anxiously, hoping for a miracle.

On the dock below, the men were now soaked in sweat. Inside the cargo bay, the magnet descended and secured itself onto the container, jarring the lift. The men were startled but suspected it was just a shift in the container's contents. They began pumping, but the container didn't move. Baffled and frustrated, they backed away, swearing as they contemplated what had failed.

Mike rotated one of the knobs and pressed "start." Tisch glanced back and forth from Mike to the container below. Mike backed away and let the system operate independently.

The container was lifted into the hold and steadied. A platform slid underneath, and the container was lowered onto it. The platform then retracted with the container into the cargo hold, where another device locked onto the top of the container. It was then transported it to its designated storage position as per the programmed parameters in the computer. This location matched the delivery information in the database so that it could be retrieved at the correct time and location for offloading. The assembly then reset and all parts returned to their 'start' position. The magnet positioned itself for the next container. At that point, the 'start' button would begin the sequence all over again.

Wilmer, Julian, and Geezer waved excitedly and blew kisses to Mike. The next container was immediately positioned underneath the cargo bay for pickup. "You did it, Mike!" Tisch shouted.

Mike held his arms out for a hug, but Tisch suddenly froze. "Come on, Tisch, it's just a hug."

Tisch panicked again and blurted, "I'm... I'm so sorry." She rushed out of the cab and down the corridor. Mike punched the wall of the cab and cursed several times. Tisch became teary-eyed, knowing that she had blown it again.

With its delivery completed, the *Blue Eagle* departed Gamma-5 on its way to Galleon-IV ahead of schedule. The bridge was unusually quiet. Geezer operated the controls while Tisch scrolled through their database of cargo. Wilmer reviewed the ship's critical functions on the computer and ran diagnostic checks on the vital systems. Julian plotted their course and relayed the coordinates to Geezer.

Julian became annoyed and chided Tisch, "I hope you're happy with your decision to let him leave." Tisch ignored him. Geezer and Wilmer glanced at each other with sly smiles.

"I can only surmise that when Gemini gets done with you, Julian might be your boss," Wilmer taunted.

Now Tisch's ire rose. "When pigs fly!" she shouted.

"Or when you get laid," Julian countered derisively. "They're both long shots, if you ask me." Tisch leaped out of her seat and rushed at Julian.

Wilmer knocked his chair over and nearly fell, interceding between the two. He pinned Tisch's arms to her side and tried to calm her down.

"I got you out of prison, and I can take you back," she warned Julian.

Julian scoffed at her and turned his attention back to his work station. Wilmer eased her away and advised her to go with him down to the galley and cool off. She reluctantly agreed. Geezer shook his head at them in disbelief for riling her up.

Mike sat alone in the galley, drinking from a bottle of water. He considered that maybe he should have left for Tisch's sake. When Wilmer and Tisch entered the galley, Tisch was stunned when she saw Mike sitting there. Wilmer remained at the hatch while Tisch sat at the table across from Mike. "What are you doing here?" she asked, curious. "I thought you left us."

"Where am I gonna go?" he replied. "I have no home, and my shuttle is a mess."

Tisch couldn't believe her good fortune. "You're still welcome here. You saved my ass with that onloader."

Mike responded coyly, "It's an ass worth saving."

Tisch wasn't sure if she should be offended or flattered by his comment. She frowned and remarked, "I'm sure you can do better than that."

"I can. Let's start over and talk about what's bothering you, particularly with me."

Tisch went to the refrigerator and returned with two beers, one for each of them. They popped the caps on their bottles, and each took a swig. Mike waited patiently for her to speak.

"So, you and Wilmer were Special Forces," she started.

"We were, and so was Gemini."

Just hearing Gemini's name ruined Tisch's mood. "I'm sure the three of you had a lot of fun together," she sniped at him. "What happened?"

Recalling his heartbreak, Mike looked down humbly and explained, "We had fidelity issues, and I left her."

Tisch needed to know more. "And now you're interested in me," she remarked boldly. "How convenient."

Mike was saddened by her reaction to him. "That's not it," he replied somberly. I haven't been with anyone in a while. A broken heart takes a lot of healing, and, in my line of work, it'll get you killed."

Tisch suddenly realized there was more to Mike than she had thought. "Why did you stay with your mercenary career for so long if you were in such a vulnerable state?"

"Honestly, I wanted to die to forget the pain," he confessed.

"Well, you know I have a problem with Gemini, and having you on board just made it a lot worse," she reminded him. "Imagine if we ever got involved. There'd be hell to pay."

"That's part of the problem, Tisch," Mike said. "I have to be careful what people know about me, not just for my safety but for the safety of everyone I get close to."

Tisch understood what he meant but couldn't resist taking a shot. "I'm sure that includes what you reveal about Gemini," she mentioned smartly.

"Yeah," he admitted reluctantly. "Even Gemini."

"Then you two are over?"

"We are. Trust issues can't be fixed. Unfortunately, I still have to deal with her from time to time."

"Nothing worse than a woman scorned. Are you to blame why she..."

Mike slammed the table with his fist, interrupting her. "Do you really think I spend my time chasing girls' asses?"

"Just Gemini's ass," Tisch shot back. "Seems you went right back to her for a job when she called."

"Maybe you're upset because I'm not on your ass!" he shouted angrily.

Julian barged in and interrupted their conversation. Mike was disappointed that Tisch had assumed he was to blame for his divorce with Gemini.

"While you two are cajoling, we have pirates approaching in two cruisers."

"Pirates?" uttered Mike.

"Thieves," replied Tisch. "Empire will do anything to disrupt Gemini's business, which, unfortunately, I'm part of."

"Then it's time for a lesson," he suggested. They stood, staring at each other for a brief moment, and then left the galley. Julian was left alone, muttering, "Why me?"

Mike followed Tisch to the turrets. She knew he was eyeballing her ass and taunted him, "Like what you see?"

"Maybe," Mike quipped.

"Isn't that what got you into trouble in the first place?"

Mike grew irritated and countered, "Why do you assume it was my fault? You have no idea what happened."

"Oh, I know all right," she remarked cynically and climbed the ladder for the topside turret. "Stay on the bottom where you belong."

"Well, I'll make it simple for you," he shouted up the ladder.

"I'll stay away from you. You stay away from me."

"Fine," she shouted from her turret. "Now shut up and get down to your turret." Mike swore and climbed down the ladder into his turret.

Geezer, Wilmer, and Julian manned their stations on the bridge. Geezer glanced at the monitor and cut in. "All right, children. Two heavies coming from the port side. Get ready."

"I got it," replied Tisch. Mike said nothing.

The conversation from the turrets came across the intercom, making the crew nervous. Geezer turned to Wilmer and commented over Mike's silence, "I'm not feeling good about that."

"Me neither," Wilmer answered. "Mike's not going to fire."

Two well-armed cruisers approached the *Blue Eagle* at a high rate of speed. Geezer attempted to contact them several times but with no luck. Julian returned and took his position. "Anything I need to know before we get pummeled?"

"Nope," replied Wilmer. "Mike and Tisch have it under control."

Julian turned to them with a less than serious expression. "I don't think there's a lot of trust between them right now. The last argument was about asses—Tisch's and Gemini's."

"Excuse me, gentlemen," interrupted Geezer. "Focus!" The men became attentive.

The ship rocked violently as several pulses pounded the hull. Everyone's demeanor grew somber as they realized the severity of the situation. Geezer programmed the force field to the port side.

Cannon fire spouted from the topside turret and peppered one of the cruisers, steering it away. The second cruiser circled over the top and fired relentlessly at the freighter. The impact of several close blasts slammed Tisch against the already cracked side of the turret. "I need help, Geezer! Where's that shield?"

"I can only cover one side of the ship at a time," he replied frantically.

"Mike, how about you get in the game?" she challenged. Mike didn't respond.

Tisch realized what he was doing and grew more determined. "All right, jackass! I can do this without you."

Mike watched the attack unfold from the lower turret, refusing to operate his cannons. Tisch fired at the second cruiser, scoring several hits, but the cruisers were significantly more durable than the fighters and sustained minimal damage from the cannons.

Once the pirates realized the only turret operating was the topside one, they came from opposite directions and pounded the freighter with pulse blasts. One cruiser targeted Tisch's turret while the other repeatedly fired at the cargo bay hatch.

Mike sensed that the damage to the *Blue Eagle* was becoming significant and targeted one of the cruisers. The captains of the cruisers sensed that the *Blue Eagle* was easy pickings and made the mistake of approaching the hatch from the same direction. Their objective was to blow the cargo hatch, board, and pillage. Tisch's turret alone could do little to stop them.

"Damn it!" shouted Geezer. "Our shield is down to forty percent. Stop screwing around, you two!"

"I don't need his help," Tisch replied sarcastically.

"The turrets are going to shut done very soon, Tisch," warned Geezer. "You got a plan for this?"

"Yeah. We're going down fighting."

"Oh, no, we're not," Geezer grumbled. The ship lurched as he veered toward the two cruisers. "All right, Mike. It's your game. We're heading right at them."

"Thanks, Geezer," replied Mike. He carefully targeted the noses of both cruisers and fired two short bursts. The well-placed shots appeared to inflict little damage, but they disabled the firing systems for both cruisers. "That's how we do it in the real universe," he taunted. "Have at it, Tisch. They're sitting ducks."

Tisch screamed in rage over Mike's arrogance. On the bridge, Geezer and Wilmer laughed over the conversation and its insinuations.

"This is what I was afraid of," complained Julian. "Listen to them."

Tisch fired at the cruisers repeatedly until they turned away. "Follow them, Geezer!"

"Are we going after the cruisers?" Wilmer asked Geezer.

"No. We need to get to Galleon-IV. Tisch will thank me later."

"I hate you, Colby!" Tisch shouted over the intercom.

"No, you don't. You hate losing," he replied.

Geezer turned off the intercom. He peered at Wilmer, and the two men burst into tears, laughing so hard.

Mike climbed up the ladder to the deck and waited. Tisch climbed down from her turret. When she turned around, they were face-to-face. She tried to retain her anger, but then Mike placed his hands on her waist and his lips close to hers. "Try me," he whispered.

Tisch felt panic set in but held her ground. "I want to but..."

"Then stay right here with me until you're sure."

They stared into each other's eyes for several seconds, and then Mike kissed her. Tisch felt her knees weaken. She placed her arms around Mike and held him tightly. When they finished their kiss, Mike asked politely, "Was that okay?"

"It was...great," replied Tisch in a trembling voice. "I want more." They kissed again with incredible passion between them.

After their kiss ended, Tisch smiled coyly and remarked, "That's your view of the top. I even included a little dialogue for you. Enjoy it because it's as close as you'll ever get." She slapped his cheek gently in mocking fashion and walked away.

Mike balled his hands into fists and gritted his teeth. "She is such a bitch!" he muttered to himself.

CHAPTER VI
CONSEQUENCES

When Mike and Tisch arrived on the bridge, the three crewmen pretended not to notice them. Tisch approached Geezer and sat next to him. "Why did you go to Mike for direction without my authorization?" she questioned him irately.

Geezer turned his chair toward her and replied, "You were out of control. You were going to get us killed. How's that?"

"Don't ever go around me like that again, Geezer."

Geezer stood up and informed her, "I quit."

Tisch was speechless as he left the bridge. "Wait!" she pleaded, but he didn't return.

"Nice shooting, Mike," Wilmer complimented him. "You bailed us out."

"Well, somebody else doesn't think so," he remarked coldly, staring at Tisch.

"I hope you're both proud of your behavior because it cost us the atmospheric integrity of our cargo hold," Julian chided. "When the hatch blew out, we lost the man-lift and Mike's shuttle. Imagine that."

"What?" exclaimed Mike. "My shuttle's gone!"

"Nah, just kidding," taunted Julian. "Now who wants to get... how do you say... assed up?" he remarked sarcastically and left the bridge.

"You screwed up my ship!" Tisch shouted at Mike.

"How's that look from the top?" he replied cynically and left the bridge.

Tisch turned to Wilmer, waiting for his comment. Wilmer shrugged his shoulders and turned away. Mike sat alone in the galley, regretting that he had stayed on board the freighter. No matter how hard he tried, there was no pleasing Tisch.

Geezer entered and stood by him. "You look like you could use a friend."

Mike was surprised to see him. He gestured for Geezer to have a seat. Geezer took a beer from the refrigerator and sat across from him. The two tapped bottles in a toast as Geezer announced, "To your shooting and your strategies, my friend. I was impressed."

Each took a sip of beer and were silent. Finally, Mike looked up and confessed, "I never meant for things to get like this. I'm sorry, Geezer."

"Don't sweat it. Maybe this is what Tisch needs to get over her issues."

"So, what now?" Mike asked.

"When we get to Taurus, I'm leaving. I need a change of scenery."

"I guess I do too. Screw the shuttle."

Julian entered the galley and sat with them. "If the hull around the hatch is unrepairable, it could be the end of her," he commented.

"The ship or Tisch?" questioned Mike.

"Both."

Mike pondered their predicament and suggested, "Let's make our stop at Galleon-IV anyway? Then we can inspect the damage and decide what's best."

"We could," replied Geezer, "if we wanted to."

"It couldn't hurt," added Julian. The three men bumped fists.

Geezer returned to the bridge and took his seat. Tisch sat somberly in her captain's chair, fighting back tears. She was surprised to see Geezer back.

"Me and the boys decided we'd take what's left of the ship to Galleon-IV and finish the run."

"I appreciate that."

"Do you really?" Geezer asked sarcastically.

Tisch turned away from him, embarrassed by her loss of control of the situation. Wilmer massaged her shoulders from behind and suggested she take a break and get something to drink. Reluctantly, she left the bridge.

Geezer and Wilmer discussed the damages and contacted the dispatcher on Galleon-IV to schedule maintenance support. Julian and Mike arrived on the bridge and joined in the conversation. Geezer then contacted Gemini and informed her of the damages sustained in the attack. She promptly put the blame on Tisch's poor skills as a captain. To their surprise, she agreed to provide help in replacing the hatch and repairing any damage once they returned to Taurus.

When they arrived on Galleon-IV and inspected the ship, the men were pleased to see that the onloader wasn't damaged. They were able to transfer their cargo off, while taking on new cargo with no delay.

An engineer and two technicians studied the hull and determined that the damage wasn't severe enough to inhibit a full repair. The ship did, however, need a new hatch. A makeshift hatch from steel beams was installed to prevent the loss of any cargo or equipment during transport. While the cargo bay would still not have atmospheric integrity, it would be enough to get them back to Taurus. Only the outside temperature of space would impact the cargo.

Once they departed Galleon-IV, Tisch remained absent from the bridge. Geezer and Julian handled the *Blue Eagle* as it traveled at half speed to protect the cargo. Mike pitied Tisch, having no intention of taking over her ship. Wilmer suggested he speak with her and come to some sort of understanding about where they stood.

Tired of the topic, Julian pressed Mike to help him gain new employment. Mike's concern was that Tisch was losing her crew because of him. He left the bridge and sought out Tisch. Her quarters were empty, so he checked the other cabins.

When he reached the last one, he noticed the nameplate on the door. It read "Captain John Mallory." After knocking several times, Mike actuated the sliding door and entered. Tisch was curled up on the bed in tears. Pictures were strewn across the floor, and the bureau was bare. Several men's knickknacks littered the floor nearby.

"Leave me alone," she blurted.

Mike sat on the floor next to the bed. "Come on, Tisch. Let's talk."

Without making eye contact with him, she responded dejectedly, "You won. You got the ship, you got the crew, and you got my dream. What else is left - my soul?"

"I didn't want any of those," he replied. "I only wanted you. Was that so bad?"

Tisch summoned her courage and opened up to Mike. "I'm always saving someone's ass. Look at my crew. That's how I got them. They didn't volunteer."

"And you saved mine," Mike added. "I won't forget that."

Tisch explained, "I need someone to lean on, someone who will give me strength."

"I can be that person," replied Mike compassionately, "if you just let me." Tisch looked away from him. Mike became frustrated and demanded she explain further.

"I can't babysit you and Gemini," she responded.

"You're afraid, and you're using her as a scapegoat," Mike challenged her. "I told you, we're over. Gemini burned that bridge several times, and it can't be saved."

Tisch slapped the table with her hand. "Gemini has to pay for what she did to my father, and your involvement with her complicates everything."

Mike offered to help her solve the mystery of her father's death if she would stop blaming Gemini until she knew for sure who was responsible. Tisch blurted out angrily, "Gemini is baggage! She's your baggage, and until you lose that baggage, I can't be with you."

Mike became annoyed but remained diplomatic. "Somehow, I'll prove to you who is responsible, and I'll get you your freedom from Gemini. Once that's done, I'll be out of your life forever. In the meantime, you have a ship and a crew to run."

Tisch was surprised that Mike would still help her after her outburst. Mike summoned Wilmer to work on the shuttle with him. He was resigned to resuming his mercenary life.

Tisch returned to the bridge and apologized to the crew. She resumed her position as captain of the ship but said very little. She was humiliated over how she had let her emotions destroy everything she had. She never had this problem before until Mike came into her life. Why, she couldn't understand.

The journey back to Taurus was uneventful and quiet with Mike and Tisch avoiding each other. When the *Blue Eagle* docked on Taurus, everyone gathered to see the damage to the ship. Tisch was embarrassed that she had allowed her ship to suffer such significant damage.

Wilmer and Julian left the bridge, leaving her with Geezer for an awkward moment of silence. Geezer stood and took in the bridge area for what he expected to be the last time. Tisch knew she needed to speak with him before he left. With her head hung low in shame, she requested, "Before you leave, Geezer, I'd like to talk."

"There's nothing to say, Tisch. Thanks for the memories," he said somberly and walked to the hatch.

"Wait!" she called to him. "I screwed up. I know that. I'm sorry."

Geezer hesitated and turned around. "We could have died because of you."

"Yes, we could have. I can't change what happened. What I can change is that it will never happen again."

"What are you saying?" he inquired, hoping that she would admit her real fear - Mike.

"I'm asking you to stay. I'm asking you to give me another chance, please."

Geezer considered her request and countered, "Why do you think I should stay?"

Tisch placed her hands on his arms. "You got me this far. I couldn't have done it on my own. I hit a wall this time, and it took more than you to get me through it."

"And did you?" he asked.

"I've been humbled. I lost control of everything I care about in the heat of battle."

"And how about Mike? Have you sorted out your feelings?"

"Yes. No. I don't know," she answered, baffled by her thoughts.

"You're out of sync with reality. He's a good man, and he covered your ass."

Tisch turned and paced the floor. Geezer knew the real answer to her problem but said nothing more. She returned to him and pleaded, "Give me another chance, Geezer. I won't let you down." Geezer, against his better judgment, agreed to stay. Tisch kissed his cheek and left the bridge.

Mike, Julian, and Wilmer exited the *Blue Eagle* and crossed the dock. Three technicians approached and questioned them about the required repairs. Several forklifts approached the open cargo bay, and the loadmaster operated the onloader remotely by pendant to offload the cargo.

Gemini pushed her way through the crowd toward Mike. Julian spotted her immediately and warned, "Here she comes, Mike, horns and all."

Mike sighed. "I'll handle her."

Tisch exited the freighter and joined the men. Unaware that Gemini was approaching, she hooked her arm in Mike's and suggested they discuss their situation over a drink. Before he could respond, Gemini interceded. "Michael, I am so proud of you," she lied as she hooked Mike's other arm in hers. "I believe we need to discuss some monetary matters."

Mike immediately became suspicious of Gemini's motive. "Does this monetary matter have anything to do with a hundred thousand credits for a task performed?" he asked.

Gemini whispered in his ear, "Everything's on the table, and I mean everything."

Tisch took exception to Gemini's possessive nature and slid between them. "If you have something to say to any of my crew, which includes Mike, you can say it in front of me."

Gemini got right into Tisch's face and informed her, "Since you mention it, I'm fining you ten thousand credits for insubordination. You disobey my orders again, and you'll lose your ship." She glanced at the battered craft and then added sarcastically, "Or what's left of it."

Geezer left the ship and, sensing an altercation, hurried over to calm Tisch down.

"He called for help and we rescued him," Tisch reminded her. "It's that simple."

Gemini gave her a smug grin. "And I told you to stand down, which you didn't. It's that simple." She tugged Mike's arm and led him away.

Tisch's face turned red. She clenched her hands and was about to pursue them when Geezer and Wilmer grabbed her by both arms. They escorted her back toward the ship and reminded her of the consequences of crossing Gemini.

Gemini entered a code into the elevator security pad. Mike took note of the code instinctively from his military training and memorized it. She glanced at Mike and smiled seductively as the elevator took them up to the Executive Level at the top of the station.

Mike leaned against the side of the elevator with his arms folded. Gemini eyed him coyly and pulled herself close to him. She remarked, "I knew you'd handle those Scrat."

Mike pushed her back gently and chastised her. "I could have been killed. You gambled with my life."

Gemini was entertained by his anger. She touched his cheek affectionately and attempted to kiss him. The elevator doors opened and three security personnel waited for them to exit. Across the hall, a man in a suit and tie watched them suspiciously. Mike noticed but said nothing.

"Oops," kidded Gemini playfully. She hooked her arm in Mike's and led him toward her suite.

"Look, Gem, all I want is my money, and I'll be out of here," he informed her sternly. "I'm not in the mood for your games."

"Patience, Michael," she responded.

They entered the conference room and approached the wide, curved window with a view to the docks and lobby below. Mike stared down at the activity around the *Blue Eagle*. Gemini massaged his shoulders and hugged him from behind. Mike lifted her arms off him and moved away from her. "My money, Gem," he reiterated.

Gemini pointed to one of the chairs and gestured for him to sit. She poured two bourbons and brought them over. "I guess we'll get down to business," she relented. "That's what you want, right?" Mike studied the contents of the glass and waited for her to talk facts with him. "Come on, Mike," she urged. "Loosen up."

"My shuttle is destroyed. I almost died. The Scrat are hunting me. How's that for loose?" he blurted.

"Look, I need a partner, and I'd like it to be you," she explained. "I can't run this business by myself anymore."

Mike laughed and chugged his drink. "You've got to be kidding, Gem!" he scoffed. "You and I are poison together."

Gemini was insulted. "What do you want? Tell me, and I'll give it to you."

Mike grew frustrated with her. He repeated, "I want my money and then I'm leaving."

Gemini sipped from her drink and stared blankly at the wall. Mike knew she was stalling; she didn't have the money. The two stared at each other for a long moment before Gemini offered, "I'll get you a new shuttle."

"I don't want a new shuttle, Gem. I want my money."

"I need time to gather the rest of it," she responded, embarrassed. "I'm a little short this cycle."

Mike stood and paced around the room, pondering his next strategy. Gemini hoped he would bend and see things her way. He paused at the window and stared down at Tisch's damaged freighter. He knew this was the time to bargain.

"Since you can't pay me, here's what I want: The *Blue Eagle* and her crew go free to operate as independents. I get a new shuttle, and then we part ways."

Gemini slammed her glass on the table. "How dare you insult me like this!" she shouted. "I thought there was more between us than blackmail."

"There was. It was a man you screwed on our anniversary," he replied coldly.

"You self-righteous prick!" she shouted.

Mike had heard enough. He stood and went to the door. Gemini was frustrated but wouldn't quit. "Wait! Perhaps we can work something out," she suggested.

"You heard my terms, Gem. I'm not playing around."

Gemini knew something was up between Mike and Tisch when he requested that she release the *Blue Eagle* and its crew. As he opened the door to leave, she asked cynically, "This wouldn't have anything to do with that cold fish of a captain, would it?"

Mike shook his head at her in disbelief. "You are a real piece of work," he chided and closed the door behind him.

"You son of a bitch!" she shouted and threw the glass at the door, shattering it. Shards of glass scattered across the floor. Gemini paced back and forth in a rage. She seethed at the idea that Mike would prefer Tisch over her. After three drinks and some serious thought, she called Sara and requested she stop by for a favor.

When Sara arrived, Gemini was intoxicated. She sat in her personal area on her couch and cried. "What's wrong?" Sara asked in a concerned tone.

"I need you to do me a very big favor," she replied.

"Yeah, I got that already," replied Sara, suspicious. "What is it?"

"I need you to find Mike and seduce him."

Sara was stunned by her request. "Now that's a favor I can live with," she kidded. "What brought this on?"

"I have to know if he's screwing the *Blue Eagle's* captain."

Sara laughed hysterically. "Why do you care who he screws?"

"I don't," replied Gemini sarcastically. "Only when it comes to that woman."

"I see. And you want me to find out if he's faithful to her."

"Exactly. And if he is, make him unfaithful."

Sara now understood Gemini's motive. "That's cruel, Gem."

"You told me more than once that you'd do anything to get him in bed."

"But that was girl talk. Besides, what makes you think he'd go for that?"

Gemini stood and approached her older sister. She ran her fingers across the front of Sara's blouse, tracing the outline of her breasts. She then ran her hands down her hips and grabbed Sara's ass.

"This is as good as it gets, and you have it, big sister. No man can say no to this body."

Sara was amused by her sister's drunken behavior. Since she really did fantasize about bedding Mike, it was worth a try, just to see what would happen. "No promises, Gem, but I'll give it a go."

"Oh, and I need to know about a device he took from the Scrat ship."

"Why the concern?" Sara inquired, wondering what she knew of it.

"The Scrat have been relentless in pursuing them. It's got to be important."

"I'll see what I can do. Again, no promises."

Gemini hugged her affectionately. Sara felt uncomfortable with her sister's behavior. It was very unlike her, erratic.

Mike stepped off the elevator and entered the lobby. As he crossed the artificially landscaped reception area, he noticed Wilmer at the main desk. He was perched against the desk with his elbow supporting him as he spoke with a pretty, dark-skinned woman whose name tag read "Shannon."

Mike walked behind him and whispered, "Not bad for an old dude."

Wilmer turned around, surprised that Mike had found him. "Who you callin' old?" he asked playfully.

"I need to speak with you about something," Mike said. "I'll be at the pub when you're...," he paused and smiled at Shannon, "... finished." Mike left them to continue their banter and went to the bar. Wilmer rolled his eyes and returned to his conversation.

Tisch studied the upcoming schedules and was relieved that hers was modified to accommodate the repairs to the ship. She was pleased to see that they had received bonus pay for coming in ahead of schedule but then noticed in her account that she was docked ten thousand credits. As angry as she was over the penalty, she knew she deserved it. To calm her ire, she reminded herself that it was worth it to piss off Gemini in such a fashion.

Julian and Geezer arrived on the bridge and interrupted her thoughts. "The repairs are going well," announced Geezer.

"The new hatch will be in place by tomorrow," added Julian.

"The hull still needs a few days of work, but we should be out of here in three days."

"That's great news," Tisch replied gleefully. "How about we go out for drinks? I'm buying for atonement."

"Well, I can't argue with that," remarked Julian.

"It's settled, then," Tisch responded cheerfully. "Let's get out of here."

Mike sat at the bar and drank beer from a mug. He considered what Gemini's eventual response to his offer for Tisch's independence would be. More importantly, would it smooth over Tisch's emotional issues over Gemini that interfered with their relationship?

Sara entered the bar and noticed Mike immediately. She wore a short, black skirt, a white blouse with ruffles, and high heels. The top three buttons on her blouse were undone, leaving an adequate view of her cleavage. Sara had met Mike once, just before he married Gemini. She envied her sister for having a catch like Mike but was upset when she heard Gemini's infidelity ruined their marriage. *How could Gemini be so foolish?* she often asked herself. She approached Mike and posed seductively in front of him. "Well, hello there," she said coyly. "Anyone sitting here?"

Mike was sure he had met her before but couldn't recall where. "I believe you are," he answered, elated by her company. "Can I buy you a drink?"

"I'd like that," Sara replied and cozied up to him. Perhaps this would be easier than she had thought. Mike held up two fingers to the bartender. The man nodded and poured two beers. They exchanged introductions and tapped their glasses in a mock toast to friendship.

Wilmer approached the bar from the lobby corridor. Tisch, Julian, and Geezer approached from the dock in the opposite direction. They entered the bar together and sat at a table. None of them saw Mike at first.

After sipping from her beer, Sara leaned forward and kissed him passionately. Mike was pleasantly surprised. "Wow, I didn't see that coming," he remarked. Sara smiled and kissed him again. With one eye open, she saw Tisch at the table. She recalled a description of Tisch from Gemini's message and assumed that was her.

When the waitress stopped by the table, Wilmer requested four beers. The waitress nodded and left them. Tisch searched the bar until she saw Mike kissing Sara. Her face reddened. "What the hell?" she uttered. The men turned around and saw Mike with Sara.

"Uh-oh," muttered Wilmer. "Perhaps we should go."

"No, I'm okay with this," she lied. Julian, Geezer, and Wilmer rolled their eyes at each other.

The bartender set two beers in front of Mike and Sara. Sara sipped from hers and studied his face. He was everything she remembered, and so far, there was no indication that he was with Tisch. "Word on the street is you took something from the Scrat and might be looking to pawn it," she mentioned.

Mike leaned back in his seat, amused by her remark. "You can't believe everything you hear," he responded, growing suspicious of her interest in the module.

Sara looked past him at Tisch. It was obvious now that Tisch was watching them. "Is that your girlfriend?" she asked.

"And what girlfriend would that be?"

"That girlfriend," she replied and nodded toward Tisch.

Mike turned and saw Tisch with the men at the table. He turned back to Sara and explained, "I only work for her."

"Then she won't mind this," Sara whispered, then took Mike's head in her hands and kissed him hungrily. Mike didn't resist, but thoughts about Tisch and what they could be as far as a relationship went through his mind.

Tisch seethed over Mike's behavior. Wilmer, Geezer, and Julian were impressed. "Damn, he's good," quipped Julian. The waitress set four beers on the table and left. Tisch eagerly took one mug and chugged half of it.

"You pretend you aren't interested," Wilmer commented. "What's he supposed to think?" Tisch ignored them. She stared into her mug with rage growing inside her.

"I told you, grasshopper," Julian taunted her.

Tisch pounded the table with her fist. "Shut up, jackass!" she shouted at him.

Wilmer and Geezer sipped their beers and looked away, sensing trouble.

Mike noticed Tisch's reaction. He pushed back from Sara, disappointing her. "Look, Sara, I don't think this is a good idea."

Sara sensed that she was losing this battle. "It's simple, Mike. Are you with me or not?" Undecided, he drank from his mug. Sara grew impatient with him.

At the table, Tisch chugged her beer as she watched them angrily. "Come on, Tisch," Geezer urged her. "Let it go."

"I'm fine!" she blurted.

"No, you're not!" he responded angrily. The bar became silent again as everyone stared at them. Tisch settled down at the table, embarrassed by her behavior.

Sara conceded that Mike wouldn't be hers tonight. She sipped from her beer, frustrated, and then asked, "Why are you here with me when it's obvious you should be with her?"

"It's complicated," he replied, unsure of what to do about Tisch.

Sara slipped a business card into his pocket and whispered into his ear, "I know people who will pay well for that module. Call me." Mike stared at the card, surprised by her offer.

Tisch chugged another beer and slammed the mug on the table. She wouldn't look in Mike's direction, but she was visibly upset with him. Julian and Wilmer tried to coax her away from the table.

Mike noticed and became concerned by Tisch's reaction. "I'd better leave before this gets ugly. Thanks for understanding."

"Maybe next time," Sara relented. Mike kissed her cheek and circled around the back of the bar toward the door. Sara strutted into the ladies' room, confident he would call about the module.

Wilmer and Julian each took one of Tisch's arms. She resisted and pulled away. "Let's go," ordered Wilmer. "You'll thank us later."

Tisch shoved them away. Wilmer persisted and nudged her toward the door. "Come on, Tisch. You've had enough."

Tisch looked for Mike at the bar, but the seats were empty. "Son of a bitch!" she cried. "They're gone." Wilmer escorted her out of the bar while Julian stayed to finish his beer.

Gemini appeared from the back corner of the bar and greeted Sara when she exited the ladies' room. Julian watched curiously to see what transpired next between them. Gemini handed Sara an envelope. Sara peeked inside and smiled. It contained three gold bonds. The two women hugged and left the alehouse together. Julian was impressed over how well the women had played Mike and Tisch.

CHAPTER VII

BAIT

On the bridge of the *Blue Eagle*, Wilmer sat across from Tisch at his engineering station. Julian sat at the navigation console and ran diagnostic checks on the ship's systems. Tisch sat in the captain's chair and studied the proposed schedule on the monitor. Next to her was a note from Geezer. She read it, and a tear welled up in her eye. He had decided to leave after all. Tisch crumpled the note and tossed it at a trash can next to Julian's station.

"What's the status of the repairs?" Tisch asked Wilmer. "I'm anxious to get out of here."

Wilmer scrolled down several screens and stopped at one. He read the notes and replied, "They're pressure-testing the new hatch as we speak. They should be finished in a few hours."

"Where's your boy toy?" taunted Julian.

Tisch turned toward Julian, red-faced. "If I come over there, I'll carve that bald head of yours like a pumpkin," she warned in a low-pitched voice.

Julian frowned and turned his attention back to his work station. Wilmer got up and walked toward the hatch. Tisch inquired without looking, "Where are you going, Wilmer?"

"Back to the bar," he replied somberly. "There's something I have to take care of."

Tisch resumed her task and thought nothing more of it.

Mike sat at the bar with a mixed drink in hand. Next to his glass were three empty shot glasses. Wilmer entered and took a seat by him. "Mind if I join you?"

"Not at all," replied Mike. He ordered a beer and a shot for Wilmer.

To their surprise, Julian entered. He approached them and inquired, "Would you have room for one more?"

"It's a public place," replied Mike somberly. "Have a seat."

Julian pointed to his beer and held up one finger to the bartender. Mike divulged his offer to Gemini for their freedom and revealed that he expected her to concede before they left the station. The men were excited by the news.

"You know Gemini pulled one over on you," Julian quipped.

Mike looked up at him, bewildered by his remark. "I mean the woman Gemini paid to put on that little exhibition in front of Tisch," Julian continued.

"I was set up?" exclaimed Mike in total surprise.

"You sure were," Julian affirmed. Wilmer burst into laughter.

"That bitch!" Mike blurted. He glanced at the card from his pocket, and then it hit him. "That was Gemini's damn sister!"

Wilmer's eyes widened with surprise. "Now I remember her. She was at your wedding!"

"You mean 'funeral,'" grumbled Mike.

Tisch entered the bar and ordered a beer. When the bartender served her, she approached the men. "I thought I'd find you drunks here," she remarked arrogantly. "The hatch passed. We're leaving in an hour."

"Mike has something to tell you," Wilmer commented, hoping to break the tension.

"Oh, the lapdog wants to say something," she responded sarcastically, staring him down. Julian became annoyed with her attitude and left them.

"Come on, Tisch," pleaded Mike. "You're making this into something it's not."

"Then how about this?" she shouted and threw her beer in his face. She stormed out of the bar, leaving Mike seething mad. Wilmer tried to conceal his laughter but couldn't. The bartender tossed Mike a towel and left them with a broad grin on his face. Antics like this were rare on the station.

Mike dried himself off and looked down dejectedly. Wilmer urged him to let it go. "There are other women out there," he reminded Mike.

Mike shouted at him, "Like who - Gemini?"

"That's not what I meant," Wilmer replied apologetically. He got up and patted Mike on the shoulder. "I'll see you on board the ship."

Mike ordered another drink. The bartender returned and spoke for several minutes with him about strangers asking a lot of questions regarding Captain Mallory's new crewman - him. Mike was interested and pressed for more details. He learned that the word was out about a valuable piece of equipment that belonged to Empire Shipping, and that they were anxious to get it back. Mike found it odd that the story seemed to pertain to him, but what he had taken belonged to the Scrat, not Empire. Then he considered that maybe the Scrat were working with Empire and that the module was built by Empire after all. Mike tipped the bartender for the information and left the bar.

As he approached the dock, the announcement was made that the *Blue Eagle* was departing. He rushed to the ship's bay, but it was too late. The hatch sealed, restricting his access. The magnetic mooring had released, and the berth opened to space. Mike stood dejectedly with his hands on his hips. This wasn't how it was supposed to go.

Tisch stood at the center of the bridge, staring at the central monitor on the wall. The bay gates fully opened, and the *Blue Eagle* departed. Wilmer stood and approached Tisch. "You're making a mistake," he warned her.

"Shut up and take the controls. You helped drive Geezer out of here, now you can do his job."

"But, Tisch, Mike..."

"Mention his name again," she interrupted, "and I'll throw you off this ship next."

Tisch then turned to Julian, who claimed the fifth, saying nothing. Wilmer shook his head in disbelief that she could be so bullheaded.

Gemini sat in her chair at the end of the conference room table with a drink in her hand. Captain Tieg entered and informed her that the *Blue Eagle* had departed the station without Mike. Pleased by the news, she finished her drink and held the glass out for Tieg to refill. As always, he dutifully obeyed her wishes. "I expect Colby will be here any time," she announced. "When he arrives, please leave us to discuss some things."

Captain Tieg lowered his head and walked to the door. Gemini suddenly had an idea and called him back. "Have two of your men on standby outside the door," she instructed. "Colby is to be arrested when he leaves." Tieg was surprised by her order, but he affirmed her instructions and left the suite.

Mike exited the elevator and approached Gemini's office. He was pleased with himself for remembering the code to access the Executive Level. Captain Tieg passed him and gave him a suspicious glance. Mike disregarded it as a sign of general disrespect for him, emanating from Gemini. When he reached her suite, he hesitated and wondered if he should just leave the station and pursue his mercenary opportunities on a leased shuttle.

Before he could decide, the door slid open. "Come in, Michael," Gemini called to him.

Mike was wary of the fact that she had expected him. He entered and paused as the door closed behind him. With her perfora in one hand and her glass in the other, Gemini offered, "Would you like a drink? I have some of that fine rum that you like so much."

Mike responded despondently, "Sure, why not?"

Gemini made him a drink and pointed to one of the chairs. He sat and eyed her as she returned to the table. She was always so seductive and dressed the part well. While looking slutty, she was anything but - except for that one time. If Mike hadn't walked in on her, he might have eventually forgiven her. The image of her with the other man, an older man at that, haunted him.

"So, what's Sara got to do with all this?" he inquired stoically.

Gemini feigned surprise. "Why would you bring Sara into this?"

Mike revealed that he knew he had been set up at the pub and pressed to know what Sara's role was for Gemini. She was bored with the topic of Sara, but did explain that she was merely a consultant with contacts for the industry. Mike assumed that Sara was more than that; maybe even Gemini had no idea who she really worked for.

"Enough about Sara," Gemini said. "Now let's discuss us."

Gemini leaned forward on the table, displaying a bird's-eye view of her cleavage. "There was a time when you found me irresistible," she reminded him and blew smoke at his face. "Don't you miss that?" She turned off the perfora and set it down on the table.

Mike hated to admit that he did. He swatted the smoke away and sipped from his glass. In a frozen stare, he couldn't take his eyes off of hers. They burned into his soul like hot irons.

"Now what was it you wanted to talk about?" she inquired and walked around the table toward him. Mike hesitated as he briefly lost his train of thought. Regaining his composure, he answered, "The money you owe me for delivering your terms to the Scrat."

Gemini leaned over him and placed her hands around his neck, her lips almost touching his. Mike's knees weakened; he felt defenseless against her seductive allure. "Here's what you need to know," she announced defiantly. "That man I slept with was Tisch's father."

Mike was horrified. Gemini dropped down in the chair next to him. She could hardly contain her joy, watching him suffer. "It was the only time I ever cheated, but, what the hell. You might as well know who it was."

"Did you kill him?" Mike asked.

Gemini laughed at how naïve he could be. "Of course not, you fool!" she replied giddily. "He was my meal ticket."

Mike was crushed. Gemini then explained, "I really did... I mean do love you, sweetheart. While you were gone, I became depressed and fell into an addiction to some powerful drugs. I was a mess."

"I had no idea," Mike responded compassionately.

Gemini stood and walked around the table, recalling the past. "John helped get me clean and brought me in as his partner. His company had expanded so much, and Tisch wasn't ready."

Things began to make sense now to Mike. He finished his drink and stared blankly at the table. Gemini so savored the moment, watching his heartbreak. "When John was killed, I continued building his shipping company. It wasn't easy, and I learned to be a cold-hearted tyrant."

"I'm sure that wasn't hard," chided Mike.

Gemini approached him and stared him down. "It's different for a woman, but you wouldn't know about that, would you?"

Mike stormed to the door. Gemini laughed again as he departed her suite. She felt some vindication knowing that she had just crushed the life out of him. When Mike left the suite, Captain Tieg's men immediately arrested him and took him down to Level D, where prisoners were kept in holding cells until their fates were determined.

Mike was stunned, not understanding what her latest motive was for the incarceration. Gemini took two more of her pills and chased them down with bourbon. A devious smile crossed her face. Captain Tieg returned, patiently awaiting her next order. Gemini pondered for several minutes how she could do more to negatively impact Mike's life.

"Captain Tieg, contact General Asher for me, will you?" she requested.

Tieg was perplexed as to why she'd want to speak with the Scrat leader. "Yes, ma'am," he replied and left the suite.

A short while later, Tieg returned to Gemini's suite and announced that General Asher was waiting to speak with her. Gemini grinned, feeling she had the advantage at this time and would exercise her opportunity to leverage the Scrat into a deal. She activated her communication set, and then General Asher's alien face appeared on the wall monitor.

Asher announced abruptly, "I was about to send you a message that we will destroy your station first. Consider yourself honored."

Tieg cringed, fearing Gemini was playing a dangerous game. She was good but also arrogant, and he feared she bet too much on Colby's success. Gemini maintained her poise and responded, "Easy, big boy. You want Mike Colby and the module. Well, I'm going to tell you exactly how to get them both."

"I'm listening," he replied in a gruff voice.

"First, I want your assurance that you'll support me against my rivals."

"When I have my module, then we'll talk," he countered. "Now stop wasting my time."

Foolishly assuming that he would agree to help her, she revealed, "One of my ships, the *Blue Eagle*, is on its way to Alpha-5 for a delivery. I will arrange for them to allow your soldiers to board for a weapons inspection."

"I'm growing tired of your games, Gemini," he remarked.

Gemini forced a smile and sipped from her drink. Asher grew irritated with her nonchalance. She continued, "Take the captain of the ship hostage. I will inform Colby that you want your property for her life. That's the only way he'll give it up."

Asher considered her offer and then responded, "If this is a trick, I will personally deal with you."

Gemini smiled and held up her glass to him in a mock toast. "Have a great day, General." She terminated the transmission.

"Are you sure this is a good idea, ma'am?" Tieg inquired.

"Oh, it's not a good idea, Captain. It's a great idea."

"But how?" Tieg asked, fearing her overconfidence in the gamble.

"When I win over Asher's trust, the Scrat will do my bidding," she explained. "Then I will put an end to my rivals and their threats!" Gemini laughed hysterically.

Tieg knew she was betting on a lot of variables and was concerned that she had overstepped her bounds with this latest ruse.

The *Blue Eagle* reached the halfway point of their uneventful journey to Alpha-5. Wilmer and Julian barely spoke to Tisch, and she had little to say to them. Julian eyed Tisch as she sat in misery at the controls.

Wilmer finally broke the silence and asked, "Can we talk like civilized people?"

Tisch peered at him suspiciously, knowing this had something to do with Mike. "Maybe," she replied. Julian listened eagerly, hoping for a thaw in the tension. Wilmer took a deep breath and summoned his courage to start the discussion. "Mike arranged for Gemini to grant you and the *Blue Eagle* independence," he announced.

"Oh, stop it, Wilmer. I'm not buying your 'Mike was looking out for me' bullshit," she responded sarcastically.

Julian shook his head at her, signaling that she was wrong. Tisch looked away, fearing she had made another mistake with Mike. Julian looked to Wilmer, prodding him to continue.

"Why did you fall for Mike in the first place?" Wilmer questioned her.

Tisch recalled the moment when she had first laid eyes on Mike in the cargo bay. There was something about him that had attracted her. She noticed Julian's keen interest in her response as well but disregarded the intrusion. "He was interested in me - in my life," she explained, "and what mattered to me. Only my father ever cared enough to ask me that."

"That's interesting," Julian remarked. Tisch waited for a sarcastic comment from him, but none came.

She continued, "I told him how I want revenge on Gemini and that I want my own ship to operate as an independent."

"Gemini is his ex-wife," Wilmer informed her. "He has to deal with her on certain things."

Tisch didn't respond. She had suspected they had some sort of relationship but never considered that they were once married. As much as she despised Gemini, she realized that Wilmer was right.

Wilmer continued, "Since she cheated on him and broke his heart, he's been alone. Sound familiar?" Tisch pulled up a chair next to Wilmer, eager to hear more.

Julian stood behind her, now with piqued curiosity as well. "How do you know so much about this, Wilmer?" he inquired.

"Years back, we were members of the Space Federation's Special Forces," he began. "I was his extractor, his 'eye in the sky' on his missions around the galaxy. That mission, I joined him on the ground for the first time." Tisch leaned forward with her hands on her knees. She was anxious to know where this was going. "We got back early for their two-year anniversary," Wilmer continued. "Mike and I walked in and found her in the act with another guy. Get the picture?"

Now Tisch and Julian both understood Mike's odd relationship with Gemini. Tisch lowered her head sadly as she now realized Mike wasn't the guilty party for infidelity. Julian looked sympathetically at her, knowing she had gone too far this time. Wilmer placed a hand on her shoulder and then turned his attention back to his station. He changed the sensors from short-range to long-range. Images appeared on the monitor from the sensor. "Tisch, you might want to see this," he suggested.

Tisch approached and looked over his shoulder. Julian joined them, anxious to see what pending danger they would encounter. A Scrat assault craft and three fighters approached at a high rate of speed.

"We're no match for them!" uttered Julian. "We need a plan fast."

"Damn, I wish Mike were here," grumbled Wilmer. Tisch slapped him in the back of the head. She felt she deserved more respect than that for her skills.

"What do we do?" asked Julian. "We have no place to go."

"I'll man the cannons," replied Tisch. "Full speed ahead to Alpha-5."

"We're at full speed," Wilmer reminded her sarcastically. "They'll be on us in minutes."

"Just do your job," Tisch ordered and left the bridge.

Tisch informed Wilmer over the intercom that she was ready to fire and gave him instructions for the battle. Wilmer contacted Gemini via transmitter and waited. Gemini responded and ordered them to stand down for a weapons inspection.

"I don't like this one bit," complained Julian.

Wilmer brought up the assault craft's specs on the database and frowned. "Oh, man," he muttered to himself after looking at their weaponry. "We can't outlast them." He rubbed his eyes with a pained expression. "Scrat assault craft are more heavily armed compared to pirate cruisers."

Tisch settled into the turret and donned the helmet. "I'm ready to fire, Wilmer," she announced confidently. "Let's see what they've got."

Julian covered his face in his hands. He knew this was trouble. Wilmer watched the monitor and bit his lip nervously. "Don't bother, Tisch," Wilmer responded. "Gemini says to let them board for a weapons inspection."

"Screw that!" she shouted angrily.

"They're a class one. They have some heavy firepower." Wilmer leaned back in his chair and closed his eyes. "It's gonna be a bad day," he mumbled to himself.

Tisch removed her helmet and set it down on the firing console. She was concerned about allowing Scrat on her ship, but considered the consequences if they fled.

Julian greeted ten Scrat soldiers in the cargo bay. He trembled over their appearance as he had never seen a real Scrat before. Carnak aimed his pistol at Julian's head and instructed him, "Turn the captain over to us, and you will be spared."

"But I thought this was a weapons inspection?" Julian responded as he realized Gemini had set them up.

Carnak grabbed Julian's chin and pressed his pulse pistol into his mouth. Julian held his hands up in surrender. Carnak lowered his pistol and asked, "Where's Colby?" When Julian hesitated, Carnak pressed the pistol against his cheek.

"He's on Taurus with Gemini," he reluctantly answered.

When Carnak shoved him forward, Julian led them from the bay. The Scrat soldiers followed him down the corridor with pulse rifles pointed ahead.

Tisch emerged from the stairwell into the corridor and was surprised by the entourage. "What the hell is going on here?" she demanded to know.

Julian stepped aside and retreated away from the Scrat. "They requested your presence," he replied sheepishly. "I'll leave you to speak with them." He hurried past her and ducked into the stairwell.

Tisch reached for her pulse pistol, but the Scrat immediately targeted her head with their rifles. Two Scrat soldiers grabbed her by the arms while another disarmed her. When she resisted, one of the soldiers punched her in the back of the head, knocking her out.

Julian peered around the corner from the stairwell. He watched sadly as the soldiers dragged Tisch away. They boarded their shuttle in the cargo bay and departed the ship. Julian was torn over helping her and risking death versus fleeing for help. He leaned face-first against the wall in shame.

CHAPTER VIII

FRIENDS AND FOES

Tapping his feet nervously under the console, Wilmer anxiously watched the monitor. He was relieved to see the Scrat shuttle leave without incident. Julian slinked onto the bridge and stood in the hatchway. Wilmer was aware of him and remarked, "I can't believe they left without a fight."

"It might be worse than that," Julian muttered under his breath.

Wilmer recognized the guilt in Julian's expression. His face became taut, and he stood slowly, poised to attack Julian. "What did you do?"

"They didn't come for an inspection," Julian whimpered. "They came for Tisch."

Wilmer stalked him with clenched fists. "Where is Tisch now?" he questioned, his temper flaring.

"They took her," he mumbled, ashamed that he hadn't done more to protect her.

"You no-good Judas!" Wilmer shouted. He lunged at Julian and choked him. Julian struggled to resist as Wilmer bounced him off the wall several times until he finally broke free and backed away.

"We have to get Mike," he cried out. "He's the only one who'll know how to get her back." Wilmer's eyes bulged with rage. He panted heavily as he refrained from another assault on Julian. Tears streamed down Julian's cheeks.

"I had no choice, Wilmer," he explained, exasperated. "They would have killed me!" Julian looked down, humiliated by his cowardice.

Wilmer charged at him and poked his finger in Julian's face. "This isn't over between us."

Feeling worthless, Julian pleaded, "I'll do anything to get her back. I swear!"

"Before this is over, you'll have that opportunity. I'll see to it," Wilmer vowed. "Now get away from me." Julian sat down at his station, saddened by Tisch's abduction.

Wilmer stared ahead, seething with rage. He returned to the main console and navigated the ship. "What are we going to do?" Julian asked humbly. "Do you have a plan?"

"We're going back to Taurus to get Mike and Geezer," he replied angrily. "Now do your friggin' job for a change!"

They changed course and headed for Taurus. Julian sent a message discreetly to a contact at Empire Shipping and informed them that Tisch was selling the module back to the Scrat. He also informed them that Mike was on Taurus and would know where the module was while Tisch negotiated the deal. He lowered his head in his hands and, unaware of the value of the module, hoped that he had done the right thing.

For four days, Mike sat dejectedly, waiting for an opportunity to escape. He was given no food, and the only drink was the water from the sink. His cell was a square room with only a steel door and a six-inch window for access. Inside the cell was a commode, a sink, and cot. He lay on the cot, pondering what to do about his dilemma.

Betrayed by two women now, he wondered if Sara was an option for an escape. At least she confessed to him that she was interested in the module.

He recalled the wedding and how beautiful both Gemini and Sara looked. He often wondered if he had picked the wrong sister.

The cell door clanked and opened. Mike sat up, wondering who was coming to see him. Two agents entered the cell, dressed in suits with pulse pistols drawn. Mike was unimpressed with them and ignored their presence.

"Get up!" shouted the older of the agents.

"Say please," Mike replied mockingly.

The second agent grabbed him by the shirt and jerked him to his feet. He punched Mike in the stomach, laughing as Mike doubled over in pain. The older agent pinned Mike's arms behind his back while the younger one punched him over and over. They dropped him on the ground and kicked him repeatedly. Mike got up slowly and staggered to the sink. He coughed and spat blood.

"Where is the teleporter module?" the older agent demanded to know.

"Kiss my ass," Mike answered stubbornly. The agents pounded his back and pummeled him to the ground.

The younger agent informed him, "We know your captain is meeting with the Scrat. Is she selling the module back to them?"

Mike grimaced. "Why would she do that?" he responded weakly as he slowly got to his feet. "And why do you care?"

The agent punched him in the gut again. "We know she wants control of Sysco," he remarked smugly. "That's not going to happen."

Mike was amused by their cluelessness. "She couldn't care less about Sysco, jackass."

The agent kneed him in the gut from the side. Mike gagged and spat more blood into the sink. Both agents mocked him. The older agent poked his finger in Mike's face and boasted, "We killed one captain from the *Blue Eagle*. I'm sure we can kill another, if you don't help us."

Mike gritted his teeth, having learned the truth about Tisch's father's death. He grabbed the water spigot with his right hand and broke it off the sink. The agents were now concerned. "Put that down," ordered the older agent.

"Make me," dared Mike.

They reached for his arms, but Mike stepped to his left and punched the younger agent in the forehead with the spigot in his right hand. The agent was dazed and stumbled backward before falling down against the wall. He had a bloody hole in his forehead and no will to move.

The older agent leaped on Mike's back and brought him down to his knees with a sleeper hold. Mike reached back and grabbed the agent's legs behind the knees. With great effort, he stood, lifting the agent with him. The agent tightened his hold until Mike's vision grew vague. He slowly succumbed to the pressure from the hold and dropped the spigot to the floor.

In an act of desperation, Mike dropped to one knee in front of the commode and threw the agent over his shoulder. The agent hit the wall upside down and dropped headfirst into the commode. As Mike backed away, the agent fell sideways, breaking the commode off at the base.

Mike looked disgustedly at them as water seeped across the floor and soaked their clothes. The agent pushed the commode aside and got to his feet. He wobbled slightly and appeared dazed. Mike was weakened from the hold and struggled to remain on his feet, as well. The two feebly traded punches before collapsing on the floor, exhausted from the battle.

As soon as the *Blue Eagle* was docked, Wilmer exited and approached Shannon, the dispatcher at the transport counter. "Good morning, Wilmer," she greeted him callously. "Can I help you?"

"I certainly hope so. We met before, if you remember?" He showed his identification tag, while ogling her. "I need to find Mike Colby. Can you check his location?"

"You never called, jerk," Shannon complained as she searched her database. After a brief delay, Shannon looked up, wide-eyed. "Mike Colby is in prison cell five on level D," she informed him. "There's no charge listed."

Wilmer backed away from the counter, mortified. "There must be some mistake!"

Shannon accessed her database again and watched the screen. Wilmer waited uneasily, watching for anyone who might recognize him. Shannon looked up and explained, "He was incarcerated four days ago by Gemini herself."

"Thanks, Shannon. I owe you one."

Shannon scribbled her contact number on a card and handed it to him. "Don't forget this time." Embarrassed, Wilmer accepted it gratefully and turned to walk away. Shannon gestured for him to wait.

"Level D is minimum security, in case you have something in mind for your friend," she told him. "Please, Wilmer, we never had this conversation."

"Of course, Honey," he responded. After pacing like a rabid animal for a few moments, he asked Shannon to locate Geezer McDavid and have him meet them in the lobby. Shannon promptly paged Geezer to report to her station. Wilmer gestured in appreciation with a wave of his hand and stormed back to the ship.

Julian exited the ship and cringed when Wilmer grabbed him by the arm and pulled him along. They crossed the lobby and entered an emergency stairwell. An alarm rang as soon as Wilmer opened the door. He reached up to the top of the doorjamb and ripped two wires out of the alarm switch. When he twisted them together, the alarm ceased. They hurried down four flights of stairs.

Mike and the older agent stood and prepared for another round of punches. "How did you know I was here?" Mike asked before they engaged in fisticuffs. "Did Gemini arrange this?"

The agent laughed at him and replied, "One of your own dimed you out."

Mike was shocked that someone he knew would do that to him. Sensing his distraction, the agent rushed at him and rammed him into the wall. Mike grabbed him in a headlock and bulldogged him to the floor. He crawled to the broken commode and broke off the horseshoeshaped toilet seat. The agent looked bewildered by Mike's actions. "You're kidding?" he remarked cynically. "Really?"

Mike glanced at the toilet seat, uncertain at first, but then had an idea. He charged and rammed his shoulder into the agent's gut. They collided against the door, slamming it closed. Now they were both locked inside. Mike smashed the agent's head against the wall, hooked the toilet seat between his legs, and then dropped him to the floor in a sitting position. The seat smashed against the agent's testicles, leaving him gasping and incapacitated. He collapsed to the wet floor in a prone position.

Mike removed the pulse pistol from the younger agent's belt and stepped back to the dry portion of the floor. When he discharged the weapon into the water, both agents shuddered as the water glowed with electricity flowing through it. Their eyes rolled back in their heads.

Drained and badly beaten, Mike dropped the pistol on the floor. He tried the cell door, but it wouldn't open. Frustrated, he smashed the overhead lights. With the room dark, Mike sat behind the door in waiting. Sooner or later, someone would come.

Wilmer and Julian paused in the stairwell at the door to Level D. In the corridor was a counter manned by the floor superintendent. His head was down on the desk as if asleep. Wilmer again tore out the wires from the alarm switch on the door. The alarm rang again briefly until he twisted the wires together, just like the previous alarm. Wilmer knew someone would come to investigate the alarms, as brief as they were.

The two men cautiously emerged from the stairwell. When they approached the superintendent, they became suspicious of the officer's prone position. Julian lifted the man's head and saw a cauterized hole from a pulse pistol in his forehead. He and Wilmer stared at each other briefly, knowing this was trouble, and then hurried down the corridor to cell five. They peered through the window, uncertain of what to do next.

"No one's in there," commented Julian. "It's dark."

Wilmer opened the door and entered. The corridor light shone on the agents' bodies. Suddenly, the door slammed. Wilmer fell sideways, while Julian tumbled backward into the corridor. Mike grabbed Wilmer in a headlock and placed the pistol against the side of his head.

"It's me," cried Wilmer. "It's Wilmer!"

Julian opened the door, and the light shone on the two again. Mike lowered the pistol and fell to his knees. Wilmer rubbed his neck gingerly.

"What took you so long?" Mike responded weakly.

Wilmer and Julian groaned at Mike and then lifted him to his feet. Struggling to walk as he clutched at his ribs, Wilmer and Julian helped him out of the cell. They paused by the stairwell to check for security personnel, but saw none so far. Mike noticed the dead superintendent and remarked, "Was that necessary?"

"That's gratitude," complained Julian.

"Just sayin'," he remarked smartly.

"It wasn't us," Julian assured him.

Wilmer then informed Mike, "I have some bad news."

"What happened now?" Mike asked in a terse tone.

"The Scrat have Tisch."

Mike was horrified and pushed him away. "How did that happen?" he shouted and fell to his knees, still in pain.

"Gemini arranged for the Scrat to board our ship for an inspection just to get to her," Julian explained.

Wilmer helped Mike back to his feet. Now he was really upset. Wilmer and Julian peered at each other, waiting for Mike to explode. And then it came. "How could you let that happen?" he uttered. "She's your captain!"

Wilmer glanced at Julian, who looked shamefully at the ground. "I should have fought for her, but I didn't," he confessed. "I hid like a coward."

"We should have known it was a trap," added Wilmer.

"All right. This is war!" Mike exclaimed.

"Then let's go," Wilmer urged and led them into the stairwell.

As they ascended the stairs, two security guards entered the stairwell at Level E behind them. "Don't move or we'll shoot," shouted one guard. Wilmer, Mike, and Julian froze.

The security guards took a defensive position and kept their weapons trained on the men. Julian approached the two guards with his hands extended innocently. The guards ascended the stairs toward him, ready to shoot. "Please, good sirs. We need your help," he urged them.

"Like hell you do," shouted one guard. "Put your hands up."

Two more guards entered from above them at the main floor, Level A. "Hands up," shouted one of them. Geezer crept into the stairwell at Level A behind the guards and shoved them down the steps.

Julian dove headfirst into the two guards at the lower landing. Mike and Wilmer grabbed the injured guards' weapons and, after a brief scuffle, shot the two of them. One guard from above grabbed Julian and slammed him against the wall. Julian dropped to his knees as if injured. The guard pressed the barrel of his gun against Julian's head and warned the others to stand down. Julian grabbed the barrel of the gun and the guard by his testicles. He shot and wounded the second guard while lifting the first over his shoulder. The guard struggled to get free, but Julian heaved him down the stairs. Julian wiped his hands as if he had just put out the trash.

"Damn, Julian!" Mike exclaimed, impressed by his bravado.

Wilmer remarked with surprise, "I didn't know you could fight."

"You never asked," he answered humbly.

Geezer waited for them at the door for Level A, the main floor. Grateful for his help with the guards, the men hugged Geezer and welcomed him back. "How did you know where to find us?" Mike asked curiously.

"Shannon told me. She also said you might need some help."

Wilmer beamed proudly at Mike. "You see, Mike, unlike yours, my women are actually helpful."

"He's got a point, Mike," Geezer pointed out. Mike sighed, realizing they were right.

Wilmer peered out the door. There were no more security personnel in sight. The four of them emerged from the stairwell and moved quickly through the crowd. As they passed the dispatch desk, Shannon saw them. "Call me, Wilmer!" she shouted excitedly.

Wilmer pointed to her and then to himself. "You and me, babe. Lunch when this is over."

Shannon gave him two thumbs up. As the men continued through the crowd, Mike whispered to Wilmer, "Like I said before, that was real smooth."

Wilmer was annoyed by the ribbing. "And like I said before; at least she's helpful."

Julian rolled his eyes at them and pushed them forward. Mike struggled to walk without support. They tried to move inconspicuously as six security personnel stormed past them to the stairwell. "Keep moving," urged Geezer.

On board the *Blue Eagle*, the maintenance shop was crowded with tools, workbenches, and broken equipment. One bench had the computer from Mike's shuttle, a magnetic coil, and an interface cable connected to a box on the wall.

Mike, Julian, and Wilmer entered the shop. Mike wore no shirt, and his ribs were taped. He labored when he walked, still in constant pain from the earlier attack. Wilmer powered up the computer while Mike and Julian watched eagerly. He retrieved the module from a box on the workbench.

Mike contemplated aloud, "The men who attacked me in the cell..." He then hesitated as he recalled the incident.

"What about them?" asked Wilmer.

"They claimed that they already killed one captain from the *Blue Eagle*."

"You think they killed Tisch's father?" asked Julian.

"I know they did." Mike explained how they suspected Tisch was selling the module back to the Scrat. He surmised how the module appeared to belong to Empire and that they wanted it back.

"But how did the Scrat get it?" asked Julian.

Mike pointed to the module in front of Wilmer and replied, "I think the answer is in that module."

Wilmer sat across from Mike and held up the module. "This little baby is very special."

"Let me guess, the Scrat can't go home without it," quipped Mike. "And their buddies can't come here."

Wilmer set the blue module close to the coil. "Magnetism is what makes it so unique."

Baffled, Mike and Julian leaned closer to view the test. Wilmer activated the program on Mike's computer and waited. A soft, red light emitted from the module in all directions. An image of the room appeared on the screen. Mike and Julian watched eagerly, wondering what would happen next. Wilmer then touched the screen in two places, locking on to Julian's figure and then the corner of the room. Julian vanished and then appeared in the corner. He trembled, not understanding what had just happened to him.

Mike stared in utter amazement at him. "You are fantastic, man!" he exclaimed. "I love you for this!"

Wilmer high-fived him and glanced over at Julian, who was still petrified. "You can come back to the table any time now," Wilmer teased.

"Friggin' assholes!" Julian replied bitterly. "How about I try that on you?"

"Easy, Julian," urged Mike. "You were never in any danger." Julian warily approached the table and sat down, wondering if this was payback for Tisch's abduction.

Wilmer explained how the module could detect and manipulate subatomic pockets of matter anywhere to teleport from one area to another, like building a bridge of energy through a pocket of least resistance. He assumed that the Scrat must have provided an enormous amount of power and magnetism for the device to lock on to a destination point so far away using the ship's own long-range sensors. He also surmised that by destroying the magnetic source, it would severely limit or even eliminate the ability to transport with the module.

Mike contemplated how they might use it to rescue Tisch without revealing that they actually have it. Wilmer continued to explore the programming generated by the module and postulated more theories. They discussed the possibility of transporting onto the Scrat ship and then back without detection. Wilmer wanted more testing before confirming the module's capability. Anxious to see the module that so many people wanted their hands on, Julian leaned closer to Wilmer. Mike pushed him back, giving Wilmer some space.

"We're going to need at least a fifty-pound magnetic coil to make this thing work on a larger scale," explained Wilmer. "I'll have to see what's available on the ship that's compatible."

Mike put his arm around Julian's shoulder. "Me and my procurement specialist will find one. Leave it to us." Julian looked confused, wondering where they'd get a coil that big. Mike then instructed Wilmer, "I need you to remove the inside of the module. Replace it with an MK9 explosive and a timer."

Both men grinned at each other. Julian was now wide-eyed with interest as Mike explained that he wanted to swap a booby-trapped module to the Scrat for Tisch. Wilmer recalled a prior mission where they had used that same trick and he was up for the challenge. Mike and Julian then exited the shop, leaving Wilmer to continue his work.

Mike sat with Julian at his workstation while Geezer waited for direction. Mike questioned him about access to Tisch's accounts for operating expenses. Geezer mentioned that he had access to one of them for minor maintenance items. Mike then instructed Julian to visit the maintenance shops in search of a transformer with a suitable coil on it. When he found it, Geezer would authorize payment, and the transformer would be delivered to the *Blue Eagle*.

"Where do you keep something like that on a ship?" questioned Julian.

"We'll need a ceramic container here on the bridge to stow it. Then we'll place the module near one of its surfaces."

Julian nodded in approval; his arms folded. "I know just where to start looking. This shouldn't take long to find one."

"You used to run a shipping operation on Aurora," Mike mentioned to him.

"Yes, and I was damn good at it."

"But you bet on the wrong horse, if I remember correctly."

Julian looked down at the floor, embarrassed. "Yeah, I did," he confessed. "I learned my lesson, though. Never mix love and business."

Mike offered to get Julian employment with Sysco if their mission was successful. Julian slid his chair toward Mike and poked a finger in his face. "If you're screwing with me, we're going to have a problem." Mike pushed his finger away. Both men stared into each other's eyes now with intensity and remained in a frozen stare for what seemed an eternity. Finally, they burst into laughter.

"So, what do you need me to do?" asked Julian. "Kidnap somebody?"

"Funny you should ask."

Julian rolled his eyes. He knew he had been duped. Geezer interrupted. "I'm here to help as well."

Mike explained the importance of the timing of their departure and the general location of the Scrat ship. Anxious to help Tisch, Geezer immediately prepared the ship for a quick departure. This entailed powering up several systems that required a warm-up period for diagnostics and charging, following a cold shutdown.

After Julian departed the ship in search of a transformer, Mike revealed to Geezer what the agents had told him. He was concerned that someone "within" informed them about his incarceration and Tisch's abduction. Geezer immediately suspected Julian and expressed his mistrust of him.

Mike realized he would need to discuss the leak with Julian personally to find out what his motive was and if he could be trusted. After further consideration, Mike decided to follow Julian and see whom he contacted.

Julian exited one maintenance shop and approached the entrance to another. Two men in suits followed him inside. Mike, dressed discreetly in his long coat and boonie hat, noticed them from a distance. He approached the maintenance shop and stepped inside the doorway.

The two men held Julian at gunpoint and threatened him for not providing additional information. Julian responded that he had requested their help for his friends, not an opportunity to sell them out. Mike was pleased by the response and refrained from intervening. The agents pressed Julian for information on the module's whereabouts.

"When the Scrat took Tisch, they took her attaché case that I believe had the module in it," explained Julian.

"What's this 'I believe' crap?" shouted the one agent.

"She was very secretive about it. I swear."

"Who else knew about the module besides her and Colby?"

"No one, as far as I know," Julian assured them. The men threatened to harm him if he didn't find out the location of the module and report back to them. Julian said nothing as he stared them down.

Mike stepped out of the shop and waited for the agents to leave. Satisfied that Julian was safe and that he had his answers, Mike returned to the ship. Julian continued through the maintenance shop until he found the technicians working on board a shuttle in the rear bay.

When he requested a transformer for the *Blue Eagle*, the technicians were amused.

"Not many of those transformers around anymore, you know," one technician quipped.

The other joked, "Not many like the *Blue Eagle* left either. Shouldn't that ship be in a museum or even a scrapyard? I saw the shape it was in after your last trip in."

"Ha, ha," replied Julian dryly. "Just get me the transformer, and I'll arrange for payment."

The first technician left them to check his inventory. The second inquired, "Who were the two suits that roughed you up back there?"

Julian sneered at him. "They were salesmen for a new program. I sent their product back after the free trial ended, and they weren't happy about it."

The technician chuckled. "I know that feeling," he related. "We get those assholes in here all the time. Very pushy."

At the lobby on Taurus, Sara approached Shannon to inquire about the three corpses on D level. She was accompanied by two men. All three wore black leather uniforms with the initials GSS on the collars, and they were armed. Shannon revealed her encounter with the *Blue Eagle's* crew and what had transpired. Sara grew concerned and left in a hurry.

GSS was more of a myth as they were seldom seen, but everyone knew to get out of their way when they were present. Galactic Security Services was greatly respected across the universe for their fierceness. When they were involved in something, it was serious.

They rode the elevator up to the seventh floor, the security level. A special key card was required for access to the floor, which Sara had in her possession. They promptly went to the surveillance room, surprising the Taurus security detail on shift. Sara demanded access to the surveillance video from Mike's cell.

The technician hadn't viewed it yet, and Sara wanted to keep it that way. When the tech accessed the video, Sara's men escorted him out of the room. She watched the fight that had transpired but was more concerned with the audio. When the footage was finished, she downloaded it onto a data disk and left the room. Her interest was in Empire's involvement in the pursuit of the module. She informed the tech that there was nothing on the surveillance video and left. The tech was surprised by her revelation and promptly informed Gemini of the event. Gemini wasn't concerned and had no idea that it was Sara who was involved.

Sara led her team to Captain Tieg's office and barged in. Tieg was reclined at his desk with his feet up. He spoke kiddingly with someone on his communication link but abruptly terminated the call to address Sara's interruption. "What is the meaning of this?" he demanded.

Sara grabbed him by the collar and yanked him to his feet. "Where's the captain of the *Blue Eagle*?"

Tieg squirmed when he saw the GSS initials on their uniforms. "You're... you're Gemini's sister!" he blurted. "You're GSS?"

Sara drew a dagger from her belt and held it to his throat. "You are going to answer my question now, and then you are going to forget that you ever saw me. Understand?"

Tieg nodded, still stunned that he had never suspected her as more than a consultant for Gemini. Sara pressed the point of the blade against his cheek. "Don't make me ask again," she warned.

Captain Tieg promptly explained how Gemini had arranged for Tisch's capture so that Mike would turn over the module to the Scrat.

Sara was shocked that her sister could be so stupid. "What the hell was she thinking?" Sara exclaimed aloud.

"She wants to win the Scrat over as allies," Tieg responded quickly.

Sara warned him once more to forget her visit. She and her men left the office in a rush. Tieg breathed a sigh of relief as he shuddered over what had just transpired.

In a prison cell on board the Scrat mother ship, Tisch was chained to the wall, hanging from shackles. Her face was bruised, and blood seeped from her busted lip. Across from her were the gurneys with the carcasses of the three Empire reps, dissected and abandoned like empty shells. They were wrapped in clear plastic for preservation and disposal.

Carnak stood in front of her and gripped her neck in a choke hold. When she nearly passed out, he released his hold on her. "If I can't have Colby to punish, then you'll have to do," he warned.

"Be careful what you wish for," she replied weakly. "If he were here, he'd kick your scaly ass."

Carnak punched her in the stomach and choked her again. General Asher entered and approached them. Carnak released his hold on Tisch and backed away. Tisch looked up, her eyes sullen and teary. "What do you want from me?" she asked feebly.

"It's not you we want," Asher responded through his interpreting box. "It's Colby and the module he stole from us."

"I don't know anything about a module. I swear."

General Asher paced in front of her. "Gemini tells me that your friend will be anxious to make a trade for you—his life and the module for yours. I believe her." He then punched Tisch in the stomach. She coughed and heaved, spitting blood onto the floor at her feet.

"Please, stop," she pleaded as she gasped for air. "I don't know anything about your module."

"It doesn't matter what you know," General Asher said as he laughed mockingly at her. "You should have learned from your father. We won't be controlled by anyone." He left the prison cell.

Tisch was stunned by his words. She sobbed and thought again about what Asher had said to her: *You should have learned from your father.* She wondered how they knew of him and what it meant.

Carnak approached her and grabbed her chin tightly. "I'll be back for more quality time with you."

As he walked away, Tisch called out to him, "What do you know of my father?"

Carnak paused and turned to face her. "So many secrets, so little time," he remarked. "He has more to do with this than anybody."

"Not anymore," blurted Tisch. "He's dead." Carnak seemed surprised. He started to speak but stopped and then left.

Tisch was more confused than ever. What could her father possibly have to do with the Scrat? Then she considered how she had left Mike without even a chance for him to explain. There was no possibility of him coming to rescue her, even if he found out where she was. She knew she had betrayed him just like Gemini did.

Mike entered the bridge and was pleased to see a ceramic container in the corner of the control room with a cable running from a power panel through a hole in its side. He unlatched the top and peeked in. To his satisfaction, there was the transformer he needed with the power cables already connected. "Damn, he's good," Mike remarked.

Mike found Julian in the galley and joined him for a beer. "Excellent job on the transformer," he said. "Now are you ready to make a play for Sysco?"

Julian sipped from his beer. "Very much so."

Mike leaned on the table with his arms. Julian waited patiently, wary of what might be asked of him. "You and Wilmer are going to be the custodians on the Executive Level of Taurus tomorrow."

Julian's face turned pale. He didn't know whether to take Mike seriously or not. "This is a joke, right?" Not buying into this, he got up to leave.

Mike remained calm and sipped his beer. "We're talking Tisch's life here, Julian. I'm deadly serious."

Julian paused at the hatch and responded defensively, "I'm no custodian. That's not the employment I had in mind."

"No shit," countered Mike. "You'll be much more than that when this is over." He kicked the chair toward Julian and nodded for him to sit.

Julian reluctantly sat down and asked, "So, what do I have to do?"

"It's simple," said Mike. "When Gemini goes to the ladies' room, you and Wilmer will kidnap her." Julian listened with renewed interest. "The cleaning cart trash can is big enough to hide her inside," continued Mike. He handed Julian a piece of paper with numbers scribbled on it. "Here is the code for elevator access to her floor."

"What's the point?" Julian asked. "I mean, why do this?"

"We need Gemini to fix this," Mike explained.

Julian extended his hand to Mike. "I believe we have a deal." The two men shook hands.

"I will take care of you, Julian. You have my word."

Julian looked at him with admiration. He believed in Mike and his ability to do whatever he said he could do.

At the maintenance shop, Wilmer assembled a dummy module, identical to the original, including the two green LEDs. The original module sat next to him on the table. Mike entered and sat next to him, waiting for his assessment. Wilmer tightened the screws on the fake module with a jeweler's screwdriver and then informed him that the fake module was mission ready.

Both men were confident they could execute their plan with the dummy module. Mike eyed Wilmer for a moment, recalling their adventures, and then asked, "So how did you wind up here?"

Wilmer paused and wore a pained expression. Finally, he responded, "When the team fell apart, I mean you and Gemini, I resigned and returned home to my family. I thought I'd have a chance to be the father and husband I never was."

Mike noticed that Wilmer became teary-eyed. He placed his hand on Wilmer's shoulder for support. Wilmer continued, "They were in a terrible accident. Since I resigned, I had no health care coverage for them. They were left to die, and I couldn't do anything about it. The Federation couldn't care less about us."

Mike apologized for everything that had gone wrong since he and Gemini split up. Wilmer shrugged it off and explained how Tisch rescued him from binge-drinking and gave him a chance to get his life back together. He then revealed to Mike that he was sensitive to his ribbing about Shannon since he, too, had been alone for some time and hoped for female companionship.

"Birds of a feather," kidded Mike. "We'll be fine. Just be patient."

CHAPTER IX

TURNABOUT IS FAIR PLAY

Wilmer and Julian departed the *Blue Eagle* and entered the Taurus lobby. They wore janitors' uniforms and wielded a cart, mops, brooms, and a large trash can. With their heads down, no one paid them any attention. Once inside the elevator, Wilmer pressed the button for the Executive Level, but nothing happened. "We need a damned security code to get on that level," he complained. "I'll bet Mike didn't think of that."

Julian removed the note from his pocket with the code on it. He smiled at Wilmer and then entered the five-digit code. The elevator doors closed, and the elevator went into motion.

"How come you have the code and I don't?" complained Wilmer.

"Maybe it's a trust issue," teased Julian.

"Screw you, asshole," Wilmer blurted. Then Julian cracked a smile and he realized it was a harmless jest.

The ride up was quiet as both men grew uneasy about what waited ahead for them. When the doors opened, they exited and pushed their cart toward the ladies' room.

Gemini's voice could be heard all the way down the corridor from her office. "Find Colby now, Tieg! And find out who those dead men are!" After another pause, she shouted, "I don't want excuses! Find him!"

Wilmer and Julian pushed the cart forward and parked it outside the ladies' room. Wilmer set up "Caution" signs in the corridor nearby while Julian mopped the floor.

Soon after, Gemini exited her office and walked toward the ladies' room. Believing they were mopping the corridor, she smirked at them as she passed. Wilmer and Julian looked both ways. No one was in sight. Julian pushed the cart into the ladies' room while Wilmer placed a "Closed—Wet Floor" sign outside the doorway.

Gemini was inside one of the stalls when they entered. Julian stood by the stall door, anxiously waiting to grab and gag her when she exited. Wilmer was ready with tape to secure her ankles and wrists.

When Gemini exited the stall, she was horrified to see custodians in there while she was present. Her eyes widened as she suddenly recognized Wilmer. "What the hell are you doing here, Wilmer?" she shouted.

Julian overpowered her from behind and covered her mouth with his hand. She struggled, but he had her at a disadvantage. Wilmer glanced at Julian, realizing this was the point of no return. Julian nodded for him to continue. She struggled and kicked frantically, but Wilmer taped her legs together at the ankles, and then her wrists behind her back. Julian taped over her mouth to keep her quiet. Gemini shook her head as they lifted her into the trash can and pushed her down. They picked up their signs and rolled the cart out of the restroom. Wilmer closed the stall door and latched it from the outside, using a coin to rotate the lock. Anxiously, they left the rest room with the cart and headed toward the elevator.

Two men, Grim and Jessup, stepped off the elevator and passed them. Jessup wore a patch over one eye and several stitches across his cheek.

"Something's not right," Wilmer commented to Julian. "Stay here."

Wilmer followed the men and watched them enter the ladies' room. Then he heard the muffled popping of pulse fire through silencers as the men fired into each of the stalls. Wilmer hurried back to the elevator.

"What did you see?" asked Julian.

"We have to get out of here fast." Wilmer pushed the button several times. Julian watched nervously for the men to return. His fears were soon realized when the men left the ladies' room and approached them. "Don't say anything to them," instructed Wilmer. Julian trembled and nodded.

The two men stopped at their cart. Grim inquired, "Did you see anyone come out of the ladies' room?" Both men shook their heads. The men groaned and hurried off toward Gemini's office.

Wilmer reached into the can under the trash and patted Gemini's head. "We just saved your life, Gem. You're welcome." Only a muffled grunt was heard from the trash can.

When the doors slid open, they pushed the cart onto the elevator. Wilmer breathed a sigh of relief. Julian chuckled, proud of their accomplishment.

On the bridge of the *Blue Eagle*, Mike sat alone and plotted their course to the Scrat command ship. Geezer was resting in his cabin, which left Mike time to ponder his relationship with Tisch. If they succeeded in rescuing her, would things be different? If not, he needed to move on. But to where? Frustration set in as he considered his options.

Grim paused outside the hatch of the *Blue Eagle*, wearing a long coat and wide-brimmed hat, with his hands in his pockets. He looked back and forth, ensuring that no one followed. The beeping sound of a large forklift, as it retrieved a pallet and reversed, attracted the attention of those on the dock. Grim took advantage of the distraction to open the hatch with the external lever and board the ship.

Seeing no one around the main cabin, he proceeded to the bridge and spotted Mike. Feeling confident with the element of surprise on his side, he approached Mike from behind with his pistol drawn. Mike noticed his shadow when it briefly blocked the reflection of the ceiling lights on the monitor. Instinctively, he rolled out of his chair onto the floor, using the chair as a shield.

Grim fired three shots at Mike with his pulse pistol, but the bursts of energy struck the underside of the chair. Mike got to his feet, still using the chair as a shield, and rushed at his assailant. He shoved the chair into Grim's face and pinned him against the wall. Grim used his knee to strike Mike several times in his injured side. Mike grimaced from the pain and wrestled with Grim's gun hand, while pinning him against the wall with his shoulder. Both men struggled until Mike broke the pistol free. He backed away, and the chair fell to the ground. Before Grim could move, Mike fired three pulses into his leg. Grim fell to the floor in agony, smoke spewing from cauterized flesh wounds on his thigh.

Determined to continue the fight, he retrieved a small dagger from a sheath on his ankle. Annoyed, Mike fired two more pulses into Grim's shoulder. He groaned in pain and dropped the dagger on the floor. Mike pressed the gun against his head. "Who are you?"

"None of your business," Grim answered defiantly, clutching at his wounds. Out of patience, Mike shoved the barrel of the pistol in his mouth. "If you don't give me answers, I'm going to put you through some very extreme torture techniques," he warned. Staring Grim down, Mike removed the gun from his mouth and waited for his response.

"Kiss my ass," shouted Grim.

"Oh, I have something better in mind," Mike remarked and set the pistol down.

Grim grabbed for the dagger, but Mike stomped on his hand repeatedly, breaking it in several places. He picked up the dagger and shoved it into Grim's groin. Grim lurched and cried out in pain. He desperately clutched at Mike's arm but to no avail. Splotches of blood formed on the crotch of his pants. Geezer stood in the hatchway and watched in horror.

Mike removed the dagger and threatened him, "Next, I'll start cutting things off." He then cut Grim's pant leg open at the crotch.

"All right!" cried Grim, now trembling uncontrollably. "Empire Shipping sent me to recover a module from you and then clean up the loose ends."

Surprised by his revelation, he asked, "How do they know about the module?"

Grim was now in serious trouble from blood loss through his wounds. He replied feebly, "You really have no idea what's going on, do you?"

"What does Empire have to do with the Scrat?" pressed Mike.

"Figure it out for yourself," cried Grim.

Mike paced the floor, debating the man's fate. He held the dagger up and eyed the bloody blade. Grim knew what he was thinking and panicked. "Please stop!" he cried out. "It's about Sysco and the module. The Scrat were never supposed to be involved. Let me go, please," begged Grim as he weakened from blood loss. "I won't tell them anything."

Mike stood over the man and asked, "Why was the captain of the *Blue Eagle* killed?"

Grim was surprised by Mike's question but answered, "He took the teleport module and used it against us."

Mike was stunned. He pressed the barrel of his pulse pistol against Grim's temple. "So how did the Scrat get here?" he inquired, somewhat baffled.

Grim stared back, despondent and ready to make his peace. "The captain of the *Blue Eagle* brought them here. He was one of us until he got the module." Mike was stunned by Grim's response. Geezer's eyes widened as he listened from the hatchway.

"Who are you anyway?" Grim asked, desperately hoping for compassion. "I'm sure my people would pay well for your services."

Mike announced defiantly, "I'm the man who's going to take down Empire." He then fired three pulses into Grim's forehead, leaving a smoldering hole. Mike then staggered backward, clutching his injured ribs. Geezer hurried to his aid and helped him into a chair. He offered to get Mike something for the pain, but Mike refused.

"You heard that?" Mike asked Geezer. Geezer nodded as he sat dumbfounded at his station. "Not a word to Tisch. Got it?" he instructed Geezer.

Geezer, still in shock over the news, replied somberly, "Who would have thought Mallory would have anything to do with this? Tisch would be crushed." Both men understood that Tisch could never know the truth that would undermine her faith in the one person who mattered most in her life.

Outside the *Blue Eagle's* hatch, Captain Tieg and four of his sentries assembled. They cautiously boarded with pulse pistols drawn. Geezer noticed the men on the monitor and ushered Mike from the bridge to his cabin. He returned and sat in the chair with Mike's knife and pistol in his hand. Tieg and his men entered and warned Geezer to drop his weapons.

"I was just about to call you guys," he announced cynically as he dropped the pistol and knife to the floor. Two of the sentries went to the corpse and examined it. Tieg questioned Geezer about what had happened and where Mike was.

Geezer was more than enthusiastic about his fantasy story of taking down the assassin. Tieg mentioned to one of his officers that, with Grim gone, it was just Jessup and Antwan whom Gemini needed to be concerned with. Geezer overheard the name Grim and wondered if there were more in this group to come.

Tieg instructed his men to search the ship while he questioned Geezer. Before they could leave the bridge, Sara arrived with her team and interceded. She instructed Tieg to leave the ship immediately and declared that this was now a GSS matter. Tieg was reluctant to be bullied again by Sara and attempted to contact Gemini for instructions. Getting no response, Sara reminded him of his obligation not to divulge her identity to Gemini. Tieg scowled and departed.

Geezer thanked her for her support and offered to comply with any requests. Sara approached the transformer and raised the casing lid for further inspection. "What might this be for?" she questioned him. Geezer shrugged his shoulders, unsure of what to say.

Mike hobbled onto the bridge and was puzzled, seeing her in a GSS uniform. Sara smiled and set the chair upright for him to sit. Mike warily accepted the seat but said nothing. Geezer nervously returned to his position at the console and resumed his duties.

"Surprised to see me again?" Sara asked coyly.

"Are you here for a drink?" Mike countered.

Giggling as she recalled their encounter at the pub, Sara inquired about the module and if Mike would be willing to part with it. Surprised that she asked, Mike wondered why she didn't use her authority to confiscate the *Blue Eagle*. "I have no module to sell or trade to you or anyone else," he replied. "Anyone who comes looking for it is wasting their time."

Sara traced her fingers along the top of the transformer, smiling all the while. "And what would you use a transformer like this for?" she teased. "I'm sure it has significant magnetic strength."

"Let's stop dancing around," Mike responded, realizing that she was on to him. "What are you doing here?"

"I need to know that the module is safe," she answered. "A lot of people are coming for it, and I can only protect you for so long." Mike appreciated her honesty and assured her that it was secure.

Sara wanted assurance that Mike would not give it up for Tisch in a trade with the Scrat. When she was comfortable with his response that the module was out of play, she wished him well and departed. Mike sighed as he watched her leave. Geezer noticed and kidded, "Damn, she's hot."

"You got that right," he replied and then added, "Boy, did I pick the wrong sister."

Geezer's eyes widened with surprise. "You mean that's Gemini's sister?"

"Oh, yeah." Both men sighed.

The main hatch to the *Blue Eagle* was open when Wilmer and Julian returned with their cleaning cart and were appalled when Tieg and his men emerged from the ship with a corpse.

"This is bad," Wilmer remarked. "Let's wait a few minutes in case anyone else is in there. Then I'll go in."

"And what am I supposed to do with her?" Julian complained. "Someone's going to ask questions when they see me standing here with this damned cart."

"Wait here," instructed Wilmer. "I'll take the damn cart."

As he pushed the cart toward the ship, Sara and her GSS partners exited the ship. Wilmer did an about-face with the cart and went back to Julian. "That was close," he blurted, his heart racing from anxiety.

"What the hell! Taurus's security! GSS!" groaned Julian. "They're all looking for Gemini!"

Wilmer gestured with his hands for Julian to calm down. He drew his pistol from inside his janitor's uniform and crept inside the ship. Julian waited nervously at the dock area, but no one took notice of him. After several minutes, he pushed the cart on board the ship, wary of any other intruders.

On the bridge, Geezer left for a mop and bucket while Mike sat at Wilmer's engineering station. In front of him on the desktop were four screws and a knife. Mike held the explosive version of the module in front of him with the cover removed. Inside the module, the slide switch was in the "auto" position. Mike dialed the timer to 00:10 seconds.

Jessup emerged from hiding in one of the cabins and entered the bridge with his pistol drawn. He crept up on Mike from behind and ordered, "Put the module down and get on your knees."

Mike lowered the module to his thigh and looked disappointedly at him. "I'm going to have to start locking that damn hatch," he complained.

Jessup stepped around in front of him and pointed at the screws. "Put it back together now!" he shouted impatiently.

Wilmer peered through the hatch and saw Jessup. He took careful aim at him and waited for his shot. When Geezer returned with a mop and bucket, he immediately took action. With one quick motion, he slammed Jessup over the head with the bucket and knocked him to the floor, dazed from the impact.

Wilmer, surprised by Geezer's aggressive action, quickly disarmed Jessup and punched him once more. Still with hurting ribs, Mike was relieved for the support from his friends. When Jessup looked up, Wilmer immediately recognized him from the ladies' room. Wilmer punched him in the bridge of his nose and knocked him unconscious.

"Great timing, fellas," Mike complimented them.

Wilmer was concerned and asked anxiously, "What the hell happened here?"

"Empire Shipping wants 'their' module back really bad."

Wilmer was stunned by Mike's remark. "So, they brought the Scrat here, not Gem!" he grumbled.

"It's a little more complicated than that," Mike explained as he secured the screws on the cover of the module with his knife.

Geezer stared down at the unconscious man with his hands on his hips. He complained to Mike, "This is becoming a habit. Every time I return after a break, there's another body on the floor." The men laughed.

"Seems like old habits die hard," Mike remarked.

Geezer and Wilmer looked concerned as they understood more about Mike's history that involved taking lives, both alien and human. Neither Mike nor Wilmer had any recollection of the assailants in any prior situation, even with Special Forces.

"How did everything go?" Mike asked eagerly.

"Like clockwork," replied Wilmer. "Julian will be here any moment."

"And that brings us to another issue. The real module needs to be programmed for the mission and positioned without anyone's knowledge."

Wilmer understood what he meant. "I'll take care of it."

Mike set the fake module on the console and waited for Julian's arrival. Geezer took the damaged chair to the incinerator in the aft compartment of the ship. When Julian entered through the hatch with the cart onto the bridge, Wilmer eagerly removed the trash bag cover off Gemini's head. Both men beamed proudly at Mike.

Mike savored the stunned expression on Gemini's face. "Well done, boys!" he complimented them.

Wilmer dumped Gemini onto the floor, and Julian cut the tape from her wrists and ankles. Eager to hear her response to the abduction, Mike removed the tape from her mouth.

"You son of a bitch, Colby!" she cried out.

"How's it feel to be a prisoner, Gem?" he taunted.

Geezer returned and stared wide-eyed at her. "Jumping Jesus!" he shouted. "What the hell did you boys do?" He covered his eyes briefly and frowned, wanting no part of this.

Wilmer pointed at Jessup and related how the two men had gone into the ladies' room to kill Gemini right after they exited. Gemini sat up, rubbing her wrists gingerly. When she saw that the assassin was Jessup, she was ecstatic. "Is he still alive?" she asked anxiously.

Mike checked him for a pulse and nodded. "Yeah, so far."

"So how the hell did they get onto the Executive Level and then know where to look for me?" she asked, concerned about her station's security.

"They probably accessed the surveillance cameras on Taurus," Julian suggested. "How else would they know you went into the ladies' room?"

Mike considered the latest development and thought aloud, "So, how is it that Empire knew I was imprisoned on Taurus? Anyone?"

Julian was red-faced with embarrassment. He replied, "I'm sorry, Mike. I thought they could help get Tisch back."

"It all worked out," commented Mike. "Just don't do it again." He was pleased that he could trust Julian to come clean on what happened.

Geezer and Wilmer stared at Julian, disappointed again in his behavior. Julian gestured with his hand for them to leave him be. He politely helped Gemini to her feet.

Gemini fixed her dress, mad as hell. "You'd better have a damn good reason for this, Colby!"

"Inside my prison cell were two bodies. They worked for the people who want the module - Empire Shipping. You know them?" he asked, waiting patiently for her response.

"My people are looking into their identities," Gemini explained.

"And this character?" Mike questioned.

"Oh, yes. I know this scumbag very well," she announced angrily.

"The first guy's name was Grim," Geezer mentioned. "Ring a bell, anyone?"

"Really?" she replied with surprise. "That means there's one more that I know of - Antwan. Unfortunately, he might be the most dangerous of the bunch."

"Empire Shipping hired them to kill us both and get the module back," Mike informed her.

"I'm sure they did," she remarked smugly. Knowing that Mike was taking down her enemies one at a time gave her the confidence that things would work out.

Jessup stirred and tried to get up. Gemini suddenly went into a rage and kicked at his head repeatedly. "Die, you stinking pussy!" she shouted at him.

When Wilmer pulled her away, she reached for his pistol and then shot Jessup twice in the head. Jessup groaned one last time and then died. Gemini was concerned, knowing that the Empire agents had access to her facility. "I have to notify my security team immediately!" she blurted.

"That's not a good idea right now," Mike warned her. She ignored him and rushed to the communication console. Julian intercepted her and winced as he sniffed the air. "Phew!" he exclaimed. "You are a little foul today."

Gemini was embarrassed, recalling how she had been abducted - from the ladies' room, no less - and treated like a commoner. She then turned her anger toward Mike and tried to punch him. "You did this to me!" she cried. "You humiliated me!"

Mike grabbed her wrists and held them tightly. Finally, she stopped fighting and fell to her knees in tears. "Get us out of here, Geezer," ordered Mike, "before we attract any more attention."

Geezer contacted the dispatcher for clearance. Overcome with curiosity, he looked at Gemini and then at Mike. "Do I want to know what she's doing here like that?" he contemplated aloud. Julian and Wilmer both shook their heads at him. "On second thought, maybe I don't."

Mike felt pity for Gemini as she fell to the floor in tears. He considered their next move and then instructed Julian, "Once we're in the free zone, make the transmission to Asher. You know what to say."

"Will do," replied Julian.

Mike took Gemini by the arm and ushered her from the bridge. The men beamed proudly, satisfied that Gemini was humbled for once.

CHAPTER X
EXECUTING THE PLAN

In his cabin, Mike sat on the bed and considered his options to rescue Tisch. He noticed a packet of pills on the table and assumed they were Gemini's. He contemplated tossing them in the trash can, but stowed them in his pocket instead. Gemini entered the cabin, wrapped in a towel, with her wet clothes draped over her arm. Mike opened the closet and took out two hangers for her clothes to dry on. Gemini thanked him and sat on the bed. Mike stared at her with sad eyes as he recalled better times. "I never thought you'd stoop so low as to do what you did to Tisch."

Gemini looked down at the floor, ashamed of her actions. "I didn't have a choice, thanks to you."

Mike walked to the cabin door and then hesitated. "There's always a choice," he reminded her. "Unfortunately, you always made the wrong one when it counted." He left the cabin, and the door closed behind him. Tears streamed down Gemini's cheeks. She wondered if he was right and things really were her fault.

Wilmer, Geezer, and Julian sat at their respective stations. Julian expressed his fears about the Scrat and what he thought about his brief encounter with them. Wilmer related how he and Mike had gone into the center of the Scrat Empire and destroyed their bases. He also enjoyed telling them how Mike and Carnak had slugged it out, with Mike getting a knockout over the Scrat officer.

Mike entered and pulled up a chair between them. "I see we're having story time, huh, Wilmer?"

"Just a few memories of our encounters with the Scrat," Wilmer responded proudly.

Their conversation was suddenly interrupted by an alarm. Geezer checked the sensor feedback. The monitor showed a ship moving toward them. "We have company closing in," he announced. "A cruiser from Taurus's security force."

"Make contact with them," ordered Mike. "We don't need their presence out here right now."

"Check that," Wilmer continued. "There's another ship at a distance. They seem to be watching. No approach."

"Somebody is very interested in us. Keep an eye on them."

Julian returned to his station and verified their coordinates. The transmitter beeped, and Geezer glanced at Mike for direction. Mike nodded for him to respond.

A man's voice crackled from the transmitter, and his face appeared on the monitor. "*Blue Eagle*, this is Captain Tieg. Prepare to be boarded. You and your crew are under arrest for the murders of two civilians and three officers."

Mike hustled over to the console and responded, "That's not a good idea, captain. We have an important meeting with the Scrat, so unless you want a war, I suggest you stand down."

Tieg grew impatient and inquired, "Where is Gemini?"

"Relax, Captain. She's safe with us."

"We'll take her from here. Stand by for boarding," he repeated.

Mike grew annoyed with him. The others stood by their stations, anxious to see the outcome. "You have bigger problems back on Taurus," Mike informed him. "Empire Shipping has placed mercs in your facility."

Captain Tieg expressed his doubt and repeated his orders. Mike left the console and pulled Jessup's corpse in front to be seen. Captain Tieg recalled Jessup being a bloody mess from an earlier meeting with Gemini. Mike dropped the corpse and took his seat. "One of several mercenaries we've encountered on Taurus," he responded and then added, "from Empire. They tried to kill Gemini outside her own office, but fortunately, my partners were there to rescue her."

Mike gestured for Wilmer and Julian to dispose of the body. They grumbled as they dragged the corpse off to the incinerator.

"Enough with the theatrics," shouted Tieg. "You will stand down. That's an order."

"Negative," countered Mike. "If necessary, we'll do this the hard way."

Geezer, now annoyed with Tieg's arrogance, urged Mike, "Use one of the turrets. Show them who's boss here!"

"My pleasure," he replied and left the bridge.

Geezer warned Tieg about Mike's marksmanship. He advised them to return to base and await Gemini's orders. Another alarm sounded as the cruiser locked onto the *Blue Eagle*.

Geezer gave him a final warning, finishing with, "You'll be sorry if you don't leave now."

Mike strapped himself in and donned the helmet. He scrolled through the menus on the screen and pressed the power knob. The heads-up display illuminated, and he focused on the cruiser. "I'm going to fire a warning shot at our guests," he informed Geezer. "When I do, ask them once more to leave the area." Geezer affirmed his instructions and waited.

Mike targeted the nose of the cruiser and fired a single shot. A red pulse of energy streaked toward the cruiser and struck a tiny plate on the nose of the ship. A brief flicker of flame indicated that the device beneath the plate was damaged.

Geezer saw the brief flash on the monitor and grinned. The alarm silenced, indicating that Mike had just disabled their targeting system. "Consider that a warning shot," Geezer announced. "Now please leave the area."

Tieg became irate as one of his officers informed him of the damage. He replied defiantly, "Consider yourselves under arrest. We're coming aboard now."

Geezer shook his head at Tieg in disappointment. "I don't think so, Captain," he replied calmly. "That shot took out your targeting system."

"You will all be tried for treason," warned Tieg, ignoring Geezer's remarks.

Geezer suspected what was coming next and grinned. Mike targeted the bottom of the rear engine on the cruiser and fired three quick pulses. All three pulses darted toward the cruiser and struck the bottom of the rear engine with a bright flash. Geezer was amused as the transmission terminated abruptly. The cruiser turned and departed the area with only one engine functional. "That's my boy!" quipped Geezer.

Mike then turned his attention to the mystery ship. He fired a long shot in their direction as a warning. The ship turned and disappeared from their monitors. "Nosy bastards," he grumbled.

"You're aces in my book, Mike!" shouted Geezer excitedly. "Nice shooting."

Mike returned and stood in the center of the bridge with his hands on his hips while the men worked from their stations. Gemini appeared in the doorway, but no one noticed. Everyone waited anxiously as Julian contacted the Scrat general. "This is the *Blue Eagle* requesting contact with General Asher," Julian announced.

Gemini fretted, knowing that Mike would board the Scrat warship to rescue Tisch. The men were surprised by her presence but said nothing. Gemini approached Mike and stood in front of him with a dour expression.

"You can't go back to that ship," she warned. "They'll kill you."

Mike was amused by her sudden concern for him. "It wasn't a problem before."

"Maybe I feel differently now," she responded.

Wilmer rolled his eyes and grumbled, "Great. She's bipolar!"

The men chuckled. Mike placed his arm around Gemini's shoulders and explained, "I'm not worried. I have an insurance policy." He nodded to her. "You."

Gemini looked baffled by his remark. She had never imagined he would take her with him to the Scrat ship. Julian announced anxiously, "We have an incoming transmission!"

Geezer activated the receiver and waited. Still confused by his reference to her as an insurance policy, Gemini wondered what Mike had up his sleeve. General Asher's face appeared on the monitor. His voice interrupted them in a loud and belligerent tone. "*Blue Eagle*, give me one reason not to destroy you right now!"

Geezer looked to Mike for direction. Mike approached the console and spoke confidently. "General Asher, I hope you're in good health today."

General Asher touched the interpreter box on his neck and shouted, "Where is my module?"

Gemini tensed in fear, seeing the anger in Asher's eyes on the monitor. She felt her pockets for her pills, but they weren't there. Without her pills, she had no arrogance or confidence. She trembled at the thought of having no control.

Mike replied calmly, "I have it with me. Gemini has ordered me to return it, and she is coming with me to ensure I do."

Gemini was horrified, realizing this is what he meant by an insurance policy. She had had no idea that she was part of the plan. Wilmer and Geezer were elated with Mike's intentions, while Julian did his best to remain neutral.

General Asher responded, "I will allow you access to my ship. This time, my soldiers will search you thoroughly before you leave the transport area, or they will meet a most unhealthy fate."

Wilmer chuckled, drawing a sidelong glance from Mike. "I would expect nothing less," Mike responded, and the transmission ended.

Gemini slapped Mike's face. "How could you do this to me?" she cried.

Mike considered his many reasons and then replied, "I want you to see what I see, feel what I feel, when you're betrayed and left to die."

Gemini paced the floor in a panic. "They'll kill us all!"

"Maybe," he quipped.

Gemini rushed off the bridge in tears. Wilmer stood and shook Mike's hand. "I applaud your style."

Julian clapped slowly and methodically. "Bravo," he complimented Mike. "That was well played." Geezer nodded proudly with folded arms. He appreciated Mike's style.

Wilmer informed him that the location he needed was programmed into the real module and would ensure their escape. He nodded toward the container with the transformer indicating its location. Mike noticed the device underneath it, between the skids of the transformer's pallet.

Geezer glanced at the transformer and grew somber. "What the hell is this all about?" he blurted. "I sense there's something going on that I don't know about. Actually, there's a lot going on that I don't know about."

"Trust me, Geezer," Mike replied. "It's not worth the headache."

Geezer rolled his eyes and sighed. "Always the last to know," he muttered.

Mike studied the long-range monitor in front of Geezer. Ten armed freighters approached from a distance, still far off. Mike knew who they were and why they were there.

Julian stood behind him, looking over his shoulder. "You have a plan for this?" he questioned Mike. Geezer and Wilmer eyed Mike, anxious for his take on the ships.

Mike placed his hands on his hips and stared up at the ceiling for several seconds. Suddenly, his eyes widened, and he instructed Geezer, "They're Empire's ships. Contact them and find out their intentions." Geezer promptly attempted to communicate with them.

"They're not here for the party," complained Wilmer. "Why else would they send ten ships?"

"They think we're selling the module to the Scrat, and they can't afford to let that happen," explained Mike.

"We have no backup," Julian added grimly. "You scared off Tieg and his boys."

Mike contemplated how this would play out and remarked, "We don't need Tieg. This is going to be epic. The plan goes on as designed."

Geezer informed the crew that Empire's ships weren't responding. Mike wasn't surprised and reiterated that this could work in their favor. Wilmer handed Mike the duplicate module and warned him to watch his time. Julian sensed the peril of Mike's plan and the chance that he might not return. He also realized Mike was on his path to something better than a mercenary for hire.

Mike eased toward the door with the fake module in hand. "Now if you'll excuse me, fellas, my 'partner' and I must prepare for our little excursion."

Julian folded his hands on his lap and watched Mike leave. Wilmer gazed proudly in Mike's direction. "He's a heck of a guy," he muttered. "A little dumb sometimes, but brave as hell."

"I don't say nice things about people too often," said Julian somberly, "but I like him."

"I have faith in him," Geezer commented. "He'll be fine."

The crew gathered on the bridge of the *Blue Eagle* in anticipation of Tisch's rescue attempt. Mike held Gemini's arm with one hand and the fake module in the other. He showed little emotion toward her as she trembled. Just prior to boarding the shuttle, he instructed her, "When we arrive on the alien ship, you're going to hold on to the module. It'll look like you're in charge."

"Thanks for the vote of confidence," she uttered cynically.

Mike and Gemini climbed into Mike's battered shuttle and strapped themselves in. Gemini stared at Mike, expecting a sarcastic comment.

Instead, Mike glanced over and gave her explicit orders. "When we meet with the General, do not give him the module until I tell you to. I want to make sure Tisch is safe before we lose our leverage."

"I understand."

"Do you?" he countered.

Gemini smirked at him. "You don't trust me, do you?"

"Prove me wrong, Gem," he challenged her. "Just once."

Gemini stared at the control console with moist eyes and shaking hands. Mike noticed and looked away sadly, knowing this could fail and they both could die. Suddenly, she remembered that she didn't have her pills. "Mike, we have to go back!"

"Too late," he responded stoically.

"But I forgot something. I need it if we're going to do this."

"You'll be fine," he remarked. "Just do what you always do."

Gemini became irate with him. "And what's that supposed to mean?"

Mike snickered. "Just follow my instructions."

When Gemini became emotional, Mike feared that would ruin the plan. He took her packet of pills from his pocket and tossed them on her lap. She was embarrassed that he knew about her addiction and tucked them under her bra. Mike was surprised that she didn't take any, but he hoped it was a start.

"Thank you," she mumbled.

The battered shuttle emerged from the open bay of the *Blue Eagle* and glided toward the alien command ship. The *Blue Eagle* then retreated from the area. One of the shuttle's rear panels smoked. Another flashed warning lights. One of the two engines sputtered and failed.

"Is this piece of junk going to make it?" Gemini asked uneasily.

Mike rebuked her. "This piece of junk has never failed me, unlike you."

"Screw you!" she shouted. Mike didn't respond. Gemini then noticed on the monitor that the *Blue Eagle* had left them. "Michael, where are they going?" she asked nervously.

"Don't worry about it."

Tears streamed down her cheeks. "We're going to die, aren't we?" she said between sobs.

"Someday," Mike answered somberly, "but not today." Gemini fumed over his nonchalance.

The shuttle entered the transport bay of the alien ship and docked. The bay doors closed, and the bay filled with oxygen. Ten Scrat soldiers entered and waited. Mike and Gemini emerged from the shuttle. Two of the Scrat soldiers searched them, then stood back and awaited their orders. Carnak entered the bay and stood in front of Mike.

"You want this?" Mike teased and held the fake module in the air. Carnak reached for it, but Mike pulled it away three times, amused by Carnak's frustration. Carnak punched Mike in the stomach and doubled him over. Mike stood up and grumbled, "Are we going to do this again? You know what happens in the end."

Carnak snarled and reached for the module. Mike again pulled it away and warned him, "Try that again, and I'll smash it."

Carnak punched Mike in the mouth. Mike responded with a punch to Carnak's jaw that flattened him. "I told you," Mike taunted, "this ends the same way every time."

Carnak was enraged. He got up slowly, rubbing his jaw. Mike staggered him with another punch. The other soldiers laughed at their comrade. Carnak got up, ready to fight but then one of the soldiers whispered to Carnak, and he reluctantly backed off. The General wanted them in the control room now.

Mike handed the module to Gemini and led her into the main corridor. The corridor was dim, and only a few rows of flashing red lights were functional. The charred walls still gave testimony to Mike's last visit. He and Gemini walked slowly as if approaching their death sentence.

"Are you okay?" asked Mike, showing some compassion for her.

"What do you think?" Gemini responded sarcastically.

"Welcome to my world."

"Did you mess up their ship like this?" she asked, half-jokingly.

"Oh, yes, and then some," he remarked proudly as they entered the control room.

General Asher rose from his elaborate mechanical chair and looked down at them from over the horseshoe-shaped control console. Mike approached with his hand raised in mock friendship. "Greetings, my friend. Are you ready to conduct business?" he asked, faking a cheerful tone.

General Asher stared at him, wide-eyed in disbelief. Mike shrugged his shoulders at him and quipped, "Nothing wrong with a positive attitude." Gemini rolled her eyes at Mike, wondering if he had lost his mind.

"The module," demanded Asher.

Mike raised one finger, indicating wait. "First, the woman," he replied.

General Asher shouted an order to Carnak in garbled Scrat dialect, indicating his growing impatience. Carnak reluctantly left the control room.

"You, as you humans say, have balls," commented General Asher.

"Yeah," Mike quipped, "and that's why I stand up to take a leak." Gemini stared at him, stunned by his disregard for the severity of their situation.

The Scrat had no idea what he meant and were distracted by the comment. General Asher stepped down from the raised platform and stood in front of Gemini. "You have caused me great pains," he announced in a gruff tone.

Gemini summoned her courage and replied, "This man has caused me great pains as well. I hope we can put this matter to rest."

Mike reached between them and nudged Gemini back. He stood face-to-face with Asher. "The woman and our freedom for the module. It's a win-win for everyone."

"Silence!" shouted General Asher, and he threw Mike to the ground.

Mike got up and fearlessly stepped toward General Asher again. "Why are you here in this part of the galaxy?" he queried.

"Are you concerned?" countered General Asher.

"No," Mike replied cynically. "Just curious."

Carnak returned, pulling Tisch by her arm. She looked rough with dried bloodstains on her mouth and clothes. Mike saw her, and his heart broke over her condition. "Tisch!" he blurted. Gemini felt horrible, knowing she was responsible for what had happened to her.

Tisch saw him, and her eyes widened. "Michael!" she cried. "You came for me!" She felt renewed hope, knowing that Mike would make things right.

Carnak threw her to the ground. Mike knelt next to her and hugged her tightly. He glared at Carnak and warned, "You and I still have something to settle, frog face."

Carnak sneered at him as Mike nestled Tisch against his chest. Gemini seethed over Mike's display of affection for Tisch. Mike helped Tisch to her feet, and together they backed away from the soldiers. Gemini, envious as always, took the module to General Asher.

"I believe this is yours," she announced proudly.

"No, Gemini!" shouted Mike.

General Asher studied the module and was convinced it was authentic. He handed it off to one of his technicians to install on the console. Gemini turned to Mike with a scornful look and responded, "You left me no choice."

Mike shook his head in disbelief. "You did it again, Gem. I knew you'd never change."

The technician approached the console to install the module. General Asher again approached Gemini and spoke mockingly, "You fool, Gemini.

With this module, I have the power to transport my entire force here. In a few short days, you will all be dead or enslaved!"

Gemini was shocked by the turn of events. She looked to Mike for some assurance, but he only shrugged his shoulders at her. Gemini grew distraught, knowing she screwed up again.

"Before you install that module," Mike suggested, "I think we need to have a talk."

"And why would I want that?" General Asher countered.

"If you check your long-range sensors," Mike explained, "you'll see that Empire has ten armed freighters approaching."

General Asher glanced at one of his technicians. The Scrat pressed several switches and looked up with an alarmed alien expression. He responded in Scrat dialect to General Asher, who turned his attention back to Mike. "What is this ploy?" he demanded.

Mike grinned. "Looks like you have a problem, my friend."

Carnak rushed at Mike and rammed him against the wall. He and Mike exchanged several punches until General Asher let out a screeching howl. Carnak froze in his tracks, and Mike leveled him with a solid left-handed upper-cut punch.

"Tell me what they are doing here, or I'll kill all of you," General Asher demanded.

Carnak got up slowly, incensed by Mike's repeated dominance over him. Mike again smiled as blood trickled down his chin. He carefully considered his words as he explained to Asher how Empire believed they were joining forces with Sysco and would stop at nothing to prevent that. General Asher was reluctant to believe that they'd have the audacity to attack a Scrat warship with all its firepower. "Let them think that the module isn't here yet?" suggested Mike. "They won't attack if it means they will lose any chance of finding it."

General Asher chuckled gruffly. "Well played, Colby. Unfortunately for you, I'm not intimidated by Empire."

Despite Mike's suggestion, the Scrat technician placed the module on the interface surface of the console. Mike nudged Tisch back into the corridor.

"They don't get off this ship alive," shouted General Asher. The soldiers immediately pursued them.

Mike pulled Tisch into a narrow alcove in the corridor, and they vanished. A loud blast sent pieces of torn metal and shrapnel from the console across the control room. Several soldiers fell to the ground, seriously wounded. General Asher was thrown to the ground as well.

Gemini lay dazed on the floor with lacerations on her face and forehead. The fire-suppression system isolated all access to the control room, preventing additional Scrat soldiers from entering.

Mike and Tisch appeared on the bridge of the *Blue Eagle*. Tisch embraced Mike. "You saved my ass," she whispered in his ear.

Mike smiled at her and affirmed, "I'd do it again, too."

The men noticed immediately that Gemini wasn't with them. Julian grinned, thinking that the plan was for him to replace Gemini after all. Wilmer and Geezer swarmed on them with hugs and handshakes.

"You did it!" Geezer yelled excitedly.

"We did it," Mike replied proudly. Tisch gazed at her crew of rescuers with pride.

Wilmer then announced, "I'll shut the gate before our friends come calling."

"No!" replied Mike. "I have to go back for Gemini."

Wilmer, Geezer, and Julian were stunned by his reply. Tisch froze in horror with her hands on her hips. "You can't go back there, Mike," she blurted with teary eyes. "They'll kill you."

"This is part of the plan," Mike reminded them. He hugged Tisch and promised to return safe. He felt horrible for doing this to her, but it had to be done. Wilmer pleaded for him to stay, but Mike promptly stepped back into the portal and vanished. Tisch paced crazily with her hands on her head in a panic. She looked to the men for help.

"He has a plan, Tisch," Geezer remarked confidently. "He knows what he's doing."

"Like hell he does!" she shouted, frozen with fear and unsure of what to do. She didn't want to lose Mike, but she didn't want to die either.

"Then go get him," urged Geezer.

"Well, grasshopper?" Julian said with a stone-faced expression. "Here's your chance."

Tisch glared at him but then understood what he meant. She removed a pulse rifle from a steel cabinet and then pointed it with one hand toward the men. "You'd better hope I come back with him," she warned, "or else."

The men cringed, knowing she meant what she said. They started to follow, but Tisch ordered them to stay put. "I'll handle this - my way," she declared with an attitude. "Understand?"

The men nodded in unison. Tisch paused in front of the invisible portal and stared back at them once more. Wilmer stood silent, fearing the worst. Julian's hands were tucked in his pants pockets, an expression of anxiety on his face. She approached Julian and placed the barrel of the rifle against his cheek. "I'll show you 'grasshopper.' Don't shut that whatever-it-is you call it." She stepped through the portal and vanished.

Geezer groaned, "I have no idea what the hell these people are doing with their disappearing act, but it's giving me the willies."

"You don't want to know," Julian replied. "Trust me."

"Smart answer," quipped Wilmer.

Geezer took a joint out of his pocket and lit it. Julian and Wilmer stared at him condescendingly. "Hey, we all have our vices," Geezer uttered and took a long toke.

Inside the alien ship, smoke and fire filled the control room and surrounding corridors. The console was destroyed, and the sounds of alarms and a fire Klaxon filled the room. General Asher lay wounded on the floor with a portion of a metal panel from the console buried in his shoulder. Many of his soldiers were scattered across the floor, dead or wounded.

Gemini crawled through the debris. Blood smeared the floor from her face and shoulder. She called out pleadingly for Mike, but there was no sign of him. Her head rested against the floor and she cried.

Mike emerged from the alcove, but the doors to the control room were sealed by the fire protection system. He swore and then took a shot with his pulse pistol at the control box. It smoked and fell to the floor in pieces. Mike grabbed the door and pressed sideways until it budged. Soon it was open far enough for him to enter.

Smoke poured out into the corridor. He searched desperately until he heard Gemini's cries. When he found her, he gently lifted her to her feet. Gemini was elated. "I knew you wouldn't leave me," she uttered weakly. "You still care."

"No, I'm just being humane," he replied coldly and approached the door to the corridor.

General Asher saw Mike rescue Gemini and shouted orders in his Scrat dialect. Four wounded soldiers promptly cut Mike and Gemini off from reaching the corridor with rifles aimed at their heads. Mike sneered as he turned to the corridor. Again, he was cut off by three more soldiers. The sound of Scrat pounding on the closed hatches echoed through the control room, adding to the chaos.

General Asher leaned against the bulkhead for support and forced a sarcastic laugh. "It's time to die, Colby."

Mike sighed, knowing there was no way out this time. "Well, you got your wish, Gem," he commented cynically. "We're together until death do us part."

"I did it again, Mike. I betrayed you," she moaned regretfully.

"Yeah, you did," Mike replied. "I knew you would. You are what you are. You can't change." She lowered her head in shame.

General Asher dropped to his knees as his wound took its toll on him. The soldiers stepped closer with the barrels of their pulse rifles just inches from Mike and Gemini. They eagerly awaited the order to shoot. Gemini nestled her head against Mike's shoulder and confessed, "If I have to die, there's no one else I'd rather be with." Mike groaned at the thought.

Tisch emerged from the dissipating smoke and marched toward the soldiers. "Get away from them!" she ordered. Then without hesitation, she fired four shots and killed the soldiers closest to Mike and Gemini.

"Tisch, what the hell are you doing here?" Mike asked, stunned by her appearance.

Focused on the Scrat, Tisch fired at the remaining three soldiers and then approached Mike and Gemini. The soldiers fell to the floor, dead without getting off a shot. "I came to get your stupid ass out of here."

"You won't escape, Colby," groaned Asher as he reached for a dead soldier's rifle. "I'll see to that."

Tisch walked past Mike toward General Asher. She kicked the rifle away from him and placed hers against his forehead. His eyes widened with fear. "A present for you, asshole," she announced coldly. "For your generous hospitality."

"Wait," he begged with his clawed hands extended. Tisch fired three pulses into his head, leaving a smoking hole.

Carnak staggered from the smoke behind her with his pistol aimed at her head. Mike set Gemini down and retrieved a corpse's pistol. "You lose, Colby," boasted Carnak.

"It ends the same way every time, Carnak," Mike reminded him. He smiled and fired past Tisch's head. The pulse struck Carnak in the forehead, killing him.

Tisch gingerly touched her ear. It was purple from the heat of the pulse, and her hair was singed. "You dick!" she shouted at Mike. He was confused by her reaction. After all, he had just saved her.

Two more soldiers approached Mike from behind. Tisch fired two shots, one past each of Mike's ears. The pulses struck and killed the soldiers. Mike and Gemini turned around slowly and saw the dead soldiers. Both Mike's ears were red from the heat of pulses. He winced from the pain but said nothing, knowing that Tisch had proved her point.

"That's how I do it in the real universe," she informed him.

Tisch walked toward them, Rambo-style, with an attitude. Gemini cringed, thinking she was next. Tisch pressed the barrel of the rifle against Mike's jaw. "Get your ass back to the ship before I use this on you."

"Yes, boss!" blurted Mike. He lifted Gemini in his arms and hustled to the alcove. Tisch backed toward the alcove, covering them from behind.

A second door opened to the control room, and a Scrat officer entered with six soldiers. They targeted Mike, Tisch, and Gemini. "Wait, Colby. We need to talk," announced the officer named Creeg.

"You have about twenty seconds," Tisch replied. "Spit it out fast." Mike and Gemini were impressed with Tisch's authoritative attitude.

Creeg gestured for his men to lower their weapons. Mike nodded to Tisch for her to comply as well. "What do you want?" Mike asked.

"I am the next in line to lead the Scrat," Creeg explained. "I'd like a truce and some help in dealing with Empire."

"You still have weapons to defend yourself?" Mike asked.

"Some," answered Creeg. "Without our command control center, we lost the use of much of our weaponry."

Mike pondered for a moment and then inquired, "How many fighters do you have?"

"An assault craft and twelve fighters that are battle-worthy," he responded somberly. "The others can't be accessed without the main console."

Mike instructed Creeg to have them stand by to support him when Empire's ships go on the offensive. Gemini watched eagerly as Mike once again found a way to survive and come out a winner. She was ashamed by what she had lost in that one moment of weakness when she had cheated on him. Even worse, he gave her a chance to prove him wrong, and she betrayed him once again.

Creeg nodded appreciatively and replied, "We will be ready. Perhaps this will mark a new era in our history between us."

"I'd like that," Mike replied and departed through the portal. Tisch cautiously backed in behind them for protection.

On board the *Blue Eagle*, Mike, Gemini, and Tisch appeared on the bridge. "Close it, Wilmer," ordered Mike.

Wilmer quickly deselected the program that enabled the transport module to maintain the portal. Mike set Gemini on the ground and considered their next course of action.

Tish stood with the rifle over her shoulder and one hand on her hip. The two women stared at each other, more civil than in the past. Both were too weak to fight, but too stubborn to back down. Mike instructed Julian and Wilmer to get the women to the infirmary while he dealt with the approaching freighters. The women were reluctant to leave with so much at stake. Julian tried to coax them off the bridge, but they refused to exit.

"Geezer, what do we know about the weaponry on those ships?" inquired Mike.

Geezer already had their specs up on his monitor. Grimly, he responded, "Class twos. They've got a lot more than we do."

"Not for long," he barked. Mike studied the specs on Geezer's monitor.

Tisch and Gemini glanced at each other as they watched Mike in action. Curious, Tisch asked Gemini, "Is he always like this at crunch time?"

Gemini nodded. "Crunch time is his time, unfortunately."

"I can see we're going to have authority issues around here," Tisch remarked.

Gemini cracked a smile. "If you only knew. He can be one tough son of a bitch."

Wilmer stood by the three of them and relented that they weren't leaving. Julian grew frustrated at his missed opportunity to take care of Gemini. He stood by her with his hands on her shoulders, subtly nudging her, but with no success.

Geezer attempted to make contact with Empire's ships once more. This time, he got a response. "*Blue Eagle*, we know Gemini is with you," a man's voice responded. "Surrender her to us, and we'll spare your lives."

"Negative," answered Geezer.

"Tell her Antwan is here to collect," the voice continued. "She'll understand."

Gemini pushed away from Julian and stormed to the console. Sternly, she replied, "I told you, Antwan, the next time you mess with me, you'll be sorry."

Antwan's laughter was heard over the transmitter and infuriated her even more. "I know you failed to get your treaty with the Scrat," he continued. "I can only assume you lost the module as well. You have nothing left for leverage to protect your precious position. Surrender now and let the big boys handle things."

Geezer glanced up at Gemini, wondering what her next response would be. She hesitated for a moment and then replied, "I have Colby on my side. Besides, I have the Scrat on my side as well. Now get out of here before you get the same treatment Jessup and Grim got."

Geezer was pleased and high-fived her. Julian was surprised by the camaraderie that was developing with her and Mike. Their confidence was short-lived when the alarm sounded as the freighters' weapons systems locked onto them. Gemini instinctively reached under her bra for the packet of pills she had stowed there. Everyone watched curiously as she tossed them into the trash can. "Who needs that shit anyway?" she remarked sarcastically. Mike smiled at her in approval.

"Are you strong enough to man a turret?" he asked Tisch.

"Damn right I am," she replied confidently. "It's still my ship, Colby."

"Then let's get to it!" he declared confidently.

On the way to the turrets, Mike reminded Tisch about the small plate on the nose of the ships that protect the controls for the automatic firing systems. The two tapped knuckles in another sign of camaraderie. Tisch hesitated at the ladder to the upper turret and turned to Mike. He paused by the ladder to the lower turret and waited for her to say something arrogant.

"What's wrong?" he asked.

"You want to be on top?" she offered.

"Yeah," he replied, "but not now."

Tisch kissed his cheek and ogled him before taking the upper turret. Mike was inspired by her change in attitude and willingly took the lower turret. The two of them promptly targeted the nose plates and fired single, accurate shots at the four lead freighters. With the shots appearing harmless, the freighters continued to close in on them.

Geezer issued another warning, but Antwan, unaware of the damage his ships had just incurred, mocked their shooting as an act of desperation. He gave the order, and the freighters fired repeatedly at the *Blue Eagle* with many shots missing badly. His shouts of frustration were heard across the open transmission in embarrassing fashion as he threatened his captains for their incompetent shooting.

Geezer activated their forward shields as Mike and Tisch returned fire, slow and methodical to preserve power. One by one, they targeted the nose plates on the other freighters. Suddenly, Creeg's fighters appeared and positioned themselves in defensive formation around the *Blue Eagle*. The freighters held their position and continued to fire at them.

Antwan was mortified when he realized that the Scrat did come to some arrangement with Gemini. His captains were reluctant to engage the Scrat and restricted their fire to the *Blue Eagle* only.

Geezer gave them one final warning and advised Antwan to consider that none of their weapons systems' auto-fire controls were functional. On board the lead freighter, Antwan was informed by his technicians that they could only fire in manual. He became enraged, knowing that Gemini might beat him after all.

The Scrat fighters swarmed on the freighters and quickly wore down their force shields. The freighters' cannons struggled to make hits as their crews weren't trained to fire in manual. Four of the freighters were crippled badly and left the battle. The remaining six took numerous hits as their shields dwindled down with fading power.

Geezer contacted Antwan once more. "Anything you want to say, Mr. Antwan? Gemini is having a drink right now and prefers not to be disturbed."

"Screw all of you!" Antwan shouted. "This is just the beginning. We are far from done with you."

Antwan was then informed by his technicians that they had lost all firing capability due to exhausted power banks. The freighters weren't designed for battles such as this, only to repel marauders in short spats. Antwan reluctantly ordered his ships to retreat and return to base. Creeg's fighters returned to their ship as well.

Mike and Tisch met in the corridor by the turret ladders. This time, Tisch pressed him against the wall and placed her lips close to his. "Well done, Michael," she remarked.

"And you as well," he responded.

Tisch embraced him and kissed him passionately. Mike was relieved as he had feared Tisch's attitude when things calmed down might return to its earlier volatility.

After congratulating the crew on the bridge, Mike ordered Julian and Wilmer to take the women to the infirmary with no excuses this time.

When Mike and Geezer were alone on the bridge, Mike man-hugged him and complimented him on his piloting. He assured Geezer that he and Tisch would lay out ground rules so that there would be no misunderstanding of who was in charge. Geezer informed Mike that he would be proud to stay on with him as a member of their crew. Both were confident that Tisch would be a much better person than before.

At the infirmary, Julian treated the women for their injuries. Not knowing what else to do, Wilmer provided beer for each of them. Gemini frowned but then accepted the beer to show her appreciation. When Julian was finished with them, he recommended they rest. Neither woman complied; both sitting up at the same time.

"Why'd you come back for us?" Gemini asked Tisch, fearing retribution for selling her out to the Scrat. The men grew uneasy, expecting the worst between them.

"Why did you kill my father?" Tisch countered.

Gemini stared back with moist eyes. "I didn't kill him. I was in love with your father. He took care of me when I was struggling with my addiction. He saved my life. After his death, I went back to lesser drugs for strength."

Tisch was stunned by her revelation. She was embarrassed as well for her treatment of Mike, now that she knew that it was her father who had ruined his marriage.

Mike and Geezer entered in a jovial mood. Mike sensed that the women were discussing Tisch's father. Recalling Gemini's words to him about her affair, his demeanor changed to one of sadness over the thought of her cheating on him with Tisch's father. He stepped back and sat down with Wilmer and Julian.

Gemini knew what Tisch really wanted to hear and was happy to disappoint her. "Your father asked me to make sure you got the *Blue Eagle* if anything happened to him," she continued. "He said it was the key to your dreams." Tisch was speechless. This wasn't at all what she had expected. Gemini continued, "You always hated me. I never had the chance to explain."

Now Tisch felt really horrible. "I'm sorry. I just…"

Gemini gestured with her hand for Tisch to stop. "I learned something today from both of you, and I'm really sorry for what I've done." Tisch was remorseful and admitted that she, too, had learned something. She then promised everyone that she'd be a different person from now on.

"Now that things are back to normal," Mike announced, "I'll be leaving once we get back to Taurus."

Tisch was shocked. "Why would you do that? I thought we were good!"

"Are we?" he asked. "If I stay, no more nonsense, and I want your word that you won't abandon me again."

"You have it," she assured him. "I promise to make it up to you and then some."

Tisch extended her arms to Geezer, and the two hugged. "I'm so glad you came back. I won't let you down either," she vowed.

"I know you won't," he responded.

"Your father was killed by mercenaries from Empire Shipping," Mike revealed to Tisch.

"Mike took care of them for you," added Wilmer.

Tisch wasn't surprised by the news. "Asher said something to me about my father," she mentioned. "He said that I should have learned from him, since he was somehow involved with the module and bringing the Scrat here."

"And I learned some things from the Empire agents that were a bit disturbing too," Mike informed her. "We'll discuss them later."

Tisch didn't respond; she feared her father's involvement with the Scrat and Gemini could be an issue of contention between her and Mike. She didn't want to undo all the progress she had just made with him over their past. The men glanced at each other but said nothing.

"Will you honor our agreement?" Mike asked Gemini.

Gemini eyed each of them briefly before replying. "You and your crew are free to operate as independents, and the *Blue Eagle* is yours to operate as you see fit, Tisch. You earned it."

Tisch was ecstatic. She shook Gemini's hand. "Thank you so much!"

"Oh, and I'll retract the fine too," she added. "It's the least I can do for what you went through." Gemini extended her arms and hugged her. "Perhaps we can forget the past and start over." Tisch was overcome with emotion as she and Gemini embraced. Mike was proud of Gemini for doing the right thing - for once.

"And now we're even," he reminded Tisch. "I delivered everything I said I would."

"Yes, you did. And you saved my ass." Tisch approached him and placed her arms around him. "I can't believe you came for me after all I put you through."

"I heard your ass was worth saving," he kidded.

Tisch punched Mike's arm affectionately and quipped, "You bet your ass it is." The two embraced and kissed passionately.

Julian complained, "Here we go with the ass jokes again."

"Spare me," pleaded Geezer.

Gemini grew depressed and stared at the floor. She knew she would never have another chance with Mike again. Mike felt pity for her, so he announced, "Gemini, I want you to meet your new business partner."

Gemini glanced at Julian and then back at Mike. "You're kidding, right?"

Mike stood in front of them and explained, "Julian knows a lot about running a shipping operation."

Julian became anxious and added, "I handled Aurora's shipping for some time before their regime change."

Gemini glanced at Mike and then smiled at Julian. "I guess it can't hurt to give you a shot," she relented. "If you really are good at this, I'll make your position permanent."

"I won't disappoint you," Julian assured her.

Then she frowned at him. "You will pay for dumping trash on me, though."

Julian grinned sheepishly and pointed at Wilmer. Wilmer shrugged his shoulders innocently.

Mike lifted Tisch onto his lap and held her close to him. Julian escorted Gemini to the hatch but then hesitated. "Just one thing, Tisch," he began. "Doesn't this make me your boss?"

Gemini wondered what the conversation stemmed from. Tisch recalled their earlier threats to each other and responded with a sly grin. "You said that would only happen when..."

Mike quickly interjected, "That's enough, Tisch."

Tisch was proud of her conquest - Mike. This time, she felt no apprehension about him. Wilmer and Geezer laughed, knowing that Mike was still adjusting to her new attitude.

"Who'd have thought either would happen," Julian teased and escorted Gemini to her cabin.

"That man still has no morals," complained Tisch.

"Neither does Gemini," Mike reminded her. "They're perfect for each other."

Wilmer and Geezer chuckled over their comments. Tisch gave Mike a seductive smile. He got the hint and followed her out of the infirmary.

In the corridor outside her cabin, Tisch pressed him against the wall and inquired, "So what's the deal with this module? Obviously, it's a teleporting device of some sort."

"Somebody, to be determined, developed it and then brought the Scrat here to help them. Whether or not it has anything to do with shipping, that remains to be seen," Mike explained. "Like Gemini, they had no idea what they were dealing with. Somehow your father was involved in it. Good or bad, I don't know."

Tisch tugged on his arm and pulled him inside. "We have a lot to catch up on," she informed him.

Surprised by her confidence, Mike responded, "I don't want to rush things."

Tisch gazed at him with hungry eyes and asked in a seductive tone, "But what if I want you to?"

Mike was amazed by her change of heart. They kissed for several moments before pausing. "So, what do we do about Empire?" she asked.

"They'll pay, just not today."

Tisch hugged him tightly. She appreciated his understanding. Mike placed his hands on hers and started to speak. "Tisch, I..."

Tisch placed her finger over his lips. "Let's not dwell on the past," she interrupted.

They kissed again, and then Mike softly sang the words to "Time Loves a Hero." Tisch crooned along with him as they danced slowly.

On the bridge, Geezer slid his chair back and folded his arms. He looked annoyed as Wilmer stood over the console, still wearing his janitor's uniform, and spoke into the transmitter to Shannon. "Oh, I showed those aliens a thing or two," he bragged. "How about dinner? We should be back at the station in a few hours." Wilmer pumped his fist in the air as Shannon agreed to meet with him for a date.

Geezer stared at him in disbelief. Self-consciously, Wilmer looked at his uniform and then at Geezer. "Hey, I helped too," he responded defensively.

Back on Taurus, Sara stood in front of Shannon's desk as Shannon ended the transmission with Wilmer. "It's done. I'll have your module in no time," Shannon promised her. Sara handed her an envelope and smiled as she walked away.

When the *Blue Eagle* docked on Taurus, Captain Tieg and his men awaited the crew's exit. Gemini and Julian exited first and immediately debriefed Tieg over the events.

When Mike and Tisch met them, Tieg punched Mike in the mouth. "That's for the damage to my cruiser, Colby," he announced.

Mike rubbed his chin. "Not bad, Tieg," he remarked with a smile. "Not bad at all." The two men laughed as everyone else watched nervously.

Then Tieg suggested, "You and I need to discuss some security issues." Mike agreed and shook hands with him.

Wilmer exited next and hurried across the lobby to Shannon's desk. Then Geezer rambled out and surveyed the crowd. Pleased with the outcome of things, especially the resolution of Tisch's emotional issues, he went to the pub to unwind with a beer.

Mike and Tisch lay in her bed under the sheet. Tisch studied Mike's face as he gazed up at the ceiling. She had never felt as good as she did at that moment and with her knight in shining armor, nothing could ruin it. Mike pulled her on top of him and kissed her passionately.

"Aren't we getting off the ship?" she asked with a hint of humor. "I thought you had things to do."

"Not today," he responded. "Let's just stay here like this." Tisch was pleased with the idea and kissed him hungrily.

The next day, everyone met in the galley. Mike and Tisch discussed ground rules over a beer to prevent any future misunderstandings about his actions and how they impact Tisch and the crew. Mike informed Tisch that he would continue to do assignments from time to time to maintain a mercenary alias. When Tisch's face grew taut, he explained that Empire Shipping and Antwan would be back again and probably soon. Along with that, he was likely to be a target. He preferred to leave the impression that he still worked alone as a mercenary and not as a crewman on the *Blue Eagle*.

Tisch understood and assured him that she would be there to back him up. He also announced to the crew that he and Tisch were good and there would be no more issues that would affect them. The crew was satisfied, and everyone toasted to their new beginning.

CHAPTER XI

A STRANGE TURN OF EVENTS

The next day, Gemini contacted Tisch on board the *Blue Eagle* and requested a meeting with her and Mike immediately in her conference room. Tisch was curious as to why she would summon them but agreed to come. Tisch, joined by Mike, left the *Blue Eagle* and passed through the transport area on Taurus to the lobby.

Mike noticed Wilmer at Shannon's station flirting with her. He could tell Wilmer was courting her by the playful poses and silly expressions the two took on while talking. Mike nudged Tisch and giddily pointed to Wilmer. Tisch gave him a playful shove and chastised him for mocking Wilmer in his pursuit of love.

"There's something about that woman," Mike commented. "I'm not sure what, but I have an uneasy feeling that there's more to her than Wilmer's ready for."

"Are you jealous?" chided Tisch. The two laughed and continued to the elevator.

When the elevator doors opened, Captain Tieg and two of his men awaited them. Mike and Tisch entered the elevator, wondering what was happening that required their presence.

Curious, Mike inquired, "Am I going to jail again?"

Tieg smiled and apologized for hitting him earlier. He did press Mike to promise he wouldn't damage any more security ships, though. "Drinks will have to wait," Captain Tieg commented. "Priorities are changing."

"Perhaps Gemini can help with that," Mike kidded.

Captain Tieg shook his head, disappointed. "I'm on the clock. Sorry."

The elevator doors opened on the eleventh floor. The two shook hands and then exited. Tisch and the two security agents followed and were entertained by the unusual camaraderie that had developed between Mike and Tieg.

Captain Tieg requested that Mike give him a detailed report on the Empire agents and any pertinent information he had learned during their encounter. Tieg then warned Mike that they still don't know the extent of Empire's infiltration of Taurus. Mike assured him that he would do all he could to help them secure the station. Tisch was impressed with the way Mike had earned respect from Tieg and from Creeg, the Scrat officer, as well. He had even earned her respect despite her earlier misgivings about him.

They reached Gemini's conference room and parted ways with the security team. Tieg and his men returned to the elevator and disappeared. The panel door to Gemini's conference room slid open and Gemini beckoned them to enter. Tisch commented that this was an odd feeling, coming to the Executive Level, especially being in Gemini's conference room. Mike warned her not to be fooled by the luxurious decor. He kidded that it was really the spider's web, and they were the flies.

Gemini and Julian sat at the oval conference table. Julian had a tablet in front of him and entered notes from a discussion they had just completed. When Mike and Tisch entered, he immediately approached them and shook hands, followed by a man-hug for Mike. "It's good to see you again, my friend," he greeted him. Then surprisingly, he turned to Tisch and welcomed her with a hug too. Tisch grew uneasy; this was not the Julian she knew.

Gemini stood and, after greeting them, gestured for them to take seats at the table. She had her perfora in hand and politely turned it off. Julian poured drinks and brought them on a tray to the table. He handed Gemini a bourbon and set two rum drinks down in front of Mike and Tisch. He returned the tray to the bar and joined them with a fancy beer in hand. Mike was pleased to see that Julian fitted in with Gemini and her operation. At least Gemini wouldn't hound him anymore to partner with her to run the business.

Gemini tucked the perfora into her small handbag on the table. She began the meeting by thanking them for their help and for giving her a chance to make things right. With the pleasantries out of the way, she then announced her plans for expansion into the colonial regions of the galaxy.

Julian informed them that he had spoken with several of the research and mining companies who recently started colonies and learned that they welcomed Sysco Galactic Services to provide supply lines to their locations. Up to now, there had been none available, and it was expensive for them to waste resources on moving supplies when their focus was on mining ore or performing research and exploration.

Gemini offered to hire Tisch and the *Blue Eagle* to scout the colonies and report logistical data for establishing trade routes back to Julian. They would arrange for their freighters to operate the routes, leaving the *Blue Eagle* free to do "other things." They would also deliver small cargoes of goods on the first run to demonstrate their capability to deliver on their promise.

Tisch enjoyed the challenge of a scouting mission, and Gemini offered a fair wage for it. She was concerned about what "other things" meant, though. Gemini pointed out that they were an exceptional crew and ship. All they were missing was a shuttle to handle personal business with the clients.

Embarrassed, Mike reminded her that his shuttle was a wreck and still on board the Scrat command ship. Gemini offered to replace it with a new one in lieu of the credits that she owed him, if he was agreeable. Mike was more than happy to get a new shuttle, valuing his independence more than the credits. With everyone agreeable to Gemini's offer, they toasted to their future together as business partners.

After a sip of Gemini's fine rum, Mike sighed with delight and appreciation. It had always been a favorite of his and very hard to come by. Gemini commented that his lust for the good stuff was costing her a fortune.

"You mean you stock this rum just for me?" he asked, feeling honored.

Gemini held up her glass and responded, "You don't see me drinking it. Do you?"

Tieg's voice interrupted them from the intercom. "Gemini, you have a transmission from Antwan. He requests to speak with you."

"What is his location?" Gemini asked anxiously.

"We're tracking the transmission to pinpoint his location now."

Gemini glanced at the others uneasily and accepted the transmission. Antwan's face was beet red, and his temples were laced with veins, indicating his stress level. He warned Gemini that there was no place in the galaxy where she could hide from him.

"Does it look like I'm hiding from you, you buffoon?" she taunted him.

"I will deal with you when the time comes."

Mike interceded and warned, "It's only a matter of time before Empire pays for their crimes, and I'll be there to make sure you pay as well. So, why don't you go find a nice arcade where you can pretend you are someone important?" Antwan laughed at Mike's threat, not knowing Mike's background with Special Forces.

Gemini responded, "For someone who just got his ass handed to him, you're still an arrogant son of a bitch, Antwan."

"You see, Gemini, Empire Shipping is only part of your problem," he remarked confidently. "There is much more to this than Empire, and you pissed off people at a much higher level than mine."

Mike grew impatient with his bantering. "I've dismantled much bigger entities than Empire or anything else you think you're part of. You tell your buddies to stay away or Colby will come for them."

Antwan forced a laugh and shook his head in disbelief. "All you have to do is turn over the module and relinquish Sysco to us, and you can lead a profitable life anywhere you choose," he offered. "If not, then it's war." The transmission was terminated with no further response.

Gemini looked to Mike for his perspective on the call. Mike suggested that they focus on securing Taurus first. In the meantime, the *Blue Eagle* will prepare for its first scouting mission as planned. Mike offered to put together a plan to help Captain Tieg deal with Empire Shipping and their partners during the trip.

Gemini thanked him for his help and offered to provide anything they needed. The group finished their drinks and ended the meeting with hugs and handshakes. Mike and Tisch left the conference room and were escorted to the *Blue Eagle* by Tieg's men for their safety.

When Mike and Tisch arrived on the bridge, Geezer performed diagnostic checks with rock music blaring from the speakers in the ceiling. Wilmer and Shannon sat at Julian's station. Unaffected by the music, he instructed her on how the navigation system worked. When he noticed Tisch and Mike, he promptly introduced Shannon to them. "She is my recommendation for Julian's position," he mentioned, nervous about making such a bold request.

Tisch glanced at Mike for his thoughts. He nodded for her to approve Wilmer's recommendation. "Fine, Wilmer," she replied. "But you are responsible for any training she requires."

Wilmer jumped up and hugged Tisch. Shannon shook Tisch's hand and then hugged Wilmer. Mike announced, "Sounds like we need a beer and a group hug in the galley for our new crew member."

As they followed Mike to the hatch, Zenith blocked his path. Mike was surprised and commented, "Did someone leave the hatch open - again?"

"I've been waiting all day for you, Colby," Zenith replied. "You never miss a day at the pub."

Tisch glared at Mike, wondering what relationship he had with this woman. Zenith announced that she was there to apply for a job. She also had information that she felt Mike should know about. "To the galley," Mike directed everyone. He was concerned about Zenith's presence around Tisch, considering her promiscuous overtures on his shuttle after he had rescued her from her kidnappers.

They entered the galley and took seats. Wilmer served beer to everyone, while Tisch waited patiently for an explanation. Mike reminded her about her pledge to be better than before. Tisch countered by asking, "Should I be worried?"

Mike patted her knee and focused on Zenith. He asked what brought her there and what information she had that was so important. She informed them that she was interested in joining their crew.

"I thought we covered that before, Zenith," Mike reminded her.

"A lot of things have changed since then." She related that she had an engineering education and trained the technicians maintaining her father's ship. Then she added, "Besides, this is Captain Mallory's ship, not your shuttle." Mike groaned and rubbed his temples. He felt a headache coming on quickly.

"Sounds like you had it good, working for your dad," Tisch commented. "Why come here?"

Zenith looked down, somewhat embarrassed. "My father... He treats me like property and is determined to control my life for his benefit," she confessed. "I can do better without him."

Tisch was impressed by her directness and honesty while Mike remained suspicious over her presence. Zenith went on to explain that her father, Dax, was planning to pursue a merger between Hellfire Fuels and Sysco Galactic Services. Mike still didn't see the value of the information until Zenith mentioned there was an investor whom she claimed offered Dax additional capital to make sure the deal happened.

"So, who was this investor?" Mike inquired.

"A guy named Antwan," answered Zenith. "He was very bossy and mentioned consequences if Dad couldn't make the deal happen." Mike and Tisch glanced at each other, concerned.

"What do you suppose he meant?" asked Tisch.

"I think they would either buy him out or force him out of the company even though it's his. The man sounded determined."

"When are they proposing to make this deal happen?" Mike inquired.

"Dad told him it would take time because arrangements needed to be made and vendors notified."

Mike felt that there was no urgency yet and assured her that they would handle it when the time came. Zenith looked uneasy by his lack of concern, but said no more about it. As far as her employment, Mike left that up to Tisch. Tisch raised the concern about how the men would behave with, not just one, but two young women on the ship. Both Zenith and Shannon promised to do what they could to help maintain discipline.

Tisch then offered the engineering position to Zenith so long as she understood Mike was off-limits. Zenith was disappointed but agreed to be an asset to the crew as well as a pipeline for any information from her father to Mike.

Wilmer suddenly realized that Zenith had just taken his position. "What am I going to do?" he asked frantically. "That was my job!"

Tisch contemplated for a moment and then responded, "You are in charge of training our new recruits, and, more importantly, you will assist Mike with whatever he needs. Understood?"

Wilmer was stunned by her offer. "Sure, that would be... great!"

Mike suggested to Wilmer that he take the responsibility to in-process the women on Taurus and get them situated in their cabins on the ship. When Wilmer gave them a thumbs-up, Mike and Tisch ended the meeting and left the galley. As they proceeded down the corridor, Tisch asked Mike in a concerned tone, "Are you sure this is a good idea?"

Mike chuckled. "Absolutely not. But it'll be fun."

"It's going to be one hell of a crew," joked Tisch.

"You want Julian back?" Mike kidded.

"Uh, let's give the girls a chance, shall we?" she responded playfully. "So long as they can perform their responsibilities with no drama, I'm okay with them."

The next day, Mike boarded the *Blue Eagle* with Wilmer. They placed the transformer from the bridge onto rollers and moved it down to the cargo bay. They hoped to find a more subtle installation that would have proximity to the module when it was installed. Mike discussed the possibility of a permanent installation of the module into one of the ship's systems to prevent it from being mobile to prevent its theft.

Wilmer agreed with him and took Mike to the power distribution room located directly above the cargo bay. The cooler temperatures in the cargo bay kept the room's temperature moderate. He suggested it to be the ideal location due to its proximity to the transformer in the cargo bay below. It was also an unlikely place for someone to search for it. He pointed out that a module like this was more likely to be found installed near communications interface equipment in a controlled environment, not a power distribution room. Content that their location was appropriate, they agreed to wait until the ship was underway before installing the module.

Tisch arrived and informed them that Gemini requested an urgent meeting with the crew. Wilmer reported to her that the girls were in-processing at the station and Geezer was at the pub, placing bets on a sporting event. Mike and Wilmer were more than happy to take a break from the ship and hoped to indulge in Gemini's expensive stock of liquors. When asked, Tisch replied that she had no idea what the meeting was for, but it sounded important. They promptly left the ship for the Executive Level on Taurus.

When Mike led them past security to the elevator, Tisch commented to Mike, "Are you special or something?" Mike wore a smug grin and entered a five-digit security code. He was surprised when the elevator didn't respond. "Something wrong?" she chided. "I thought you had privileges."

Mike placed his hands on his hips and complained, "She had the security code changed. What a bitch!" They returned to the security desk, and Mike requested entry to the Executive Level. The desk sergeant summoned two sentries to escort them to Gemini's conference room.

Now it was Wilmer's turn to jest with Mike. "Had your special privileges revoked for bad behavior?"

"Oh, shut up," grumbled Mike.

When the elevator stopped on the eleventh floor, they exited and followed the sentries to Gemini's suite.

The first sentry opened the door and announced their presence. Gemini instructed the woman to let them in. Mike entered and was surprised to see Dax Jensen, Captain Tieg, and Julian at the conference table with Gemini. Then he noticed that Gemini and Dax were holding hands on the table!

Gemini saw his expression and smiled. She felt a degree of satisfaction now that Mike knew she had finally moved on from him. After short greetings and introductions, Gemini informed them that their presence was required because something important had come up involving the *Blue Eagle*.

Captain Tieg began the meeting by discussing several security concerns, including one regarding his men and their loyalties. He was concerned that some had been approached by strangers and offered compensation for information on the *Blue Eagle* and Gemini's interaction with Hellfire Fuels. Mike pondered what the importance of that last item was.

Dax spoke next and announced the details of his contact with Antwan. He revealed that Empire was part of a parent company named Kronos Enterprises, which wanted a merger between Hellfire Fuels and Sysco Galactic Services.

Mike was surprised to hear the name Kronos and sensed that this was the link to the module he was looking for. Julian suggested that Kronos might take control of Hellfire prior to the merger by replacing the board members with their own people, which, if executed, was a prelude to a takeover of Sysco via a merger. Dax mentioned that three of the eleven board members had already mysteriously disappeared.

"So where does the *Blue Eagle* come in?" questioned Tisch.

Dax revealed that Hellfire Fuels had developed a new engine and a fuel-regenerating process. "We have four of these engines and would like to install them on the *Blue Eagle* to prevent Kronos from getting their hands on them," he divulged. "In addition, the fuel regenerator can also be installed, which will allow you to fly ten times longer without refueling."

Mike, Tisch, and Wilmer glanced at each other, stunned by Dax's revelation. "Where and when will this installation take place?" asked Mike.

Gemini informed them that the installation and testing would be done on Taurus and that the equipment was already in route from Hellfire Fuels. She then explained that increased security would be needed during the retrofit of the *Blue Eagle* and announced that GSS would be responsible for that.

Out of curiosity, Mike inquired, "Who or what do we know about GSS other than that they are a high-tech security organization?"

"Not much, I'm afraid. Their reputation is impeccable, and they contacted me about helping us out."

Mike glanced at Julian and then Wilmer. They were aware that Sara was involved, but obviously Gemini wasn't. Tisch suspected there was a motive to Mike's question but said nothing.

Mike then asked, "Does any other corporation know about the new engines or the fuel regenerator?"

"Only our scientists know that it has successfully been completed," Dax replied. "Nano chip trackers have been installed in the base of their necks for monitoring. If anyone attempts to divulge any details of the technology, they are nullified instantly."

Wilmer chuckled. "Nullified—the politically correct word for exterminated." Only Mike found his quip funny.

"So, you want to move your new technology onto the *Blue Eagle* before these people find out about it, assuming they don't already know," Tisch surmised aloud.

"Yes, I do," answered Dax somberly. "I invested too much into these projects to see these criminals steal them from me." He went on to explain that the other board members took a buyout for fear of their lives, but not before agreeing to liquidate the company. "We obviously had a unanimous vote, which offset the issue of the missing three members," he concluded.

"When does the retrofit start?" asked Mike.

"As soon as you give the okay," answered Gemini anxiously.

"And the engines are on their way?" questioned Mike, suspicious.

"Of course," replied Gemini. "That was the first thing on our list." Dax nodded in agreement as proof of their unity on the issue.

Tisch looked to Mike and Wilmer. Each nodded in approval. "Then go for it," she responded. "And what about training on the new equipment?"

"Tomorrow morning, on the fourth floor," Gemini answered. "You and Wilmer will receive training on the engines and fuel regenerator. These changes won't affect Geezer's duties."

"What about me?" blurted Mike, feeling left out.

"Oh, I almost forgot," Gemini commented giddily. "A new onloading system will be installed as well; my present to Tisch for what I did to her with the Scrat. It has four subsystems on it, increasing your capability to transfer cargo much faster. You'll be trained on maintenance and operation of the whole system." Mike looked disappointed and rolled his eyes.

"Suck it up for the team," chided Tisch.

"Yeah, yeah," he grumbled.

Gemini stood and inquired, "Any other questions?"

Mike raised his hand, exhibiting a disappointed expression. "Why'd you change the security code for the elevators?"

Gemini snickered. "To keep uninvited jackasses off my floor." Tisch and Wilmer both punched Mike in the arms and laughed at him. "Oh, Michael. I forgot to mention," Gemini added. "Your new shuttle is in Bay 17. Try not to destroy this one."

Mike's eyes reflected his excitement at the news. "I'm going to check it out right now."

Julian stepped away from the table and spoke quietly into his communicator. He returned to the table and informed them, "The *Blue Eagle's* upgrade will start immediately. Expect to see GSS and technicians around your ship by the time you return to it."

"Will we still have access to it?" Tisch inquired.

"Of course," replied Julian. "Just try not to get in the way. We're on a very tight schedule."

Mike and Tisch glanced at each other uneasily, noting the urgency to start the upgrade.

CHAPTER XII

BAIT AND SWITCH

Mike arrived at Bay 17 and was surprised to see two GSS officers standing at the entrance. He showed his ID and was allowed access. One of the officers mentioned as he passed, "Sara sends her best, Mr. Colby."

"I'm sure she does," Mike responded sarcastically. Inside the bay was a beautiful late-model shuttle. As he eyed it, he noticed the name *Self-Righteous* painted professionally in Edwardian script on the hull.

"Oh, that bitch," Mike mumbled to himself. Then he laughed as he realized that Gemini still held a grudge over their resolution. She had always hated to lose.

Inside, the shuttle was equipped with the latest technology including force shields, and light weaponry. Mike sat in the pilot's seat and watched the tutorial on the shuttle's computer. It was long and tedious. He became bored and pondered for a moment that Gemini actually came through for him with the shuttle. *There has to be a catch*, he thought to himself. *She doesn't give anything away for free.*

A short while later, Wilmer entered and took a seat next to him. He opened a lunch bag and took out the module. "I thought you might want this since strangers will be crawling all over the *Blue Eagle*."

"That was clever, putting it in a lunch bag," Mike remarked. He took it from him and inquired, "Can we install it on the shuttle?"

"Why not?" he responded. "I just have to verify that we have a magnetic source on board strong enough to operate it. After that, I just have to interface it to the computer." Mike gestured with his hands for Wilmer to have at it. He resumed the painful task of viewing the tutorial while Wilmer inspected the technical documents for the module's interface on a second monitor.

Wilmer found his answers in the documents and then contemplated the changes to the ship, the crew, and, more importantly, his relationship with Mike. Having Shannon and Zenith on board would take up a lot of his time. Things would surely be different.

After several minutes, Mike threw his hands up in frustration and blurted, "I need a break!"

Startled, Wilmer replied, "So do I. What are we going to do?"

Mike thought for a moment and then grinned deviously. "How about we go for a ride and try this baby out?"

Wilmer was pleased with his suggestion and hurried to the flight deck. He glanced back through the hatch at Mike, wondering why the hesitation. Mike contemplated where they should go and hated to waste an opportunity to do something spontaneous. Finally, he joined Wilmer and powered up the shuttle's systems. Next, he contacted the control center and informed them that they were exiting the station. After a few moments, he received a response authorizing their departure.

Outside the shuttle, red lights blinked around the bay and the sound of a siren filled the air. Thirty seconds later, the gates on the interior side of the bay sealed and the oxygen was removed, creating a vacuum. As soon as the vacuum was complete, the outer bay doors slid open vertically and the bay became ambient with space, void of gravity. The magnetic latching device released, and the shuttle drifted free of its mooring. Mike started the engines and piloted the shuttle out of the bay and away from Taurus.

"So where to?" inquired Wilmer curiously.

"I was thinking about visiting our friends on the Scrat command ship," answered Mike as he transferred the coordinates from the computer to the navigation system. "Damn, this is smooth," he added. "I guess I owe Gemini for this. She did me well."

Wilmer only stared in astonishment at Mike. "Why the hell would we go back to the Scrat ship after everything that happened?"

Mike chuckled. "The Scrat and I are cool now. We're like best friends, and I have an open invitation to come back to see them." Wilmer groaned, knowing there was more to this that he was unaware of.

During the trip, Wilmer set up an interface port for the installation of the module and designated a card slot in one of the racks. The module was designed smartly by the Archaeneans for use like a standard PC board, anticipating the humans' application of the module. Wilmer then programmed the computer to communicate with the card slot when the module was installed, for programming coordinates of locations.

The new shuttle was much faster than his old model, and they made quick time getting to the Scrat command ship. Mike contacted the ship and spoke with Creeg, the Scrat commander. Creeg was glad to hear from him and invited them to dock in the ship's transport bay.

Wilmer wondered how Mike had a way of turning the worst situation into a favorable one. This time it really puzzled him. "What happened to Asher?" inquired Wilmer.

"Oh, there was a bit of a regime change while we were there. The new leadership is much more hospitable."

Wilmer shook his head in disbelief as Mike docked the shuttle. He opened the locker and removed two pulse pistols. Mike turned and looked at him with a surprised expression. "Put those away!" he ordered. "They are our friends!" Wilmer was embarrassed but complied.

They left the flight deck and exited the shuttle. Creeg welcomed them and led them to the control room. Several of the Scrat technicians worked on repairs under the console and grumbled at the sight of Mike. Mike waved to them in a friendly gesture and took note of the damaged console. He turned to Creeg and asked, "How bad is the damage?"

"You did quite a number on our control system. It will take some time to repair."

"I'm sorry it had to go down that way," Mike replied apologetically.

"It had to be that way for change." Creeg led them from the control room to an office at the end of a corridor. Mike hadn't been to this part of the ship before and was curious of its design. Creeg closed the door and gestured for them to sit.

Wilmer was amazed that they were guests on a Scrat ship and was speechless. Mike inquired if they should address him by rank as they did General Asher. Creeg responded that it wouldn't be necessary. Only his people would do so.

"Is something wrong?" Mike asked, noting that Creeg's demeanor had grown somber.

"I have a very important request of you," he replied. "I know it's asking a lot."

"I'm listening," Mike responded.

Creeg explained that he needed to get back to the Nebula Galaxy and inform the Scrat command that the plans have changed and that there will be no invasion. He wanted them to understand that there would be peace between the Scrat and Sysco Galactic Services.

Wilmer inquired as to why the peace would be specific to Gemini's corporation only. Creeg revealed that Kronos Enterprises was behind Empire's interference with the shipping routes and was a threat to everyone, including the Scrat.

Mike understood what he was asking and considered the risk of revealing that he still had the module. "How can I help?" he asked.

Creeg requested that the three of them transport with the help of the module to the Nebula Galaxy. He would contact the Scrat command from there and see their reaction. If it was favorable, they would meet with them. In addition, he needed to acquire some components for the repair of his ship. If the Scrat command's reaction was not favorable, they would return without any further communication.

Wilmer looked apprehensive over Creeg's request, but Mike was willing to give it a shot. "I trust you, Creeg, and I hope we can have a lasting friendship between our people. We'll do what we can to help."

Creeg was pleased and provided them with the coordinates. Wilmer was hesitant until Mike urged him to get moving. "We haven't tried the module out on the shuttle yet," Wilmer cautioned. "I don't even know if it will work."

"I have faith in you," Mike said confidently. Creeg spoke with one of his officers in the control room and informed them that he would be gone for a short time to avoid any misconceptions about Mike's presence. The three of them left Creeg's office and returned to the shuttle.

Wilmer removed the lunch bag from a locker in the rear of the shuttle and installed the module in the navigation control panel. Mike questioned Creeg about his knowledge of Kronos Enterprises and Empire Shipping regarding the module.

Creeg's knowledge was limited to the fact that John Mallory, Tisch's father, had come to them for protection from Kronos. "Asher believed it to be a trap, but Mallory gave him the module in good faith to protect all of them from Kronos," explained Creeg.

Mike and Wilmer were stunned by the information. They had assumed that Mallory stole it from Empire Shipping.

Creeg continued, "When Mallory realized that he would be imprisoned by Asher after he demonstrated its use, he took advantage of Kronos's attack on our ships to escape. Asher had the module and didn't really care that Mallory fled. We fought a short but significant battle with Kronos and, thanks to the module, wiped out their entire force. We had some casualties, but nothing we couldn't recover from. Soon after, someone from Kronos contacted us and warned that they would be back for revenge. That's the last we heard of them."

Wilmer installed the module and returned to the flight deck. "Mission ready, I think," he announced nervously. Mike started the shuttle and piloted it out of the transport bay. When they reached open space, Wilmer activated the module and cringed. Mike held his breath, while Creeg remained unnerved. Nothing seemed to change. They waited for a few moments, and finally Mike asked Wilmer, "Did it work?"

Wilmer shrugged his shoulders. He wasn't sure what to expect in this situation. On board the *Blue Eagle*, he physically witnessed Mike disappear and reappear with Gemini and Tisch. Here, he had no indication, and the monitor appeared inconclusive.

Mike turned to Creeg for his thoughts. Creeg attempted to make contact with the Scrat command but received no response. "We need to get closer," he instructed them. Mike nodded to Wilmer, who reprogrammed the module through the shuttle's computer. He activated it and waited for a response. Now the monitor had clarity, and they recognized their position in the Nebula Galaxy. The shuttle was positioned between two large planets, and Mike recognized one of them as the home of the Scrat military command from his mission a few years ago.

The short-range sensors were activated, showing close-ups of the planet's surface. Mike and Creeg were stunned by the destruction they saw on the monitor. The Scrat facilities were a mass of smoking rubble as far as the sensors could see.

"What the hell happened here?" blurted Mike. Creeg was dumbfounded. He tried to contact other sources on the planet, but there was no response.

"Can we take the shuttle down?" Creeg requested. "I need to see if there are any survivors to tell us what happened."

Mike complied and landed the shuttle just outside the ruins of the city. Wilmer remained on board the shuttle while Mike and Creeg searched the rubble. They found many Scrat corpses among the rubble and then encountered the wreckage of several Scrat warships. The heat from the flames and plumes of smoke indicated that the attack was recent and that there were likely no survivors.

Creeg climbed through the wreckage into one of the ships, while Mike waited uneasily outside for him. He fretted over what kind of armada could destroy a force as powerful as the Scrat.

Mike recalled his mission to the Scrat planet, where his objective was to destroy a manufacturing facility and two bases suspected of housing advanced warships called Starships with weapons capabilities never seen before. The Scrat never recovered from the destruction he had left despite their vast military strength.

Creeg returned with a case containing several components necessary for the control system repairs on their ship. Still searching for evidence of the attackers, they climbed over one of the Scrat ships for a better vantage point.

A short distance away, they found what they were looking for. Two wrecked warships with the symbol "KE" on the hulls lay smoking on top of two collapsed buildings. "KE. Kronos Enterprises," grumbled Creeg. "They did this."

Mike was shocked that Kronos had the kind of firepower that could decimate the Scrat world like this. "We have a really big problem," commented Mike. "We need to get out of here fast!" They hurried to the shuttle and fled the planet. With the aid of the module, they quickly returned to the Scrat ship.

Wilmer inquired how Creeg would explain to his people what had happened to their planet. Creeg lowered his head in shame and answered that he would just tell them the truth.

Mike suggested that they move the Scrat command ship to Taurus, where Taurus' technicians could help them make the necessary repairs. Creeg acknowledged that they were at the mercy of Sysco Galactic Services, with no place to go and not enough resources to make all the repairs on their own. Mike offered to make arrangements for them to join Sysco and make Taurus their home. Creeg was willing to present the idea to his troops for consideration.

When they returned to the Scrat ship, Creeg promptly addressed their findings with his troops. The Scrat officers and sentries were enraged and demanded revenge. Creeg proposed that they join Mike's team against Empire Shipping and Kronos Enterprises. He informed them that their only option was to move the ship to Taurus for repairs so they could retaliate at some point. They reluctantly agreed. Creeg instructed them to repair all weapons systems and fighters before anything else. He wanted the capability to respond in case they were attacked on Taurus.

With limited power available, Mike offered to help tow the big ship, since his new shuttle had significantly more power than his previous shuttle. It would be slow, but they would get there. Wilmer was uncomfortable with the idea of bringing a Scrat command ship back to Taurus but acknowledged that it could be done. To do so, he needed to make adjustments to the drive system for lower speed and more thrust. They made the necessary preparations and began the journey back to Taurus.

On Taurus, a ten-wheeled crawler transported four large containers to Bay 11, where the *Blue Eagle* was docked. A dozen armed Taurus security guards escorted the vehicle as it approached Bay 11. Ten GSS agents verified the identities of the men before they inspected the crates and verified that they were untampered with.

Tarik, the lead GSS agent at the interior gates to Bay 11, contacted Sara and received permission to move the crawler into the bay. A muscular man, he was tall, with shoulder-length, dark hair, a pointed beard and a mustache. The sentries were not happy about GSS taking over their responsibilities inside the station despite Captain Tieg's orders and were reluctant to turn over the crawler to them. Tarik contacted Sara again and requested backup.

One of the sentries, a lieutenant with a scarred face, demanded to know what was so important that they couldn't move the crawler inside the bay. Tarik explained that the containers were designed for sensitive cargo and were to be loaded to verify they would adapt to the *Blue Eagle's* onloading system. He added that Sysco Galactic Services was looking to increase the *Blue Eagle's* load capacity, which required altering the dimensions of the shipping containers to accommodate the onloader. The precautions were to ensure no one could sabotage the *Blue Eagle* before its departure in the morning.

Convinced that the story was true, the lieutenant ordered his men back toward the neighboring bay's gates to stand by. He reluctantly turned over the crawler to GSS. Tarik's men took a defensive position while he opened the gates to Bay 11. Several bystanders stood by to watch, but the GSS agents moved them back a significant distance.

GSS's mission was to hide the activity on and around the *Blue Eagle* to prevent word from getting out that they were upgrading the ship. When the gates opened just wide enough to accommodate the crawler, Tarik took the controls of the cargo vehicle and brought it into the bay himself.

Inside the bay, numerous technicians worked on the *Blue Eagle's* frame and three of its control panels that were staged on a workbench. The *Blue Eagle's* four engines lay on a large rack in the corner of the bay.

The lieutenant approached the GSS agents and demanded to see the *Blue Eagle*. He challenged Tarik, calling him and his men impostors sent by Empire Shipping. Tarik denied him access, which led to a pushing session. Other sentries got involved, and the GSS agents were forced to retreat toward the gates. The lieutenant then saw that the engines were removed and that the *Blue Eagle* was incapable of flying in the near future, despite Tarik's earlier claim. He drew his pulse pistol and ordered his men to attack.

Pulse fire erupted and sent the bystanders scrambling away. The GSS agents took cover behind several crates and returned fire. Tarik called in the emergency to Sara. Soon, additional GSS agents arrived and took position behind staged cargo at Bay 11 in support of them.

Captain Tieg and several of his men took position in front of bay 13, behind the sentries. Tieg felt confident they had the intruders trapped from both sides and could contain the situation. "Stand down!" he ordered. The traitor sentries then turned their fire upon Tieg's men.

Overwhelmed by the traitors' heavy pulse rifles, they were forced to retreat further, unable to help Tarik's team. Tieg was perturbed that the traitors had been issued high-powered rifles from someone compared to the light weaponry his men had. He then realized that their enemy was well-funded and had access to advanced weaponry from other parts of the universe. Five more of Captain Tieg's men turned traitor and joined the strangers against GSS. Tieg now feared that this wasn't going to end well.

On the Executive Level, six men in suits attempted to storm Gemini's conference room. Gemini, Julian, and Dax retreated to Gemini's suite, anticipating the assailants would gain entry. Sara and three GSS agents quickly responded and exchanged fire with the strangers. One of the men tossed a grenade in their direction and sent Sara's team scurrying for cover. The explosion wounded two of her agents badly. She returned with the other and continued the battle.

Outnumbered badly, Sara and her remaining partner had difficulty returning fire against the lopsided number of shooters and stayed hidden. Her communicator buzzed and distracted her from the firefight. She continued to fire randomly while taking the call. Captain Tieg informed her that they were battling traitors but were outnumbered. She ordered him to initiate a lockdown of the station and related her dire position as well.

On the fourth floor, Tisch was engaged in classroom training for the safety overrides of the new engines. The alarm for lockdown startled her, and the announcement clarified what she feared. The station was under attack. She attempted to leave, but all doors were secured until the lockdown ended. Panic set in as she felt helpless to do anything. Her instructor attempted to get additional clarification on the events but with no success.

On board the shuttle, Mike contacted Sara to get instructions for the arrival and docking of the crippled Scrat warship. Wilmer was anxious to hear her response as he thought this was the craziest idea Mike had ever had. Mike tried three times to contact her and thought it strange that there was no response. He tried once more.

The communicator buzzed for the fourth time, drawing a profanity-laced tirade from Sara before she answered. "What is it?" she shouted. "I've got my hands full!" Mike and Wilmer were stunned by her reaction. Sara never lost her cool, especially under pressure.

"What's going on?" Mike asked. Sara warned him to stay away and quickly summarized the predicament. Mike requested the location of the attackers and a bay in a strategic location to support her.

Sara resigned herself to the fact that he wouldn't listen and directed him to Bay 7. She contacted Gemini and instructed her to get Mike access to the station, despite the lockdown. Gemini, baffled by Sara's voice, obeyed.

When Gemini contacted Mike to allow access to the station, he surprised her with his strange request. "Gem, I need a place to dock a Scrat command ship!" he exclaimed. "Can you help me?"

"What the hell are you up to, Mike?" she demanded.

"I'm bringing in reinforcements, but they need a place to dock."

Gemini glanced at Julian, who was dumbfounded by Mike's revelation. Dax was clueless as to what was going on and said nothing. "Bay 24 is the closest that will accommodate a ship that size," she replied. "Tell me you got the Scrat to take my alliance!"

"Not exactly. It's more complicated than that."

Gemini shook her head and remarked, "It always is with you."

Mike chuckled and ended the transmission. He turned to Wilmer, and the two men burst into laughter. "We need to use the module to get to Taurus now. They're under siege and need us."

"I'm on it," replied Wilmer. "You know, Mike, she's right."

"What about?" he asked.

"It's always complicated with you."

"Don't I know it," he said as he contacted Creeg to advise him of their situation. He instructed Creeg to take his men to Bay 11 after they dock and help defend it. Creeg understood and waited eagerly for their arrival on Taurus. It would be their first taste of revenge for what Kronos had done to their planet.

Wilmer programmed the module and activated it. Suddenly, Taurus appeared on their monitor. Mike released the shuttle from the Scrat warship and allowed it to drift and moor against the gate for Bay 24. Ships that size didn't enter the bay but docked outside and moored against pylons which supported the outer gates. There was an alternate access for boarding and loading operations for large ships at Bays 24 to 30.

When the shuttle docked inside Bay 7, Mike and Wilmer each took two pulse pistols and exited. The corridor was eerily empty as anyone not involved in the firefight had fled the area. Mike contacted Gemini again and requested the code for the elevator, while reminding her that "jackasses" are important too. As soon as he had the code, he complained, "Next time, you'll keep me in the loop." Gemini sighed and ended the transmission. He always wore her out with his persistent preaching.

When Mike and Wilmer arrived on the Executive Level, Sara was the only GSS agent left, and she fought valiantly to hold the intruders off. With the element of surprise, they quickly took out four of the attackers and diverted some of the pulse fire from the others away from Sara. When the last of the suited men was killed, the remaining traitor from Taurus Security surrendered.

Mike and Wilmer were stunned when Sara approached the man and shot him in the forehead. They hadn't seen that side of her before. "I hate traitors!" she grumbled as she checked for survivors among her fallen men.

Creeg's men, twenty in all, approached Bay 13 and immediately identified who were Empire's people by the defensive position of Tieg's men. Creeg called out to Captain Tieg and announced their presence. Tieg gestured for them to approach from behind the crates.

Creeg disregarded his instructions and led a rush toward the attackers. Their uniforms were resistant to pulse fire, which did little to deter them. Firing as they approached, they forced the traitors into a panic and then pursued them as they fled. Waiting for them at the opposite end of the transport area were another dozen Scrat soldiers. They were more than happy to execute the men as part of their thirst for revenge against Kronos.

From behind one of the crates near Bay 12, a bearded man in a maintenance jumpsuit spoke quietly into his communicator. "Antwan, the *Blue Eagle* is here and the upgrade has started." He ended the message and slipped away from the area unnoticed.

With the siege over, Sara immediately assessed what resources were left and instructed Mike and Creeg to meet with her in her secured facility on the seventh level.

Meanwhile, the crawler was positioned next to the *Blue Eagle* and the four containers staged by crane on a second rack next to the old engines. These were the new engines from Hellfire Fuels.

CHAPTER XIII

WHAT'S UP?

Jim Sykes sat down at Dax's oak desk and leaned back in the comfortable leather chair. He imagined how things would be when he became the new president of Hellfire Fuels. Just as he was about to light up a cigar, Antwan entered and approached him. The grim expression on his face indicated there was trouble. Sykes set the cigar down and sat upright. "What can I do for you, Antwan?" he asked politely.

"I need a tour of the factory now," he demanded.

Sykes was surprised by the request. "Any particular reason why?"

"Just take me there—now!"

Sykes quickly got up from his desk and made a call to the attendant downstairs. He finished the call and led Antwan down to the lobby. A limousine glided to a stop in front of the building, and a well-dressed gentleman opened the rear door for them to enter. Sykes allowed Antwan to get in first and then followed. The limo sped away toward the factory on the other end of the vast site.

"You assured me that the new engines were still at the factory," Antwan commented.

"They are," assured Sykes. "You'll see shortly."

The limo arrived in front of the factory and parked. The lot was eerily empty except for three vehicles. "Something's wrong!" exclaimed Sykes. "There should be over a hundred employees here today." He rushed to the entrance and was met by two security guards. "Where is everyone?" Sykes shouted frantically.

One guard explained, "Operations were shut down for a week for maintenance work on the building."

"We need to go inside," he instructed the security guard. The second guard promptly unlocked the doors and allowed them to enter. Sykes took Antwan through a corridor and a series of doors before entering the plant area. He was horrified to see that it was empty. There was only an empty warehouse where there was once a whole production and assembly line of machines and equipment. Even worse, the new engines were missing.

"Where are the engines!" screamed Antwan.

Sykes was dumbfounded and stunned by the turn of events. "I... I don't know," he mumbled, knowing he was in big trouble.

Antwan reminded Sykes that he had trusted him and would have rewarded him well for performance. He removed a short dagger from under his jacket and stared at the blade. Sykes extended his arms toward Antwan to plead his case, but Antwan slit his throat before he could utter a word.

Antwan took out his communicator and announced somberly, "Jack, the engines and fuel regenerator are gone. Hellfire Fuels is cleaned out."

A male voice responded, "Handle this or else."

Antwan stowed the communicator and tossed the bloody knife aside. He rushed out of the building and walked away. One of the security guards grew curious and entered the building. The limo driver was oblivious to Antwan's departure on foot. The security guard rushed out and used his communicator to summon medical help for Sykes, but it was too late. The limo driver preferred to stay out of whatever mess got Sykes killed and drove off. The two security guards looked at each other with baffled expressions, wondering what was going on.

Creeg's troops returned to their ship at Bay 24 once the battle was over. Mike met Creeg in the corridor and requested he join him to meet with Sara. As they walked, Mike inquired how the Scrat were able to outflank Empire's agents when they'd never been on Taurus before. Creeg stopped and stared at Mike, surprised that he would ask that question.

"I have to know," explained Mike. "Kronos could do the same thing you were planning. How ready were you to invade us?"

Creeg revealed that the purpose for their ship's presence in the sector was to detail every space station and satellite to expedite a quick and decisive victory. They expected that the humans would never know what had happened, that it would be over quick.

Mike questioned him about the size of the fleet they thought they needed to accomplish that. He was surprised to learn that there were over seventy Scrat warships in the armada. They had planned to destroy all Sysco and Empire freighters first and then methodically take over each station. Creeg reminded him that every one of those ships was now just wreckage, thanks to Kronos Enterprises.

Mike assured him there would be payback when the time was right. Creeg commented that he believed the Scrat command underestimated their situation and should have considered using the humans to bolster their military against Kronos. Mike agreed but was concerned about who Kronos Enterprises really was. The two were developing an odd friendship that neither could have ever imagined.

They rode the elevator up to the seventh floor to meet with Sara. Mike chuckled as he realized how helpful it was for him to have the elevator security code after all. *Who is the jackass now?* he thought to himself, remembering Gemini's cynical response to him.

When they arrived at the door, Mike pressed an intercom button and announced their arrival. The door slid open, and they entered an antechamber. The door closed behind them, and they waited. Creeg remarked, "We didn't anticipate this."

"Neither did I," replied Mike. "It must be new." A blue light from a scanner in the ceiling covered them briefly, scanning for weapons, and then a green light flashed. The next door slid open and allowed them entry to the central security facility.

Seven technicians operated a variety of security equipment, including sensors, scanners, and cameras. Sara appeared through another doorway and gestured for them to follow her. They no sooner had sat at a conference table when one of Sara's technicians interrupted on the intercom. "Gemini requests entry into the facility, ma'am," he announced. "She says it's urgent." Sara instructed him to escort her in.

"This should be interesting," she remarked and stood with folded arms. Mike and Creeg glanced at each other, wondering what Gemini's reaction would be, learning that her sister ran GSS.

Mike inquired about the safety of Tisch and the rest of the crew. Sara explained that the station was placed into lockdown as soon as the attack began. Seeing the concerned expression on Mike's face, she mentioned that his friends were secure in their classrooms except for Wilmer. Mike was relieved; he already knew that Wilmer was in the shuttle, waiting for instructions.

Gemini entered the room and stood with her arms folded, like her sister. Mike refrained from chuckling as the two women looked like carbon copies of each other despite their hair color, standing there with cold stares. The technician closed the door behind Gemini, leaving them to their privacy.

Not one to miss the spotlight, Gemini blurted, "My sister runs GSS, Mike sits here with a Scrat officer, and there's a Scrat warship docked in my station. How many other secrets have you all kept from me?"

Sara responded first and informed Gemini that GSS had been watching her back for some time and it was for her own good that she didn't know about it. Gemini was embarrassed that she had spoken so many times and requested favors of her sister yet never suspected she had operated GSS. "Very impressive, sis," remarked Gemini. "You never cease to amaze me."

Gemini turned her attention to Mike. "And what brought on this unholy alliance? I seem to remember being the pariah for wanting this very relationship with the Scrat."

Creeg was amused as he considered all the events that had occurred, leading up to this moment. Mike introduced Creeg to Gemini and Sara. He explained how Kronos Enterprises had decimated the Scrat on their home world, and how Creeg offered to work with them against Kronos and Empire Shipping. Gemini was pleased, knowing she had gotten what she wanted all along - an alliance with the Scrat, or what was left of them.

Sara was anxious to know what Mike's intentions were for the Scrat warship. Mike explained that they needed to help repair the ship's weapons systems first and then the remainder of the ship. Once that was completed, they had to find out where Kronos Enterprises was located. Gemini was more concerned about Empire Shipping, her immediate threat.

"Where are Julian and Dax?" asked Mike.

Sara assured him they were safe for now. She then revealed that Dax's finance guy, Jim Sykes, was working with Antwan to steal the engines and the fuel-regeneration technology. Mike raised his hand in cynical fashion to question where Hellfire's equipment was. Sara gestured for him to wait. She deferred to Gemini for further explanation. Gemini revealed that the engines were already there and ready for installation on the *Blue Eagle*, as was the fuel regenerator.

"So, Dax's stuff was already here when we last met to discuss this," Mike mused.

"For security reasons, we wanted Empire's spies to think the engines and fuel regenerator were still at Hellfire Fuels," she answered.

"During the attack, one of the agents saw the *Blue Eagle* through the open gates and reported to Antwan," explained Dax. "Antwan went to Hellfire Fuels to find out for sure. When he realized we had played him, he killed Sykes and vanished before we could apprehend him."

"And what does Dax get out of this?" Mike questioned Gemini.

"There is no merger," Gemini replied. "Dax and his people were absorbed into my corporation, as was their technology. Hellfire Fuels is no longer a valid company."

"Then the cat's out of the bag about the engines," Mike commented.

"But it bought us the time we needed," she explained. "The *Blue Eagle* is nearly finished."

Creeg remarked, "I never realized how conniving humans could be. I applaud your creativity." Everyone laughed at his attempt at humor.

Sara pressed Creeg to explain what his expectations were and what allegiance they could expect from him. He reminded them that the Scrat had no place to go; all they cared about was getting revenge on Kronos. Sara was pleased with his response and asked if he had a problem working with their group to accomplish that. Creeg was fine taking orders so long as the Scrat weren't taken advantage of. Everyone agreed that it was a fair expectation.

"What is our next move?" asked Mike.

Sara instructed Gemini to prioritize repairs to the Scrat command ship in case of another attack. She requested Creeg to supply a dozen of his soldiers to guard Bay 11 during the *Blue Eagle's* upgrade and to expect another attack. As soon as the *Blue Eagle* upgrade was complete, she wanted it away from Taurus.

Gemini informed Mike that she had an assignment for them as soon as the ship was ready. Mike was surprised when he learned that the completion was expected in only three days. With all questions answered, they dispersed from the facility.

Creeg returned to his ship and assigned twelve of his troops to be sentries at Bay 11. He briefed them that human technicians would be boarding their ship to help with repairs as well as the *Blue Eagle* for the upgrade. They were to be accompanied by two guards at all times to prevent the possibility of sabotage.

Mike left several messages for Tisch that went unanswered and then went to the pub, hoping to find them. When he arrived, he was pleased to see Tisch sitting with Wilmer, Geezer, Shannon, and Zenith. Tisch quipped, "Sounds like you had quite an interesting day."

Mike shook his head in disbelief. "You have no idea." He went on to reveal all the details of the meeting and how they should expect a quick departure in a few days. Shannon updated them on the training she and Zenith had just completed and reported that they were ready to go.

Content that everything was under control, Mike recommended they turn their attention to something more entertaining. Everyone agreed and raised their glasses of beer in a toast. Afterward, it was agreed that they would sleep in the quarters provided by Gemini on the sixth floor for safety reasons. It was too risky being on or around the *Blue Eagle* right now, and their presence might interfere with the Scrat sentries' ability to monitor the technicians around the ship.

Geezer and Wilmer shared one cabin, while Zenith and Shannon shared another. Mike and Tisch elected to share one as well, knowing it would irk Gemini. In their quarters, Tisch sat at the desk, quietly contemplating all that had happened that day. Mike rubbed her shoulders from behind and assured her that everything would be fine.

Tisch turned to him with tears in her eyes and explained how she had feared the worst. She had no idea where he was when the attack started, and they were isolated in their classrooms.

"I never wanted you to be involved in this kind of life," Mike confessed.

"Well, it looks like I am, whether I like it or not," she countered. Mike coerced her to come to bed and get some rest.

Geezer and Wilmer each finished a beer in their room. Geezer commented about how exciting things had become since Mike came on board. Wilmer shook his head in disbelief and pointed out that Mike's whole life was like that, including their time spent in Special Forces. Geezer pointed out that if they didn't have Mike, these events would have happened anyway and would likely be a whole lot worse. Wilmer was in agreement.

Zenith and Shannon talked for some time, getting to know each other. Shannon quizzed Zenith on Hellfire Fuels and what she knew of it. Zenith then asked Shannon what she was really doing with them. She confessed to Shannon that she knew she was much more than just Wilmer's friend. Shannon admitted that there was more to her than she could reveal right now but assured Zenith that she was there to help and that their budding friendship was real.

The next morning, the crew met in the cafeteria for breakfast. They were surprised when Julian appeared and joined them. His expression was somber as he pulled up a chair and sat with them.

"Well, look who it is!" kidded Mike. "How are you, Julian?"

"Not bad, all things considered," he replied. "We need to talk."

They glanced around the cafeteria to determine the degree of privacy. Content that it was adequate, Julian continued, "You will be leaving for Niems, tomorrow morning."

"For what purpose?" inquired Tisch.

"I believe you'll find some of the answers that you both are looking for."

"About the module?" asked Tisch.

"Yes," Julian responded, and, after a brief hesitation, he added, "And John Mallory's involvement."

Tisch's jaw dropped in awe. This was the last thing she had expected to hear from Julian. The others said nothing but studied his expression, wondering what he had learned. To break the silence, Mike inquired, "Then what? Are we making a delivery or something?"

Julian stood and shook Mike's hand. "Consider it a favor. It's the least I can do for what you did for me." He smiled for once and then left them.

Appearing stressed, Tisch addressed the crew. "You heard him. Tomorrow morning, we're back on the road." She got up from the table and left them.

Sensing everyone's interest in the trip, Mike explained that there were things they needed to know about the module's creators and hoped for answers to what had led to John Mallory's death. The girls lost interest when they realized there would likely be no excitement on the trip. Geezer pondered aloud, "I hope we aren't chasing ghosts."

"I guess we'll find out," Mike remarked. "Tonight, we'll do an operational readiness check on the *Blue Eagle*. I assume they'll be finished with the upgrade later today if we are leaving tomorrow."

Geezer was concerned with the speed at which the engines were replaced, the fuel regenerating system added, and a brand-new loading/conveyor system were installed. He urged Mike to push for time to do a complete functional test before departing. Mike reminded him that every day the *Blue Eagle* was on Taurus was another day everyone was at risk.

Shannon excused herself from the table and left the pub. Mike recommended that Geezer and Wilmer arrange for staple items and supplies to be staged at the hatch tomorrow morning, just prior to departure. Wilmer quipped, "Does that include beer and rum?"

"Of course," Mike replied with a chuckle. "Besides, it's on Gemini's tab." Everyone laughed. When they left the cafeteria, Mike noticed Shannon standing with Sara at the end of the corridor. They appeared to be in a somber discussion by the dour expressions on their faces. Mike pretended not to notice and excused himself from his crew mates. He took the first elevator up to the Executive Level.

Julian entered Gemini's suite and took a seat across from her. "Are you all right?" he asked. Gemini sipped from a glass of bourbon and said nothing. "It's Sara, isn't it?" he asked.

Finally, Gemini responded. "All this time, I had no idea. I don't even know how long she's been with them. For all I know, she conspired with Mike behind my back."

Julian chuckled at her and then reminded her that they had all saved her ass more than once already. Mike's voice interrupted them on the intercom. "It's me, Gemini. We need to talk."

"Oh, great. Here comes my biggest headache," she muttered and then used a remote device to open the door for him.

Mike entered and approached the table, looking dead serious. Gemini gestured for him to sit. "Is this about the name on the shuttle?" she asked irritably. Julian burst into laughter.

Mike thought about it for a few seconds and then replied, "That was second on my list."

Julian went to the bar and made drinks for the three of them. Gemini finished her glass and set it aside. She stared at him, waiting for his first complaint. "What do you know about Antwan that you aren't telling me?" he asked.

"Who says I know anything?" she responded dryly.

"You seemed to know his crew intimately before we killed them."

"I did, and I hated each of those sons of bitches."

Julian set the drinks down on the table and suggested a toast to their future. Mike found that curious and, after the toast, asked him to explain *future*.

Gemini interceded and revealed that John Mallory rarely left the station; it was unusual for him to leave alone in the *Blue Eagle*. She concluded, "As to how Antwan and his goons got involved, Niems holds the answer to that. I want to know what happened as much as Tisch does."

Mike then turned his attention to Julian. Julian explained that he had a contact that was proving to be very valuable in their battle with Kronos, and the *Blue Eagle* would play a big role in defeating them.

"We need to focus on Empire Shipping first, which includes Antwan," Mike cautioned. "Then we can turn our resources on Kronos."

"And we will," assured Julian. "I believe your visit to Niems will be helpful to all of us."

"All I ask is that you keep me in the loop, even if it excludes the others," Mike requested.

Julian and Gemini both agreed, but then Gemini raised the issue of GSS and Sara. She was concerned that Sara had an ulterior motive other than sibling love for getting involved in this. Mike promised to inform her if he found out anything to support her concerns. Mike finished his drink and thanked them for their help. He then mentioned that the shuttle was exceptional, but the name would have to go.

Gemini quipped, "Truth hurts, doesn't it?" Mike smiled graciously and left them. He felt there was no reason to feed Gemini's ego further.

Julian suggested to Gemini that she had been a bit harsh to Mike, but she assured him that Mike was tough enough to take it. They tapped glasses playfully and finished their drinks.

When evening came, Mike and Tisch met the crew at Bay 11's gate. Creeg waited with a dozen of his sentries as they approached. Mike greeted him and thanked him again for his support. Creeg opened the gates to allow them access to the *Blue Eagle* and permitted them to enter. Mike cautioned him to be ready for anything, especially now.

The bay was clear of the crane and all equipment. There was no sign that the upgrade had ever been performed, other than the presence of the larger engines on the ship. When the crew got their first look at the new *Blue Eagle*, they were impressed. "Those are some big, friggin' engines," quipped Geezer.

Wilmer pointed out the additional hatches, allowing them to load four bays at a time instead of one. He promised Mike that he'd work with him to get him up to par with the system once they were under way.

Everyone but Tisch boarded the ship. She stood alone and gazed at it with a tear streaming down her cheek. *What did you get me into, Dad?* she thought to herself. Mike stuck his head out the hatch and called to her. She wiped her cheek and boarded the ship.

"Are you okay?" he asked, concerned by her delay.

"I'm fine," she replied. "Just admiring my baby." Tisch was happy to be back on board her ship and looked forward to getting back into space.

Each crew member powered up their assigned system and began diagnostic checks. Tisch reminded everyone that their survival could depend on every system on the ship functioning properly. Geezer spent time with the girls on the navigation and piloting systems. Mike and Wilmer worked with the new loading and conveyor system. By midnight, the diagnostics and preflight preparations were complete.

When they exited the bay, four pallets with containers labeled 'water' and 'perishables' were staged for them by the Bay 11 gates. Before the dockworkers could leave, Mike and Tisch discussed the fact that this was unexpected. Creeg's men stood ready in case of trouble, but none occurred. Tisch ordered the men to take the pallets back to the warehouse. They suspected that the pallets held their supplies but would look into the manifests in the morning.

Shannon stood apart from everyone and contacted Sara. She informed her of the unexpected pallets and asked for instructions. Within minutes, Sara appeared with ten men at Bay 11. She quickly confirmed that there were no manifests for the pallets, so GSS took over the responsibility and arranged for an intense inspection of the contents and their source in the morning. Meanwhile, the pallets were quarantined in an isolated bay.

Sara informed Shannon that her mission had changed. She was no longer interested in obtaining the module from Mike but instead wanted to keep the module safe. She explained to Shannon that it was too dangerous for GSS to take possession of it. Mike noticed the two women as they spoke at length. He approached and inquired what they were up to.

Sara responded calmly that she was prepping Shannon with security protocols in case of an attack. She did reveal that Shannon could reach her anytime in the event of trouble. Mike didn't quite buy her story, but he knew Sara well enough that he could trust her to have his back. When Sara left, Shannon promised Mike that she wouldn't be any problem for them; she just wanted a chance to be part of something new and exciting.

Mike stopped her before they reached the crew. "Look, Shannon, Wilmer is my friend," he reminded her. "Whatever you and Sara are up to, don't break his heart, or we're going to have a problem." Shannon placed her hand on Mike's arm and assured him that she would never hurt Wilmer, or any of them for that matter.

"Fair enough," Mike said and continued on his way. Shannon breathed a sigh of relief. Everyone returned to their quarters on the sixth floor and slept until morning.

The next morning, Mike and Tisch led the crew to Bay 11. When they arrived, the Scrat sentries searched through the expected supplies that had just arrived for loading while Sara's team guarded the gates. Satisfied that the supplies were safe, Sara ordered her men to open the gates to the *Blue Eagle*.

Gemini, Julian, and Dax approached them from the elevator. Dax went to his daughter, Zenith, while Julian and Gemini met with the others. Dax hugged Zenith and told her how proud he was of her. Zenith was cold toward him at first. He explained how he had never gotten over the death of her mother and how he meant well.

Zenith became emotional and shoved him angrily as tears streamed down her cheeks. Dax pleaded with her to understand that he tried to be a good parent. Finally, the two embraced, crying on each other's shoulders.

Mike watched while the others talked of the latest news. Sara interrupted Mike's thoughts, saying that they were lucky Tisch had questioned the presence of the pallets. He reminded her that it was Shannon who had made the call to get her involved. "She's here to help," Sara remarked. "If you waited, the pallets might have activated in the gate area and killed everyone."

"How so?" he asked.

"The containers were made to break down over a short period of time and release a poisonous gas," she explained. "Fortunately, the surveillance cameras in the quarantine pen displayed the degrading containers on the pallet before my people entered to inspect the contents."

Mike expressed his concerns about the heightened attacks against Taurus, seemingly centered on the *Blue Eagle* and its crew. Sara reminded him that this was more about the module than Taurus, although Sysco and the module both appeared to be the focus of the attacks. Before they parted, Sara warned him, "Protect that module with your life. I think there's a lot more to it than we know."

Mike promised and then returned to Julian. He noticed that Tisch and Gemini were engaged in a lengthy conversation and wanted no part of it. He shook Julian's hand and cautioned him to watch his back as well as that of his partners, Gemini and Dax.

Julian assured him that he had confidence in the contact and that she had information that might lead to defeating Kronos. "These are dangerous times that require dangerous measures," he warned bluntly.

Mike was concerned by his words. "Are you sure you are ready for this, Julian? There's still much that we don't know and it could get a lot worse."

Julian convinced him that they would take no action until they had discussed it with him and Sara. He reminded Mike that this needed to be a coordinated effort when the time came. Mike shook his hand and held onto it.

Julian sensed his concern for him and was touched. "Don't worry about me, my friend," he uttered with some sadness in his voice. "I'll do whatever it takes to protect Sysco and the *Blue Eagle*." Mike kidded him about how he was getting sentimental, and the two men laughed.

"Take care, my friend," Mike said and patted Julian's arm.

Mike called out to the crew to board and grabbed Tisch's hand, a sign of his impatience. Gemini remarked to him, "I see you didn't change the name on your shuttle yet."

Mike chuckled. "I'm beginning to like it. Maybe I'll keep it after all."

"Great," Tisch complained to Gemini. "You're feeding his already-bloated ego."

Gemini surprised them each with a hug and warned them to be careful. They parted ways with her and boarded the *Blue Eagle*.

Julian contacted the control room and instructed them to make no announcement of the *Blue Eagle's* departure as this was only a test run. He and Gemini agreed that the less that was known about the *Blue Eagle's* status, the better.

The crew gathered on the bridge, excited to depart Taurus for the first time in a long time as a group. Geezer offered Zenith the honor of piloting the ship while Wilmer deferred his navigation and engineering duties to Shannon. Mike and Tisch observed their crew proudly as they executed the departure flawlessly.

Tisch cautioned them to be alert for any unusual indications from the new engines. She also permitted them to handle their own rotations at their stations as needed. Mike invited Tisch to join him in the galley for a beer so they could discuss things. Tisch placed Wilmer in charge and followed Mike off the bridge.

Mike grabbed two beers from the refrigerator and set them down at the table. He and Tisch tapped bottles in a toast to their new journey. Tisch grew uneasy over their meeting, wondering what was on his mind. Mike opened the conversation by apologizing for placing her in the middle of a war that they still didn't fully understand. Tisch reminded him of the consequences if they hadn't rescued him and how the Scrat would have controlled the whole sector. Mike realized she was right, and the two considered what would happen if that did occur. Tisch uttered somberly, "The war would still go on, but it would be between the Scrat and Kronos. We'd be casualties, long gone."

"So the Scrat were instead the casualties long gone, and the war is between us and Kronos," he surmised. "Who made out on this deal?"

"One day at a time," Tisch remarked. "Let's focus on our part of the plan and see what gives at Niems."

Mike agreed with her and then turned the discussion to the new crew members. He mentioned that Shannon, although he believed her to be trustworthy, was much more than they were aware of. Tisch suspected there was a relationship between her and Sara that wasn't advertised. Neither one wanted to mention that they suspected she was a GSS agent. When the time was right, they were sure they'd know.

Tisch mentioned that she was excited to have a full complement of a crew for once. She hoped to add two more members to help with the loading duties, especially since they had the capability to load and unload four bays at once instead of one. Mike groaned as he realized she would pressure him to step up his time with the new systems. They could make better windows at their destinations to get in and out ahead of schedule. Tisch kissed his cheek and left the galley.

Mike looked at the empty bottles and grumbled, "That's right. Leave the grunt work and the housekeeping to ol' Mikey." He picked up the empty bottles and tossed them in the refuse container. Tisch hollered from the corridor, "I love you, Honey!"

"Yes, dear," he replied sarcastically.

CHAPTER XIV

ANSWERS WITH QUESTIONS

The rotations among the crew worked well with no complaints. Tisch was pleased with the engines' performance but often wished she knew more about the module in Mike's possession. Mike was secretive about it, and she wasn't even sure it was on board. Mike noticed and requested a private conversation in his quarters. Tisch accompanied him, wondering what was on his mind this time.

When the door slid closed behind them, he embraced her and they kissed. "I miss you," he said coyly. "With so much going on, there's been no time for us."

"There will be," she assured him. "We have a big responsibility right now, and we can't afford to fail."

Mike was amused by her words. She sounded more like him every day. "I know you're wondering about the module," he commented. "What do you want to know?"

Tisch hesitated at first but then revealed that she wanted to know everything: its capabilities; its intended use by Mike; and, most importantly, where it was. Mike started with what he knew about its origin and her father's involvement, and then he revealed that it had been installed on the shuttle and would not be used unless absolutely necessary, so no one would know for sure who had it and where it was. Tisch thanked him for his honesty and then left the cabin. Mike was disappointed by her abrupt departure. Things just weren't the same anymore.

Zenith noticed a ship shadowing them from the edge of the long-range sensors' range. Shannon was the only other crew member on the bridge, so she called for Tisch over the intercom. When Tisch replied, she mentioned the ship's presence to her. It was not a threat, but it was definitely shadowing them. Tisch returned to Mike's quarters and informed him they might have a problem. The two arrived on the bridge and were briefed by Zenith.

Shannon used the navigation system to determine that the ship wasn't there long, and that it likely came from a very small planet called Zim. After researching Zim, she informed them of her findings. Zim hosted a pirate haven called Murgatroyd's Oasis, a hub for illicit trade. "Only the worst of the worst go there, according to the shipping logs in the database," she warned.

"Let me know if anything changes," Tisch instructed Zenith. "Oh, and nice work."

Tisch approached Shannon's station and requested she bring up any data on Niems. Meanwhile, Mike sat with Zenith and studied the trailing mystery ship. Zenith was at ease with Mike by her side but was well aware that he was off-limits to her. Tisch would surely be watching them.

Zenith questioned Mike on his thoughts about what was happening and whether he thought her father had made the right decision in teaming up with Gemini. Mike explained that it was an ingenious move under the circumstances. It was a battle he couldn't win any other way, thanks to Kronos.

Zenith then mentioned that Dax always had a thing for Gemini and suspected it was motivation for him to make the deal for the engines. Mike wasn't intimidated by the possibility but turned the conversation toward Zenith. He inquired about Zenith's history with her mother and what had happened. Unfortunately, there wasn't much for her to tell. Her mother died when she was very young, so she had few memories of her, although they were important ones. He offered his sympathy, but Zenith informed him that her primary interest now was to find a good man and live a stable life.

"Patience," Mike remarked confidently. "Sometimes, the right person shows up when you least expect it." Zenith appreciated his words of encouragement.

Tisch and Shannon read over the few ships' logs that were available on Niems. Shannon suggested that she could access "other" databases to find out more. Tisch was impressed as Shannon worked her way into the GSS database. Tisch asked if that was by accident or if she had had prior training. Shannon confessed that she had considered joining GSS and that she was kin to Sara, although she didn't mention how. She also revealed that she preferred to be a crew member on the *Blue Eagle* rather than a GSS agent.

Tisch then questioned her on what training she had received from Sara thus far. She was surprised to learn that Shannon was well-versed in hand-to-hand combat and other fighting skills.

"Could we keep this between us?" Shannon requested. "I don't want to scare Wilmer off. I really like him a lot."

Tisch agreed and complimented her on her ability to adapt to ship life thus far. Shannon finally brought up the GSS files on Niems. Tisch pulled up a chair and watched intently as the pages scrolled.

Many years ago, Niems had been an outpost for an advanced group of aliens called Archaeneans. Their mission was to bring their technology to other species in a peaceful manner. At issue was a device that would change the way human races traversed the universe. The Archaeneans created one of these devices for the humans, and one particular corporation negotiated to receive the module on behalf of all the groups in the galaxy. That distant corporation named Kronos Enterprises broke their trust and forced them to abandon the outpost. No one was sure what had happened to the module after that. Niems had been abandoned ever since.

"So why is Niems suddenly an important location that supposedly has answers?" Tisch thought aloud.

"Something must have changed, or someone found out something else that made it important again," surmised Shannon. "Maybe the Archaeneans never really left."

"This whole mystery of the module gets more and more confusing by the day," complained Tisch.

"What's that?" asked Mike.

"Just thinking out loud. Nothing important," Tisch replied and winked at Shannon. Shannon was happy to have a real connection with Tisch.

When they drew close to Niems, Mike suggested that he and Wilmer take the shuttle and investigate the outpost first. Tisch was opposed to the idea and countered that she and Shannon should check it out. Mike didn't understand her power play here and why she'd want Shannon with her instead of him or Wilmer. Zenith interrupted and announced that the mystery ship was still out there but remained on the edge of the sensors' range.

Tisch was adamant and promised to stay in contact with them. Mike reluctantly agreed to her plan. The two women left the bridge for the cargo bay to board Mike's shuttle.

Wilmer suggested to Mike that Tisch wanted to know more about what her father had to do with the module and feared it could be embarrassing. Mike was more concerned about their safety *and* his shuttle. He instructed Zenith to watch the monitors closely and warned her that Empire Shipping or Kronos Enterprises were likely to make an unwelcome appearance.

Geezer arrived on the bridge and was quickly briefed by Zenith on the situation. Mike was pleased with how she had handled the responsibility of acting on the identification of an unknown ship and accurately turning over the details to him.

Wilmer paced the floor behind them, feeling like a lost soul. "Are you okay?" asked Mike.

Wilmer shook his head in frustration and complained, "We should be down there."

Mike patted his shoulder and echoed his sentiment. "I know how you feel," he said. "It's my damned shuttle." They waited anxiously for word from the women when the shuttle docked inside the abandoned station. Geezer reminded Mike that they had agreed to trust each other and work together. Mike acknowledged him but explained the guilt he'd feel if something happened to Tisch over the module.

"There's another ship approaching at a high rate of speed!" Zenith exclaimed.

"This is what I was afraid of," groaned Mike. "I'll take the top turret. How about you, Wilmer?"

"I, uh, never really fired a cannon before," he replied sheepishly.

Zenith leaped at the opportunity. "I got your back, Mike!"

Mike was surprised but had nothing to lose. "All right, Zee. Let's kick some ass!"

"I'll hail them over an open channel so you can hear the response," Geezer announced.

Wilmer suggested he handle the contact, hoping to be of some use. Geezer agreed and let him operate the comm/nav system. Wilmer made several attempts to reach them, but there was no response.

As the ship drew closer to them, Geezer recognized its shape as one of Empire's armed freighters, a class two. He relayed the info to Wilmer, who once again attempted to contact them. Out of patience with them, Wilmer announced in a cold, firm voice, "Come in, Empire freighter. This is your last chance to respond or you will be dealt with severely. This is your final warning." Still there was no response.

Wilmer contacted Tisch on the shuttle. "Are you docked yet?"

Tisch affirmed that they were just exiting. Wilmer briefed her on the situation and requested she stand by. Tisch was anxious to explore the outpost, but Shannon warned that they should be prepared in case they had to evacuate in a rush. Tisch was persistent and decided to go forward. They wore environmental suits to cross from the shuttle into the air lock.

As the freighter approached, Mike instructed Zenith on their strategy for firing. He reminded her that the *Blue Eagle* was known for having a small crew, so the word might be out that they wouldn't have enough crew to man both cannons if they had people out on the shuttle. Zenith was anxious to show her shooting skills but understood that she needed to hold her fire until the optimal moment.

Mike informed her of the small plate on the nose of the freighter that contained the firing control system. He suggested that she focus on hitting it when the freighter was close enough.

As soon as the freighter entered firing range, Mike locked onto the ship. Geezer was ready to activate the forward shields if the freighter fired. Wilmer and Geezer stood by the console, hoping for a transmission from the ship. The tension was thick as everyone waited anxiously. Then the transmitter beeped and startled them.

Wilmer accepted the call and stood in front of the three-dimensional monitor over Geezer's station. A bearded man appeared and spoke. "I'm Captain Oliver of the Olympia. We are with Empire Shipping. What do you want on Niems?"

"Why do you care?" Wilmer countered.

"Niems is property of Kronos Enterprises and is off-limits," he replied. "You are trespassing."

"I was under the impression that the outpost once belonged to someone else and was abandoned. Besides, if you are Empire, then why do you care what belongs to Kronos?"

"Regardless of what you heard, you are trespassing," warned the captain. "Leave now, or you will be destroyed."

"I believe Mike Colby has something to say about that," quipped Wilmer.

Mike opened fire on the freighter and knocked out their two forward turrets. Zenith fired at the nose but struck just wide of it. Mike frowned as that wasn't the plan. The freighter turned broadside and hammered them with cannon fire from its port and aft cannons.

Geezer activated the shields just in time, but they degraded quickly due to heavy fire. The *Blue Eagle* rumbled from the impact of the cannon fire, but the shields still held up.

"Forget the plan, Zee! Just fire!" shouted Mike. They returned fire and inflicted damage to the rear engines on the freighter. Geezer warned that the shields had dropped to thirty percent. Mike instructed Zenith to slow down and pick her shots.

The mystery ship suddenly raced toward them and fired on the freighter. Caught off guard, the freighter sustained significant damage to the forward control section of the ship. The freighter now concentrated its fire on the new ship, and both exchanged cannon fire. Each ship sustained heavy damage, but the Empire freighter was forced to eject one of its engines and flee. As it turned to escape, Zenith had a good shot at the nose plate and fired. A brief explosion indicated that she had found her mark.

"Nice shot, Zee!" shouted Mike. The crippled freighter fled the scene and the mystery ship drifted aimlessly with no power.

When Mike and Zenith returned to the bridge, the transmitter beeped, indicating an incoming transmission. Wilmer eagerly acknowledged the signal. Two crew members, a darkskinned man and woman, stood in tattered uniforms that caught Mike's attention.

"Can you help us, please?" the man begged. "Our ship is crippled, and we need help."

"How many of you are there?" Mike asked.

"We're the only two survivors," answered the woman. "Our core has significant leakage, and we have several hull breaches."

"We don't have long if we stay here," added the man.

"Do you have a way to transport here?" inquired Wilmer.

The man replied that they had a shuttle and could leave immediately. It had limited range due to a shortage of fuel. Mike agreed to take them on if they could reach them in their shuttle.

Geezer became frantic as he tried repeatedly to reach Tisch. Mike grew agitated with the recent string of events happening all at once. Wilmer questioned Mike about Tisch's situation and what to do with the newcomers. Mike considered that they could use the strangers' shuttle to transport to the outpost and back up Tisch. Mike reminded him that the ship did come to their aid, so they aren't likely to be enemies.

Geezer and Zenith remained calm, but Wilmer was nervous about the newcomers. "Did you notice their uniforms, Mike?" asked Wilmer with a note of sarcasm.

"I certainly did," he answered uneasily. "Those are the same uniforms we wore for the Federation's Special Forces." They watched the shuttle depart the derelict ship and approach.

Mike and Wilmer left the bridge to greet the guests as a security measure. Geezer and Zenith alternated in their attempts to contact Tisch.

The shuttle landed in the cargo bay, and the outer doors sealed. As soon as the atmosphere was restored, Mike and Wilmer entered the bay, armed with pulse pistols holstered at their sides as a precaution. The shuttle hatch opened, and the two survivors staggered out.

Each had minor burns on their faces and hands along with some lacerations. Mike and Wilmer escorted them to the infirmary for treatment of their injuries. The two introduced themselves as Griff and Topa.

Griff wore the uniform of a senior officer, while Topa's uniform indicated she was enlisted. After the introductions, Mike inquired about who they were and why they were following them.

Griff was curious when he learned of Mike's name. "Are you the Mike Colby who led the mission against the Scrat a few years ago?"

"I am," he answered with renewed interest. "And how would you know that?"

"We were supposed to be your backup for the mission," explained Griff. "Kronos ambushed us, and we sought refuge on this outpost."

"Those bastards boarded the outpost and hunted us!" exclaimed Topa.

"They slaughtered your team?" asked Wilmer.

"We hid in one of the ducts," answered Griff. "But the remainder of our team disappeared. No bodies, no uniforms, nor any weapons."

"The Kronos soldiers searched for quite a while and were stumped by their disappearance as much as we were," continued Topa. "Eventually, they left the outpost. We never found our team."

"Does this have anything to do with why you were shadowing us?" questioned Mike.

"Yes, it does," replied Griff. "We were hoping that you learned something about their disappearance and that led you back here."

"Well, you certainly had good timing," Mike remarked. "I'm sorry the rest of your crew didn't make it."

"There were only eight of us. Our crew members lost relatives in that battle and wanted answers, too."

"Would you be interested in boarding the outpost with us?" requested Mike. "Two of our friends are there, and we lost contact with them."

Griff and Topa glanced at each other uneasily, but then agreed to take Mike and Wilmer in the shuttle. On their flight from the *Blue Eagle*, Griff mentioned that they had been stranded for six weeks on Niems before a pirate cargo ship heard their SOS signal. He also told Mike that they didn't know how successful the mission had been against the Scrat until much later. What they did hear was impressive.

Mike joked that he was best friends with the Scrat now, or what was left of them. Griff and Topa were stunned when he explained how Kronos had decimated the Scrat world. Griff emphasized that Kronos had to be stopped somehow. Mike assured him that they were working on a plan.

Tisch and Shannon exited the air lock, each with a flashlight and a pulse pistol. The interior of the outpost was dark and appeared to have been abandoned for some time. There was a layer of dust across the floor and an eerie silence that reminded the women of a tomb.

They passed through several corridors and ascended the stairs to the control room. Along the way, Tisch attempted to contact the *Blue Eagle* but with no success. Shannon explained to Tisch that the outposts were often equipped with special shielding to deflect radiation bursts from a variety of sources as well as bombardment from pirates seeking to storm the facility. The two women sat at the controls and attempted to power up the outpost's systems.

The backup lighting illuminated, and some of the systems initiated but with low-power alarms. Tisch commented to Shannon about the oddity of the backup power still being operational, although in a limited capacity, what with the outpost having been abandoned for so long. Suddenly, the two women shook uncontrollably. The last thing Tisch recalled before blacking out was the glow of electricity over their hands.

When Tisch awoke, she and Shannon were propped up in chairs. She called to Shannon several times before she heard a response. Both were disoriented and groggy from the shock.

"What the hell was that?" groaned Shannon.

Tisch responded that they must have set off an anti-tampering device on the control console. They peered around the control room and attempted to see through the dark but with no success. "So, who put us in the chairs?" Shannon asked as she stood up unsteadily.

A woman's voice startled them. "Why are you here?"

"I'll ask the questions," snapped Tisch angrily. "Now tell me who you are before I get really pissed!"

The glowing figure of a woman appeared in front of her. "You are trespassing on my outpost. I will ask the questions, and you will answer them."

"Fine," Tisch relented and then related where they came from.

Meanwhile, Shannon used the distraction of the conversation to rush at the ghostly figure. She was stunned when she waved through the woman as if she wasn't there.

"What are you?" shouted Shannon. "Some kind of apparition?"

"I am an Archaenean," she replied, unconcerned with Shannon's interruption. "I am the keeper of the outpost."

"Why would you attack us like this?" questioned Tisch. "We mean you no harm."

The figure laughed at them. "Kronos Enterprises betrayed us once. That will never happen to us again."

Shannon explained that they, too, had no love for Kronos. Tisch then added that they were sent there for answers about the module. The figure took a solid form as a human woman and asked if John Mallory had survived.

Tisch was stunned that the woman knew his name. She revealed how he had died and that she sought answers as to how he was involved with the module.

The woman sat in a chair opposite Tisch and Shannon. She explained that they had been asked to build the module for peaceful purposes; Kronos would determine how it would be implemented. A very important person contacted them about Kronos and their true intentions. The Archaeneans were advised to give John the module and help him escape. After Kronos attacked, the Archaeneans abandoned the outpost by transporting back to their home planet.

The woman introduced herself as Denia and demanded to know who had the module. Tisch informed her that it was safe from Empire Shipping and Kronos Enterprises for now, but they were determined to find it at any cost.

Mike crept up the stairwell with Wilmer, Griff, and Topa. They caught part of the conversation before entering the control room. "Tisch!" he called out as they approached with pulse pistols drawn. The woman stood alert and returned to her ghostly form.

"It's all right, Mike," Tisch responded calmly. "Stow your weapons."

Mike nodded to the others, and they complied. The woman took her human form again and sat down. Tisch introduced them and urged Denia to continue their conversation. Denia studied Griff and Topa for a moment and then spoke to them. "You were here some time ago with others."

Griff's eyes widened with hope. "You remember us!"

Topa asked anxiously, "What happened to the others?"

"They are with us now," answered Denia. "They have been cared for and are part of our plan to defeat Kronos."

"Can I see them?" asked Topa anxiously. "I have to know that they are okay. My brother was among them."

"They are safe. All will be revealed in time," answered Denia. "We needed to know that the module was secure before we proceeded with our plans against Kronos."

Griff pressed Denia to tell them where their friends were, but she only repeated part of her last phrase. "All will be revealed in time."

"So, what are we supposed to do, just leave?" Mike complained.

Denia stood and took her ghostly form. "Ramses-3," she whispered softly. "When the time comes, you will be part of the plan." She then vanished, leaving them in the dark.

Tisch chided Mike. "You should have stayed away. I had this under control."

Mike got in her face. "No. You should have listened to me. Now get back to the shuttle." The two stared each other down before leading the others back to the shuttles.

When they arrived on board the *Blue Eagle*, Tisch met with Mike, Griff, and Topa to discuss what had happened during her absence. Mike briefed them on the recent events with Empire Shipping and how little they knew about Kronos. Griff suggested that they return to Murgatroyd's Oasis on Zim. Mike recommended to Tisch that they take Griff's advice. She wondered if she might find more answers about her father at the pirate haven and agreed that they should check it out.

Mike insisted that they try out the new fuel regeneration system and replenish the fuel on Griff's shuttle. Wilmer hoped to avoid the drama that was growing with Tisch and Shannon, so he offered to help. Griff and Topa were curious about fuel regeneration and agreed to try it. Mike led the effort to remove the thirty fuel rods from Griff's shuttle, one at a time, and insert them into the chamber. Each rod took about fifteen minutes to regenerate and then was re-installed.

Once finished, Mike was pleased with the results and considered that they could regenerate the fuel on his shuttle as well, when needed. Initially, they believed that the process could only be performed on the ship while its power generation was active. Griff's shuttle was in cold shutdown.

When they located the facility on Zim, Mike suggested that he and Griff check it out. Just like before, Tisch insisted that she and Shannon investigate first. If there were more details about her father, she wanted to be sure she found them.

Frustrated with Tisch's insistence on putting herself in danger, Mike relented. He and the new crew members, Griff and Topa, would still go, but in Mike's shuttle, and would see what they could find out about Kronos. Tisch frowned at the idea but took Griff's shuttle anyway. Wilmer and Zenith weren't thrilled about being left out again but remained on board with Geezer.

During the short flight to the station, Topa expressed her displeasure with Denia. Griff added that he felt Denia was hiding something and that they both wanted to know the true fate of their comrades after that fateful battle. Mike assured them that they would get to the bottom of it in time and urged them to be patient.

As they approached the pirate haven, the monitor revealed a number of dilapidated ships with no markings on the hull or tail. They had the appearance of abandoned wrecks, but Mike knew better. This was the perception that pirates preferred to keep, hoping to be underestimated by their enemies. The shuttle docked in a bay at the far end of the transport section to avoid being noticed. Once the shuttle was secure, they departed from the shuttle and entered the station.

Mike was surprised at the condition of the station as a "pirate haven." It was much more advanced technologically and very respectable from what he could tell. Griff took the lead and led them into the station's pub. It was reminiscent of a large beer hall with a variety of races clustered in groups at the tables. The hall was divided by rope partitions into five areas: Parts, Commodities, Staples, General, and Arms.

When they approached the bar, an elderly man with a handlebar mustache intercepted them and stood in front of Griff. The two men stared each other down for several seconds, and then they burst into laughter. They man-hugged and shook hands. Griff introduced him as Kellen, a former member of his unit. They sat together at an empty table near the corner of the hall in the General section. Mike and Topa said nothing while the men talked of past escapades.

Then Griff introduced Kellen to Mike and Topa. Mike expressed his interest in the pub hall and inquired about the rope partitions. Kellen explained to him that the sections were designated to facilitate trade. The Parts section involved equipment or anything that could be used to build or repair a ship. Commodities included anything like precious metals, jewels, or fuel. Staples included food, drink, or medical supplies. General was for the drinking population with nothing to trade. The Arms section was self-explanatory. Kellen warned them that it was a 'no questions asked' zone regarding the procurement of any of the materials up for trade. He mentioned that there were a number of rooms on the second floor for private negotiations as well.

"Quite the industry," Mike remarked.

The bartender, a bearded man in his late years, brought a tray of ales to the table and served them. Kellen glanced around the hall for a moment to ensure their privacy and then discussed Kronos's presence in the area. Then Mike inquired about Empire Shipping. Kellen informed him that the word among the pirates was to leave Empire's ships alone, if they were encountered. They believed that Kronos was the parent company and would respond with extreme prejudice against all pirates in the area. Mike found that interesting.

Finally, Topa spoke up. "Has anyone learned of the fate of our comrades on Niems?"

Kellen grew uneasy and again glanced around the hall to ensure no one was eavesdropping. He whispered that they had heard from strangers that the aliens who owned Niems might have taken prisoners to a distant planet called Ramses-3, where they were forced into slave labor. He emphasized that it was rumor with not enough detail to know for sure if there even was a planet called Ramses-3.

Griff and Topa were concerned over Kellen's version of the team's fate and grew more determined to get to the bottom of the mystery. As they spoke, Tisch and Shannon entered the hall and approached the bar. The bartender served each of them an ale and inquired what area they preferred to sit. Sensing they were new, he recommended the General section and pointed to several open tables. Mike watched subtly as the women sat ten tables away from them.

Griff revealed to Kellen that Mike had led the mission against the Scrat three years ago. Kellen's eyes widened with surprise and he asked excitedly, "How did you succeed against them? Your team had no backup when we were overtaken on Niems."

Mike inquired how Kellen himself had survived the attack. Kellen explained that he had played dead and was tossed in a bin with other corpses. He escaped and hid on the ship until it docked at Fermi, the space station that hosted the headquarters for Empire Shipping at the time. From there, he hopped a ride with a small ship carrying tools from station to station.

Mike related his story and how the Scrat were the latest victims of Kronos' aggression. Kellen felt an indebtedness to Mike for failing to back up his team during the mission. He pledged to help if Mike ever required it. Mike suggested that any information on Kronos's operations and presence in the area would be appreciated. They raised their beers and toasted to Special Forces.

Tisch paid them no attention and pursued her own means of questioning. She overheard a conversation about Empire Shipping and a bounty from a man named Antwan. There were five men and three women at the table. They appeared to work in the shipping industry based on their conversation. "What do you think, Shannon?" she asked.

"Let's give it a try," she responded.

The women approached the table and asked to join them. The crew seemed disinterested in their presence, but one man gestured for them to take a seat. During a pause in their conversation, Tisch inquired if anyone was familiar with Niems. She quickly drew several stern looks from them. They resumed their conversation without acknowledging Tisch any further. Shannon suggested she let it go and try elsewhere.

Tisch didn't appreciate the treatment and slammed her mug on the table to get their attention. Mike cringed as he watched the scene unfold. Griff and Topa continued their discussion with Kellen, unaware of Tisch's presence nearby. Mike stood and started toward Tisch.

One of the men at the table held a knife to Tisch's throat and warned her to shut up and leave before she brought trouble on them. Shannon attempted to nudge Tisch away from the table, but Tisch insisted on knowing why they wouldn't help her. The man sat down and resumed the conversation with his crew, ignoring Tisch and Shannon once more.

As Mike approached, he was cut off by a dark-haired woman in a cloak, who blocked his path. Under her cloak, she wore a black leather bodice and pants with several knives in a thigh belt and two pulse pistols holstered, one on each hip. Mike suspected the silver balls at the end of her long dreadlocks were flash devices or even miniature grenades. He was curious to know more about her until she held one of her knives up to his throat and instructed him to walk toward the opposite corner of the hall. He reluctantly complied and took a seat at her table. "What do you want?" he asked impatiently. The woman gestured to one of the barmaids to bring two ales.

"I'm saving your life, you idiot," she responded coldly. "What the hell do you want here?"

"I'm looking for information," he replied.

"That will get you killed in a place like this. Start talking," she ordered, holding a pulse pistol under the table aimed at his groin. Mike related the details of their trip to Niems and the search for the missing commandos. The woman was disinterested in the conversation and seemed relieved when the barmaid arrived with two beers.

Mike asked who she was and why she was interested in helping him. She laughed and then chugged one of the beers. Mike reached for the other beer, but she grabbed his wrist. "That one's mine too," she remarked arrogantly. "Get your own."

Mike held his hands up innocently, meaning no disrespect. She inquired if this visit had anything to do with an Archaenean device. Mike replied that he wanted to know what role John Mallory had in it.

"His role was what I told him to do," she said. "Make the pickup and get out of there. Why do you care?"

Mike was surprised by her revelation. He informed her that his partner was the daughter of John Mallory and that John had been killed over the module. The woman looked disappointed by the news. "And the device?" she asked.

"No one knows," he answered innocently. "I've heard it was destroyed in the explosion that killed Mallory."

A bearded man in raggedy clothes came to the woman and spoke softly, "Marina, beware. Kronos soldiers just arrived here." Marina nodded to him and he left. Mike heard the man address her as Marina but said nothing.

"What is your involvement with Kronos?" she asked him and then sipped from her beer. Mike revealed everything that had happened and how he hoped to form a plan to defeat them.

"Well, at least we have one thing in common," she commented. "When the time comes to deal with Kronos, you'll know. In the meantime, you'd better get your girlfriend out of here before she gets herself killed." Marina finished her beer and left the table. Mike pondered her words and then hurried over to Tisch's aid.

Three men in plain uniforms had grabbed Tisch and Shannon. Tisch demanded they release them. The crew at the table ignored them and continued their conversation. The uniformed men ushered them away. Griff noticed and followed with Topa and Kellen right behind him. Mike trailed them out of the hall and down the corridor. He called to the uniformed men and rushed to speak with them. "What's going on here?"

"None of your business," replied the biggest of the men. "Now beat it, or you can join them."

"What authority do you have to arrest anyone?" Mike demanded to know.

The men laughed at him until the big man answered again, "Kronos is our authority. Need I say more?"

Mike lowered his head and feigned sadness. Suddenly, he threw an uppercut and knocked the man out. The second man drew his pistol, but Mike knocked him out before he could fire. The third man backed away with his pulse pistol drawn. "You have no idea what you just started!" he shouted.

Mike walked toward him, ready to fight, and taunted, "Why don't you show me?" The man aimed at Mike's head, but before he could fire, Griff shot him from a distance.

Griff, Topa, and Kellen arrived and urged them to hurry to the shuttles. Tisch remarked sarcastically, "We had everything under control, but once again..."

Mike interrupted her and warned her that they would finish the discussion later on the ship. They hurried to the transport bay, and the shuttles were soon on their way back to the *Blue Eagle*.

When they exited the shuttles, Kellen spoke to the women sternly. "You can't walk into a place like that and make a scene!"

"And why not?" countered Tisch.

Kellen shook his head in disbelief and explained that Kronos had agents there searching for rebels. He then pointed out that she had endangered every person in there with her actions. Mike added that Kronos was now aware of their presence since they killed one of their agents.

Shannon was embarrassed for their ineptitude and said nothing. Tisch realized they had made a big mistake and stormed out of the cargo bay. Griff explained to Mike that they needed to leave the area fast before Kronos could identify their shuttles or the *Blue Eagle*.

Mike instructed Geezer to get them back to Taurus right away. He then informed Shannon that she was banished from any future excursions until he told her otherwise. Wilmer arrived in the cargo bay, anxious to hear what had happened.

Shannon joined them and attempted to apologize. Mike chastised her for her foolishness and mentioned his encounter with Marina. Visibly upset with the way things went, he instructed Wilmer to take the crew to the galley, and he would meet with them shortly. Wilmer sensed the urgency of the situation and promptly led them from the bay.

Mike sat in the open hatch to the shuttle and held his head in his hands. He thought he was past this with Tisch, but obviously not. Shannon took advantage of the discord among the crew and sent a coded message to Sara, updating her on their findings.

CHAPTER XV

THE BIG ONE

On Taurus, a class-four freighter by the name *Carnage* requested an unscheduled stop for repairs. The transport supervisor permitted them to dock at Bay 29, a short distance from the Scrat warship at Bay 24. With the *Blue Eagle* gone and the Scrat assisting GSS with security, there was a period of calm at the station.

Sara arrived at Gemini's suite on the Executive Level to update Gemini, Dax, and Julian on information she had recently received from Shannon regarding their stop at the pirate haven on Zim. Sara started the meeting by announcing that there were other groups that were attempting to organize against Kronos Enterprises. She also mentioned that they needed to find out more about a planet in the Strontarian Galaxy called Ramses-3.

Julian questioned the value of this information to them and how it impacted their security measures. Gemini was more interested in the *Blue Eagle's* experience on Niems. Dax took notes on the meeting and attempted to tie the bits of information together. "Too many questions and not enough answers," Sara remarked unhappily.

"Or we have the answers, but don't know the questions," complained Gemini.

Sara surmised that Kronos would become more visible in their part of the galaxy, whether it be through Empire Shipping or directly by them.

If they were aware of a mounting threat by rebel groups, then they would likely seek to eliminate them, one by one, to deter the others.

Julian pointed out that due to their success in fending off Empire's previous attacks, they would surely be the primary target as 'something bigger'. If they were defeated, other groups would back down. Sara agreed and decided that they needed increased security measures on the station, but traitors and mercenaries were still a concern.

When the conversation turned to Niems, Gemini pointed out that Antwan's crew was terminated. Antwan appeared to be the only survivor from the Niems incident and, coincidently, the leader, at least in this part of the galaxy. She was certain that he was the one person they needed to focus on for now. "Find him, and you've cut the head off the snake," Gemini told them. "And if you do find him, I'd like to do the honors."

Sara was concerned that someone had the technology to build a module with the capability to travel across the universe in a few seconds and that they could make more of them. The Scrat had already proved what could happen with the module in the wrong hands.

Dax finally spoke up. "How do we find out who our unknown allies are?"

Sara's only response was that they would know or be informed when the time came. Dax gestured in futility, his hands in the air. "That does nothing for us," he complained.

Julian offered to contact old acquaintances from his days with Aurora Shipping. Sara suggested that she, too, would reach out to old contacts to find out what was going on. They considered that the information they had received was merely rumor or misinformation and that they were on their own against Kronos Enterprises.

Sara was perplexed by the woman Shannon mentioned who had spoken with Mike. The name Marina sounded so familiar, yet she had no idea who she was. *Perhaps she is just a pirate making a name for herself,* Sara thought. *Or maybe someone of great significance.* This was no help to her.

Their discussion was interrupted when Sara received a message from the transport supervisor. She looked panicked and contacted him directly by transmitter. The expression on her face indicated something terrible had just occurred. Sara ordered the supervisor to deny the unscheduled ship any moorage until they could verify its identity and owner. She grew red-faced when the supervisor revealed that the ship was already docked at Bay 27. "No one else comes in or out of this facility!" she shouted at the supervisor. Her transmitter beeped again and she looked pained while answering it. Creeg informed her that containers were already being offloaded from the freighter bearing the markings KE-427. He noted to her that it was a Kronos ship and was concerned by the urgent offloading of the containers.

Sara ordered him to summon all his troops and prepare for a major attack. "They're here!" she announced to the others in the conference room. "Get ready for war!" Sara instructed them to arm themselves and secure the floor if possible. If not, they were to barricade themselves inside the suite. After ordering Gemini to have the security center place the station in lockdown, she stormed out of the conference room and into the corridor.

Sara waited for the elevator with five of her agents. They took a defensive position away from the doors, expecting intruders. The elevator doors opened, and seven mercenaries with pulse rifles targeted them before they could react. After a short burst of pulse fire, each group suffered casualties. Sara and her two remaining agents were forced to retreat back toward Gemini's suite.

Ten containers had been offloaded by the time Creeg and Captain Tieg arrived. The area was cordoned off and the containers surrounded. There was an eerie silence in the transport area as the sentries waited nervously for whatever was to occur next. Suddenly, panels slid open on the sides of the five containers facing them, and a barrage of pulse fire erupted toward them. The five rear containers opened, and a large contingent of soldiers in dark uniforms emerged and took cover. The pulse fire was incredible as thirty mercenaries now battled Captain Tieg's men and Creeg's troops.

The battle was stalemated for a lengthy period until grenades were launched from behind the containers. The security teams retreated back toward the smaller bays. The invading army seemed to disregard Creeg's troops and were instead determined to push Tieg's team in the direction of Bay 11 with heavy pulse fire and grenades. Captain Tieg attempted to contact Sara for additional support but with no success.

When the security team reached Bay 11, the pulse fire stopped, and an eerie silence returned. Finally, one of the assailants shouted, "Give us the *Blue Eagle* and Gemini. You have my word: we'll let you live."

Captain Tieg and Creeg glanced at each other, baffled by the request. They both knew the *Blue Eagle* wasn't there. Tieg suggested they play along and use that misinformation against them. "This is as far as this goes," responded Tieg to the soldiers. "Leave now, and you will be spared."

"Then you will all die," the leader responded, and the pulse fire resumed.

The *Blue Eagle* approached Taurus and paused outside Bay 11. Geezer requested entrance to the bay from the transport supervisor. He was informed that the station was under siege and in lockdown. He had orders not to allow anyone in or out. Geezer summoned Mike to the bridge and informed him of what had happened.

Mike ordered the supervisor to give them access or else they would blast the outer bay doors off the station. The controller warned him that he would be reported to GSS when this was over. Mike laughed sarcastically and replied that it was the least of his concerns right now. The supervisor reluctantly complied, and the outer gates opened, allowing the *Blue Eagle* to enter Bay 11.

Tisch arrived on the bridge and demanded to know what was going on. Mike instructed her to man the turret and await his instructions. Tisch argued that this was ridiculous, and she would not fire a cannon inside the station. Mike was about to explode with anger and poked a finger at her face. "When this is over, so are we," he declared coldly. "I'm tired of this game you're playing."

Mike instructed Geezer to keep the ship powered up in case they needed to escape in a hurry. By now, everyone had arrived on the bridge. Mike ordered them to arm themselves and wait for further instructions. He left the bridge and rushed to the upper turret.

Tisch blurted out, "What the hell does he think he's doing with my ship?"

"Saving your ass!" Wilmer shouted angrily. He led everyone to the weapons lockers and armed them with pulse rifles and grenades. They split into two groups, with the women guarding the personnel hatch, while the men rushed to secure the cargo bay hatch.

Tisch complained to Shannon that this was the problem she had with Mike before. She hated when he pulled rank on her in critical situations. Zenith commented that this was Mike's area of expertise and that perhaps she should work with him. Tisch would have none of it, though. "We'll play his game this time, but he's done on my ship after this," she uttered bitterly.

Shannon and Zenith looked uneasily at each other. Topa wasn't thrilled with the childishness of Tisch during battle either. She studied the surrounding area and designated locations for the women to take cover in case of a breach.

As the men reached the cargo bay, Wilmer contacted Mike and asked, "How serious is this?"

"What?" Mike said. "The attack or Tisch?"

Wilmer considered his response and shrugged his shoulders. "Both."

"Critical," Mike quipped. "Don't do anything until I tell you."

Out in the corridor, the battle waged on. Both sides incurred heavy casualties, and the security team could no longer hold them off. They retreated, giving the attackers access to Bay 11. The soldiers formed a defensive line in front of the bay, facing the security team as the inner gates were opened.

Mike was stunned to see a large, organized assault team in the transport area. He waited until the gates were fully opened and fired one shot. The soldiers had no idea the turret was manned, and one blast from the cannon wiped out more than half of them. The remainder rushed at the ship to get under the turret's range. Mike fired once more and killed several others. Unfortunately, the sealing edges of the inner gates were mangled, and the supporting frame was warped from the heat of the cannons.

Captain Tieg ordered the security team to close the bay gates and contain the assailants. They were shocked when they approached and saw the *Blue Eagle* inside. Now containing the attackers in the bay wasn't an option.

Mike instructed Geezer to contact the transport supervisor and have him close the gates. He then warned the crew to be ready for a breach. The inner gates functioned but would not close completely due to the damage. Mike instructed Geezer to request the transport supervisor to open the outer gates of the bay. Geezer grinned, realizing what Mike's plan was.

Captain Tieg panicked when the gates failed to fully close. He feared that the soldiers would capture the *Blue Eagle*, and, in their escape, the outer gates would open to space, thus sucking out the air and anyone close to the gates with it. Even worse, he could not let the remaining invaders escape with the *Blue Eagle* and the ship's new technology along with it, no matter what.

The ten attackers attempted to enter through the personnel hatch on the *Blue Eagle*. The external 'manual override' allowed them to open the hatch. As soon as it opened, Tisch ordered the women to fire. After a brief shootout, the soldiers were forced to retreat. Geezer, seeing the "personnel hatch open" indication, closed it once more from his console.

The soldiers attempted to enter through the cargo bay, again using the external 'manual override' for the cargo hatch to open it. Again, they were met by pulse fire from the men. Mike left the turret and hurried down to the cargo bay. The cargo bay hatch was half open, and the pulse fire was intense between the two groups.

When Mike reached them, he saw that they were still outnumbered. He contacted Geezer and repeated his earlier order to have the transport supervisor open the outer bay doors. Geezer raised the man on the transmitter and shouted, "Open the outer doors now!" The supervisor monitored the fighting by surveillance camera and feared opening the outer gates with the inner gates and the ship's cargo hatch partially open.

The soldiers rushed to the *Blue Eagle's* personnel hatch and set up explosive charges on it. Geezer watched on the monitor and saw that the outer doors hadn't moved. He contacted the transport supervisor and threatened to beat him to death if he didn't get the doors open. Red lights and a Klaxon sounded as a warning that the outer doors were about to open to space. Finally, the outer doors opened.

Upon hearing the Klaxon sound for the outer doors, Captain Tieg ordered his men to retreat from Bay 11. The attackers panicked and attempted to charge through the cargo bay hatch. Four were quickly gunned down by Mike's team. Suddenly, the bay filled with a powerful vacuum force as the outside doors opened and broke the containment seal. The remaining soldiers were pulled away from the hatch and ejected into space. Mike's team held on desperately, waiting for the cargo bay doors to close.

As soon as Geezer saw the soldiers sucked out of the bay, he ordered the transport supervisor to close the outer doors quickly. He immediately closed the cargo bay hatch from his console. It seemed like eternity before the cargo bay hatch and the outer gates closed and sealed.

Inside the cargo bay, the men were exhausted, extremely cold, and panting heavily from the lack of oxygen. Mike heard Geezer's voice over the intercom calling his name. Mike responded, much to Geezer's relief. He was anxious to know that the men were safe. Mike offered to come up and kiss him for handling the gates and hatches so well. Geezer politely declined.

Tisch and the rest of her team returned to the bridge. Geezer was eager to explain how Mike's plan worked and how the invaders were defeated. Tisch was less than thrilled that, once again, Mike was right.

As soon as the bay had reached a safe oxygen level, the men left the ship through the cargo hatch and crept through the damaged inner gates. Mike instructed Wilmer to remove the explosive charges, whose detonators had not yet been activated. They were soon met by Captain Tieg, Creeg, and the few remaining Scrat and GSS agents. Mike was appalled at the damage and loss of life inside the station.

Captain Tieg immediately informed Mike that they were unable to reach anyone on the Executive Level. Mike expressed his concerns to Captain Tieg and Creeg that it was unlikely that Empire's mercenaries would attempt to capture Gemini using the same tactics as last time.

Tieg suggested they ride the elevators at the opposite ends of the corridor to the Executive Level and box them in. Mike disagreed and recommended taking two teams through the air shafts and then determine the best method of attack. Creeg warned that the elevators would likely be rigged to explode unless they were locked out for a late escape. Tieg sent two men to find out if any were operable. He then gave Mike the security codes for the emergency stairwells and accesses between station sections during lockdowns. Meanwhile, Mike instructed Wilmer and Griff to accompany him to the tenth floor by the emergency stairwell.

Tieg's men returned and informed him that only one of the four elevators was inoperable. They had locked it out on the twelfth floor to access the shaft. There were explosives found in the shafts of the others with detonators wired to the open-door-limit switches. Captain Tieg concluded that the soldiers' plan was to get in and get out fast using the locked out elevator. Tieg instructed his men and Creeg's troops to secure the class-four freighter and seize any personnel on board. He tried once more to contact Sara but with no success. For once, he actually hoped that Mike was successful.

Tisch questioned Geezer about where Mike was and what he was up to. Geezer frowned and informed her that the Executive Level was still under siege and that Mike was working with Creeg and Captain Tieg to come up with a plan to end it. Tisch grew frustrated as she realized she had put herself out of the picture over her obsession with Niems and her father. She asked Shannon for an update about what was happening. Shannon recommended they stay put and protect the *Blue Eagle* in case there were more insurgents in waiting. Topa said nothing, hoping that the drama would end. Her thoughts were on Niems and the fate of her former team.

Zenith listened without saying anything until Tisch had finished with Shannon. Zenith then spoke up and asked why Tisch had recurring issues with Mike over his suggestions. Tisch approached her with a wicked scowl on her face, ready to explode on her, but Zenith continued before Tisch could speak. She commented on what a great team they were when they worked together and an even better couple after the job was done. She also remarked how envious she was of Tisch for all her successes as a captain and for having a great man in her life. Tisch quickly regained her composure and patted her shoulder. "You are so right, Zenith, but sometimes, that man drives me crazy," she explained. "It bothers me that he's right not once or twice but every single time!"

"Consider the alternative," Zenith said. "Imagine if he was reckless, unreliable, and unfaithful."

Tisch understood where Zenith was coming from and thanked her for her wise words. She promised to try harder to work with Mike without creating all the drama the crew had to endure once more. Zenith hugged Tisch and reminded her how much she appreciated the opportunity to join the crew. Tisch thanked her and hugged her back.

Shannon entered the bridge and informed them that she could not contact Sara, which concerned her. Tisch asked if she thought they were overrun and captured or killed. Shannon shrugged her shoulders and lowered her head sadly. Tisch pondered a moment over what action they should take, but then she recalled the conversation she had just had with Zenith. Tisch instructed them to take defensive positions at the hatches in case of an attack.

Geezer continued to watch the monitor displaying the bay's inner gates and personnel entrance for any intruders. His responsibility was to warn everyone if any unauthorized personnel were spotted entering the bay.

Thanks to the security codes provided by Captain Tieg, Mike led his team to the tenth floor by way of the emergency stairwell. They accessed one of the computers in an engineering office to review the ductwork to the eleventh floor, particularly around Gemini's suite and the conference room. Mike was sure they had everything figured out and removed a duct cover. He led his team into the air duct and shimmied up to the eleventh floor. When he reached the top of the vertical shaft, his progress was impeded by dampers much smaller than he had expected. He tried to break off some of the vanes but with no luck.

"What's going on?" asked Wilmer from below him. Mike informed them that the plan had failed. With no other option, they retreated back to the tenth floor. Griff suggested they try the elevator shaft since that elevator was locked out.

Mike realized that the assailants needed that one elevator to escape, unless they had access to the stairwell. He ruled the stairwell out because it was eleven floors and would leave the mercenaries vulnerable at each floor. The elevator was their only option, so they rushed to the shaft for the disabled elevator.

Wilmer and Griff forced open the doors on the tenth floor, allowing Mike to enter the shaft. He climbed up the service ladder to the eleventh floor and tried to pry open the doors. With the use of only one arm while holding on to the ladder, he struggled but with no luck. Wilmer propped the door open on the tenth floor, allowing Griff to climb up the ladder. He slid under Mike, and the two pulled on the doors together. The doors budged, but barely.

Wilmer requested they come down and give him a try. Mike chuckled at the idea but had no other options. He and Griff climbed down and left the shaft. Wilmer eagerly climbed up and studied the door's operation.

Sara and her two agents were cornered outside Gemini's suite by the mercenaries. Their pulse pistols were depleted, and they were outmanned. The leader of the mercenaries, a scarfaced man named Cress, approached them with a pulse rifle aimed at Sara's head. He ordered Sara's agents down on the ground, and the mercenaries tied them up.

Sara stood defiantly and stared Cress down. He placed the barrel of the rifle against her head and ordered her to open the entrance to the suite.

Sara refused and spat on the man. He punched her in the forehead and nearly knocked her out. Sara staggered, her head spinning from the impact.

Inside the suite, Gemini, Dax, and Julian could see them on the cameras. "We have to help her," Gemini blurted, concerned. "They'll kill her."

Julian explained that Sara was protecting them, and if they opened the door, they were all dead. Dax lowered his head, feeling useless. Gemini stared at the monitor and counted how many soldiers were outside the suite. "There are only five out there," she commented. "There are three of us with weapons."

"If we go out there, make your shots count," warned Dax. Julian advised her against it but conceded he would follow whatever her orders were.

Cress dragged Sara to her knees and pistol-whipped her head and face several times. "Open the damned door now!" he shouted.

Sara still refused. Cress stowed his pistol and took a hunting knife from his belt. "I'll ask you one more time, and then I'm going to cut off fingers, and after that... perhaps your face." he threatened.

Sara resigned herself to the fact that she was going to die. Cress knocked her to the floor and knelt on her wrist. He held his knife over her left thumb and threatened her once more. Sara cringed, awaiting the pain that was to come.

Watching on the monitor, Gemini, Dax, and Julian were horrified at how far the mercenaries would go to achieve their goals. Gemini bit her lip as she wrestled with the decision of when they should interfere. Julian suggested. "It's now or never, Gem."

"Let's go," she replied defiantly. "This is my company, and it's time to fight for it!"

Cress pressed the knife down on Sara's thumb, slowly increasing pressure. Sara still refused to cooperate. Julian turned off the security override and pressed the 'open' knob. Gemini led them into the corridor and caught the mercenaries by surprise. Gemini took out Cress with three shots to the head while Dax and Julian shot the others. One of the soldiers got off a shot and struck Dax in the abdomen.

Gemini and Julian hurried to Sara's aid, unaware of Dax's injury. Sara got up slowly, looking like a frightened child, and hugged Gemini. Her thumb had a deep laceration but was still intact. For once, Gemini had saved her life. Then Gemini saw Dax lying on the floor in a pool of blood. His eyes were glazed over, and he shuddered. She rushed to him and knelt beside him.

Julian shouted for someone to get help while she cradled Dax across her lap in her arms. He squeezed her hand and smiled briefly. Tears streamed down Gemini's cheeks as she hugged him tightly. Captain Tieg arrived and quickly authorized access for the medics to help Dax.

Wilmer found the limit switch that activated the elevator door. He triggered it, and the doors slid open. He motioned for the others to follow. Mike humbly apologized for doubting him. Now on the eleventh floor, the four of them rushed toward the suite, hoping to catch the mercenaries by surprise. They were stunned to see Sara and Julian standing over the dead mercenaries. Then they saw Gemini kneeling on the floor with Dax in her arms, and they grew somber.

"A little late for the party, aren't you, Colby?" chided Gemini tearfully. The medics arrived and placed Dax on a gurney. Gemini grabbed one of them by the arm for his assessment, but the medic could only promise to do what they could to save him. Gemini released her hold on him, and he joined the others in moving the gurney.

Mike shook his head in disbelief over the odds they had overcome. "How'd you manage to do it, Sara?" he asked.

Sara pointed to Gemini and Julian. "They get the credit for this one," she replied weakly. Sara lowered her arm to her side. Blood dripped from her thumb and pooled on the floor. Julian retrieved a first-aid kit from the conference room next to Gemini's suite and promptly dressed her wound.

Sara's first concern was the status and casualties from the attack. Mike caught her up on what had happened down at the transport center. She contacted Creeg and was informed that they had taken control of the class-four Kronos freighter. The crew was already in custody. Sara instructed her people in the security center to override the elevator lockouts and to remove the explosives from the shafts. "I need to rest," she muttered and left them.

Reluctantly, Mike and his team took the emergency stairwell down to the transport lobby on the ground floor. He was eager to board the Kronos freighter and search its database. During their descent, he contacted Geezer and informed him that the siege was over but to be aware of any stray mercenaries lurking about.

Geezer relayed the information to Tisch. Tisch, Shannon, Zenith, and Topa were anxious to leave the ship and assess the damage. They met with Captain Tieg and learned how the events had unfolded. Tisch noticed that there was no sign of Mike, and then Topa disappeared from her group as well. She rolled her eyes and complained, "Here we go again."

Shannon urged her to relax and maintain her composure. Tisch sighed and settled down. She considered the fact that Shannon and Zenith had been a help to her in handling her emotions and was thankful. In the past, she had Wilmer, Julian, and Geezer to deal with. Having women to share her feelings with was beneficial to her.

Captain Tieg was curious as to how the *Blue Eagle* had returned to the bay without anyone knowing. Shannon joked that it was a good thing the station personnel didn't follow security protocols.

"I'll make sure that doesn't happen again," Tieg remarked sarcastically. He was especially concerned that an unidentified ship was permitted to dock without authorization and then allowed to unload cargo containers before security could take control.

On board the Kronos freighter, Mike and Griff questioned the crew. At first, they were uncooperative, but when Mike threatened to turn them over to a Scrat group that was anxious for revenge, they had a quick change of heart. Sara arrived, still shaken from the firefight, and was content to let Mike handle the questioning. Creeg stood by, ready to inflict fear into the crew if they became uncooperative.

The ship's captain explained that they had been paid handsomely by a man named Antwan to bring the containers to Taurus. The captain was okay with the idea so long as there weren't any explosives that jeopardized his ship. He never suspected he was hauling an armed mercenary army. He then revealed that he was due to contact Antwan with an update on his delivery shortly.

Mike informed him that he would speak with Antwan when the contact was made. When questioned about his employment with Kronos, the captain admitted that they had hired him through a third-party service and paid him through Empire Shipping. Part of the deal included bearing their markings on his ship for his own safety.

Sara requested from Captain Tieg that reserve security personnel be engaged and sent down to the freighter. She was undecided on what to do with the crew, but she instructed one of her technicians to scan all the computer files to determine all prior destinations and contacts. For now, the crew would be held in custody until their personal histories could be verified.

The ship's captain initiated contact with Antwan as planned. When his face appeared on the monitor, Mike slid his chair in front of it. Antwan was stunned to see Mike on his monitor. "Where are my men, Colby?" he shouted.

"It's over, Antwan," Mike replied calmly. "And now you really pissed me off."

"What do you want?" Antwan asked. "Name your price. Kronos has deep pockets."

Mike laughed at him. "We're way past that. It's personal now and I'm coming for you." Antwan panicked and terminated the transmission. Mike was disappointed that there was no response after his threat. He and Sara agreed that it would be a while before they heard from him again. This had to be a significant setback for Kronos in this part of the galaxy. In the meantime, there was a lot to be done to improve the security of the station.

Captain Tieg was more than grateful for GSS assistance after the recent attacks. He knew they were not equipped to handle well-trained mercenary attacks on a scale like this.

Believing Dax was dead, Mike met Zenith at the personnel hatch to the *Blue Eagle* and informed her of her father's condition. When Zenith became teary-eyed, Mike hugged her. He praised her father for being a good man, even if he was lacking in the skills of fatherhood. Zenith wiped her tears away and muttered, "Life sucks. So be it."

Mike offered to spend time with her if it helped. She felt that the time away from Taurus would be sufficient to help her get over it. Mike commented that no one ever gets over the loss of a loved one and promised to be there for her if she needed someone. Zenith kissed his cheek and boarded the ship. Feeling sorry for her, he considered how far she had come from the person she once was.

Tisch assembled the crew on the bridge of the *Blue Eagle* and informed them that the ship was grounded until the inner gates could be repaired. Until that time, the outer doors were de-energized and would remain shut. She added that GSS had brought in extra security to protect the station, as well as the *Blue Eagle*. During that spell, she arranged for additional training for everyone. When she finished, Mike announced that he was leaving, and so was Griff and Topa. Tisch was shocked by the announcement. Zenith stood and announced that she would leave as well. They left the bridge, leaving Tisch speechless.

Wilmer commented that he was only staying because of Shannon and would limit his presence on the bridge as much as possible. He gestured for Shannon to join him, and they left the bridge too.

"What the hell just happened?" Tisch exclaimed.

Geezer reminded her of what had fractured the crew in the past. He suggested that she speak to them when everyone was calm and things were back to normal. Tisch broke down in tears and left the bridge for her cabin. Geezer shook his head and grumbled, "There goes my backup. Damn!

And that Zenith had so much potential." He powered the ship down and departed the bridge.

Mike met with Sara and discussed taking Kronos's freighter on a fact-finding mission to learn more about potential allies against Kronos. Sara recommended against it, but she also expressed her frustration that all her avenues were exhausted and she had nothing as far as intel on Empire or Kronos. Mike promised to contact her if he found anything of importance and thanked her for her support. He gathered his new team and added Kellen. They departed Taurus and headed for Murgatroyd's Oasis on Zim.

During the trip, Mike announced that he intended to take out any of Kronos's personnel on the station. Kellen was wary of making a scene like that but was sure he could rally many of the pirates to join them. By accomplishing this, Mike hoped to force Kronos to reveal their location and how big their military was. He realized that any information would be a start since, as of now, they had nothing to go on. No one knew where Antwan was or the location of Ramses-3. They also had no idea what the connection between Empire Shipping and Kronos Enterprises was. He wondered if they were one and the same or just partners. Partners can be separated.

It also crossed his mind that Ramses-3 was the headquarters for Kronos, but that conflicted with what the Archaenean woman had told them. Topa was concerned about Niems and Denia, the alien being. She needed to know why their team was taken and what they were being used for.

Griff wondered if their former team had joined a different army with no limitations like those imposed by the Federation's Special Forces. Both were bitter that the military leadership had refused to investigate the disappearances on Niems. There was no acknowledgement that the team was dead or even missing. Mike assured them that he would do his best to get answers. He reminded them that it may take time and a lot of work before they got the answers they sought.

When they departed Taurus, Griff and Topa took turns piloting the ship. Mike sat in his new quarters and came to terms with the fact that he and Tisch were done. He knew that neither of them could change, and that just made for problems between them, the crew, and even those on

Taurus. Sara and Gemini had stepped up for him and did well. Tisch's behavior while the station was under siege proved that their relationship put everyone at risk. He lay back on the bed and closed his eyes.

Zenith entered his cabin with a bottle of whiskey and sat on the bed. "Look what I found in one of the cabins," she boasted and took a swig. Mike opened his eyes and smiled at her. She handed him the bottle and commented, "I'm not sure if we should be celebrating a victory or mourning a funeral." Mike knew she was referring to his breakup with Tisch as well as the death of her father. He drank from the bottle. She joined him on the bed in a sitting position. They said little and drank much. Finally, Zenith asked the question, "Where does this leave us?"

Mike smiled as he considered her question. He responded, "Relationships are dangerous in this business. Friends aren't." Zenith took the hint and set the bottle down. She climbed onto Mike's lap and kissed him briefly.

"Friends are fine," she whispered in his ear and kissed him again. Mike limited their affair to just kissing and embracing each other. He warned Zenith that sex becomes a dangerous thing when you count on people to have your back. Then Griff's voice over the intercom interrupted their peace.

"We're pulling into the station, Mike. Any instructions?"

Zenith giggled at him and stood up. "Duty calls, again," she teased. Mike admired the outline of her body in the dim light and reluctantly got up. His response over the intercom surprised the crew on the bridge. "No instructions. Just have fun and we'll see where this goes."

"Does that apply to me as well?" Zenith asked coyly.

Mike kidded, "Especially you." She pressed herself against him and kissed him passionately.

"I'm going to like this," she whispered to him.

Mike was fine with their friendship so long as it didn't interfere with business - and Tisch. Zenith assured him there were no commitments and she would stay out of his way when it came to work. Mike was anxious to report to the bridge, and Zenith looked forward to a drink without the drama that Tisch had created.

Tisch sat in the pub alone on Taurus and sipped from a glass of wine. Tears welled in her eyes as she humiliated herself once again. She noticed Wilmer and Shannon entered the bar and sat at a table in the back. She was glad for Wilmer's happiness but angry with herself that she had thrown that same happiness away. It seemed she was cursed to suffer even if she did cause her own misery.

Once again, she was irked by the fact that it was her ship and that she always felt that her leadership was threatened. Gemini and Julian entered the pub and sought her out. When they spotted her, they came over and sat down.

"We were concerned about you," Gemini commented. "You're going through a rough spell."

Julian touched her hand with his and advised her, "Things will get better. These are tough times."

Tisch figured they knew all about Mike's departure and came to savor her misery. The bartender brought over two ales and another glass of wine. Gemini reminded Tisch that Mike was a very difficult person to live with and even harder to hold on to. Tisch finally responded to them. "This was all on me. I caused it, and now I'm paying the price. I just lost most of my crew over this."

Gemini moved next to her and placed her arm around her. She reminded Tisch that Mike drove her to the affair that she had with John Mallory, Tisch's father. It was never intended, but Mike had left her out of his life, and she was lonely. "Why do you think I named his shuttle Self- Righteous?" Gemini joked. "He doesn't get what he does to people; how he isolates himself from them and leaves them stranded on an island to fend for themselves. Then when you fail, he's there to criticize." Tisch nodded in agreement.

Julian added, "Mike is a good man, but he is obsessed with winning, especially when it comes to battle."

The three of them raised their glasses and toasted to Mike's self-righteousness. Tisch kidded that it was so ironic having this drink with Julian and Gemini over the topic. She felt naive that she hadn't understood this before. Julian was much like Mike in many ways, but he kept to himself. There were no casualties. She couldn't understand why Mike picked her to start a relationship with anyhow. Now she understood Gemini, Julian, and even Mike as clear as day. "So now what do I do?" Tisch asked.

Gemini answered sternly. "When the outer gates are nearly fixed and we set the *Blue Eagle's* next mission, you contact him and tell him to get his ass back here."

"You need to take control of him," Julian recommended. "Let him know that you are in charge. Besides, you have something that he wants."

Tisch blushed and replied, "Julian!"

Gemini laughed. "Besides that, Tisch. You have his heart. He will come back."

Tisch finished her glass of wine and replied, "I hope so. I hope they all come back."

Julian assured her that things would work out and that time heals all wounds, even his.

CHAPTER XVI

FINISH WHAT WE STARTED

The *Carnage* docked at Murgatroyd's Oasis on Zim and sent many of its clientele scrambling for cover. They feared that Kronos's ship had brought soldiers to punish them for the death of their agent at the hands of Griff.

Before leaving the ship, Mike instructed Griff to reset the security codes for access to the ship. For Griff, this was a minor program change in the system. When Mike led his crew off the ship, a few of the stragglers were quick to spread the word that it wasn't Kronos's people after all. Soon, the crowd returned. Everyone was anxious to know how Mike got control of a Kronos freighter, especially a class four. Those were expensive and rare.

Topa, Kellen, and Griff went to the pub hall in search of Kellen's contacts. Mike wandered around the station in search of the owner, hoping that the owner would seek him out first. He ascended a set of stairs to the second floor and strolled down the corridor, looking more like a lost tourist than a mercenary.

The corridor extended the length of the station and was lined on either side by doors with watertight hatches open in front of them for emergencies. He heard voices inside one of the rooms and paused to listen. Inside were a dozen Kronos agents discussing how to punish the station's visitors for the death of their comrade. They wore black, which distinguished them as members of Kronos Enterprises. Their mission was to deter and report any rebellious action to their headquarters. One of the men received a message and grew concerned.

The others, sensing trouble, ceased their conversations and listened. The man instructed them to arm up and follow him. He revealed that the *Carnage* was docked at the station and that the crew wasn't any of their people.

Mike immediately opened the next door down the corridor and hid inside. The agents left the room and rushed down the corridor to the stairs. As soon as they were out of sight, Mike opened the door and peered into the corridor. The light from the corridor illuminated the room behind him. Three computers were stationed along one wall. A communications set was staged in the corner opposite the door. Mike took note of the room number on the door and returned to the corridor.

As he passed the last door before the stairwell, the door opened. A tall, bald man with a long beard grabbed him by the back of the neck and held a pistol against his head. After disarming Mike, he pulled him into his office and threw him to the floor. "One wrong move and you're a dead man," he warned. "Who the hell are you?"

Mike introduced himself and explained that he was looking for the station's owner to discuss a mutual problem. He continued with an offer to rid the station of the Kronos agents as well. Sensing the man's reluctance, Mike reminded him that he had arrived on a class-four Kronos freighter, hoping that would give him credibility.

The man introduced himself as Korick, the station's owner, and then chastised Mike for bringing the ship there. He then reminded Mike that he had a bounty on his head and there was no loyalty among the people in a pirate haven. Korick shook his head at Mike and warned him that he should leave immediately.

Mike offered to take out the Kronos agents and provide protection for the station in return for information on Kronos and Niems. Korick laughed hysterically at him. He tossed him his pistols and warned him once more that he should get out of there with his ship before he brought the wrath of Kronos down on them. He also told Mike that if he failed to escape, he would deny ever meeting him.

Mike was baffled why Korick wasn't concerned about getting rid of the Kronos agents. Korick became impatient and explained that so long as Kronos was there, they had nothing to worry about as far as getting annihilated by their forces. If the agents saw nothing suspicious, then they had nothing to report. All was good. Mike was embarrassed for missing that. He agreed to leave the station and left Korick's office.

Mike returned to the transport area near his ship and was amused to see the Kronos agents trying to gain access. Griff had reset the freighter's security system so only he and Mike could open the hatch from outside the ship.

Marina appeared, disguised in a cloak, and watched them until she saw Mike across the transport area. She approached him and struck him in the head with her pistol, knocking him out. She then dragged him away from the dock area and instructed two passing strangers to take him upstairs and tie him up. The strangers immediately obeyed, indicating that Marina was an authority figure at the station.

Sara arrived at the pub and sat down with Tisch, Gemini, and Julian. "We have a problem," she began. "I was contacted by someone of significance about Mike."

Gemini groaned and asked, "What did he do now?"

Sara maintained a somber expression and explained, "The pirate haven is a meeting point for several of the allies against Kronos. It appears Mike docked the Kronos freighter there and is endangering their operation."

Tisch muttered, "Well, that was stupid."

"So, what do they want us to do?" Julian inquired cynically.

Sara stood and leaned on the table with a stern expression. "Go get him, Tisch, and after you do, stay the hell away from there." Sara stormed out of the pub.

Gemini offered to lend them a shuttle as the interior gates to Bay 11 were still under repair. Tisch understood what needed to be done and left the pub. Gemini remarked, "I hope she knows what she's doing."

"They'll be fine," Julian assured her. They tapped glasses and finished their drinks.

Tisch summoned Wilmer and relayed their instructions to him. She asked for his thoughts on using a loaner shuttle. Wilmer grinned and suggested they use Mike's. At first, Tisch was baffled, but then she understood what he meant. *That's where the module was installed!* She instructed him to get Shannon and meet her in the cargo bay of the *Blue Eagle*.

Tisch wondered how much longer the *Blue Eagle* would be confined to Bay 11. She considered that Wilmer could use the module to transport the ship out of there. Unfortunately, that would advertise the fact that they had the module. At least there was a chance that no one would notice the shuttle if they used the module to transport out of the *Blue Eagle's* cargo bay to another location.

Wilmer and Shannon arrived, and the three of them boarded the shuttle. Tisch explained that their job was to go in quietly, get Mike's team, and get out. No shooting or fighting.

"Finally," Wilmer commented. "A plan that I like."

In the pub hall, Marina approached Mike's friends at their table and stood over them in her intimidating style. "Which of you is asking about Niems?" she inquired coldly.

Griff half-raised his hand, sensing trouble. Zenith was nervous by Marina's presence and said nothing. Topa spoke up boldly and answered, "I am. I want to know what happened to my team and my brother."

Marina sat down next to Zenith to speak with them. Zenith shuddered, fearing that she would be the first casualty in a fight. "Who piloted the class four here?" Marina inquired. Again, Griff half-raised his hand. Marina continued, "I'll take you to your team, but it's a one-way trip. There's no coming back to this part of the galaxy."

Griff and Topa consented to her offer. She glanced at Kellen and Zenith. "Not you two," she added. "You need to go back to Taurus."

"I assume you want us to take you in the class four," Griff remarked to Marina.

"The longer that ship is here, the more likely it is that Kronos will destroy this place and everyone in it. That would be a major setback to our plans against them." She instructed Griff and Topa to meet her in an hour at the ship and then left them.

Zenith breathed a sigh of relief. Kellen understood what Marina's intentions were and offered no resistance about Griff and Topa leaving with the ship. "I'll make sure Zenith and Mike are safe," Kellen assured them. "In the meantime, I need something a bit stronger than ale."

"That woman scares me," Zenith complained.

Kellen laughed. "She scares everyone."

Mike opened his eyes and grew frantic when he realized he was a prisoner tied up in a chair. The room was dimly lit, and there was no furniture in it other than his chair. He swore as he struggled to get free. The door unlatched and opened. Mike froze, expecting to see Kronos's agents enter. Instead, it was Marina.

"Get me out of here!" he shouted at her.

Marina grabbed him by his chin and responded angrily, "Do you know how much danger you put this place in? How much you put our operation against Kronos in jeopardy?" Mike was surprised by her words and said nothing. "Bringing that class four here was about the stupidest thing you could have ever done!" she shouted and punched him in the jaw. Mike was stunned by the force of her punch and was soon spitting blood on the floor. She instructed him to stop asking questions and stay out of this war with Kronos. He was a liability.

"It's my war too," he snapped at her.

"You're wrong," she replied and punched him in the face. The force knocked him over backward.

Mike mumbled, "I'm not afraid of you. Set me free, and we'll settle this."

Marina grinned and yanked him upright in his chair. "You have no idea who I am. If you did, you'd shut your mouth while you still can."

Mike spat on her boot. "And you have no idea who I am, do you?"

Marina had had enough of his bravado and karate-kicked him in the side of the head. He was unconscious before he ever knew it was coming. Marina shook her head in disbelief at his stupidity and left the room.

When she arrived at the freighter, Griff and Topa watched as the agents attempted to override the security protocols to access the ship. They turned to Marina for direction.

Marina instructed them to wait there. She approached the agents and yanked the silver balls from the ends of two dreadlocks. She rolled them across the floor toward the men. A loud pop stunned them, followed by the acrid smell of smoke. Marina entered the smoke and disappeared from sight.

Griff and Topa glanced at each other and wondered if they should help. The sound of punches followed by grunts and groans held their attention. The smoke cleared, and Marina emerged. "Let's go," she ordered them.

Griff and Topa were stunned. Every one of the agents were down. They hurried to the hatch and opened it. Marina stepped on board first and waited as Griff closed the hatch. She contacted the transport controller for clearance, and then they departed the station.

Mike's shuttle appeared and glided toward the station. Tisch received clearance and docked at an inside bay. When they exited the shuttle, Korick met them. He instructed them to follow him to the second floor.

Tisch and Wilmer were uneasy that Korick had expected them. With their hands on their pulse pistols, they ascended the stairs behind him and paused in front of one of the doors. Korick turned to Tisch and reminded her, "You need to take your friend and leave immediately." He then opened the door and stepped aside.

Mike lay on his side, unconscious. Tisch was horrified and rushed to help him. "Was this necessary?" she cried out.

Korick shrugged his shoulders. "He must have said something my boss didn't like." Wilmer kept an eye on Korick as he moved toward Mike.

When Korick walked away, Shannon ran after him and demanded to know where Zenith was. Korick instructed her to follow him. Shannon directed Tisch to meet her at the shuttle and then hurried after Korick. Tisch trusted Shannon and focused on getting Mike back to the shuttle. When they returned to the shuttle, they found Korick waiting with Zenith, Kellen, and Shannon.

Tisch had enough of the station and immediately ordered her crew to board the shuttle. Kellen promised Tisch he would stay in touch if he heard anything of value for them. Tisch thanked him and boarded the shuttle last. Soon, they were on the way back to Taurus. Tisch instructed Wilmer not to use the module as there were some things that needed to be resolved before their return.

Zenith and Shannon treated Mike's injuries until he awoke. He rubbed his eyes and face, grimacing. At first, he had no idea where he was until Tisch explained how she came to rescue his ass. Mike complained about Marina, saying how if he saw her again, he would return the favor. Tisch got in his face and told him to shut up before she kicked his ass next. Mike sensed that everyone was quite somber.

"Did someone die?" he asked uneasily.

Tisch tried to keep her composure but lost it on Mike. First, she chided him for destroying the gates on Taurus and stranding her ship. Then she chastised him for his reckless disobedience. Mike frowned with nothing to say. Then she scolded him for bringing the class four freighter to Zim of all places. At first, he was reluctant to listen, but then he realized that things could have gone terribly wrong. Then Tisch explained that they could never go back to Murgatroyd's Oasis for any reason thanks to his recklessness. They had just lost a potential source of information.

Mike suddenly realized that Griff and Topa were gone. Tisch suggested that they had saved his ass by getting the class four freighter away from the station. Shannon then informed everyone that Sara would have more to tell them when they returned.

Wilmer became concerned about Shannon's recurring contact with Sara without their knowledge. He gestured with his hand for her to follow him to the small kitchen for a conversation. When she entered, he demanded to know what her deal was. At first, Shannon downplayed it as an overreaction on his part. Then Wilmer suggested that if she valued their relationship, she'd better open up to him and explain what she'd been hiding. Shannon was serious about Wilmer, and, despite her reluctance to expose her true identity, she informed him that she was Sara's niece, and it was her "internship" with GSS that placed her there.

Wilmer was crushed at first, feeling as though he had been taken advantage of, especially since he was responsible for her employment on the ship. Shannon explained that she preferred being with him on the *Blue Eagle* than being an agent with GSS. Her arrangement with Sara was to be their liaison for her and protect the module. She then pleaded with Wilmer to trust her, that she really cared for him and wanted to stay. She apologized for keeping things from him and hugged him. Wilmer considered the circumstances and accepted her apology. He did require some extra love to overcome his disappointment. Shannon was eager to accommodate him with all the hugs and kisses he wanted before they left the kitchen.

Zenith suggested to Tisch that she was being too hard on Mike. Tisch promptly schooled Zenith on responsibility and crew loyalty. She then revealed how their actions could have collectively ruined everything the allies were building against Kronos. She then informed Zenith that perhaps she should look for other employment when they returned to Taurus since she constantly disagreed with the way Tisch handled things. Zenith retreated to the rear of the shuttle and sobbed. She realized that she had overstepped her bounds and was too caught up in Mike to consider that Tisch was the reason she was part of the crew.

When the shuttle drew closer to Taurus, Tisch instructed Wilmer to get them back inside the *Blue Eagle's* cargo bay before someone noticed their approach.

Once inside the cargo bay, the shuttle was powered down, and the hatch opened. Sara waited with a somber expression as the crew exited. Mike was the last to exit; he looked like hell. His mouth and face were swollen, and his eye was blackened. Sara recommended they conduct their debrief on the *Blue Eagle* immediately. Tisch led them to the bridge, where Geezer slept at the controls.

Sara began by congratulating everyone for a great job repelling the mercenaries during the last siege. She pointed out that, as a result, they were now an active part of an alliance to defeat Kronos. She explained how the class four freighter could have drawn them into battle with Kronos too soon and cost the alliance a key meeting place. Then came the hard part, the tough love that they needed.

Sara reminded them that both Sysco Galactic and GSS invested a lot of money into the *Blue Eagle* and its crew. There could only be one person in charge, and that had to be the captain. She suggested to everyone that if they couldn't follow their captain, then they should leave now. Mike realized that she was referring to him. He was speechless.

Sara then revealed to him that he had had his ass kicked by the baddest warrior in the galaxy, and now she was no friend of his, nor would she ever be. She expressed her concern that they might have lost a valuable ally over Mike's cowboy antics. Then Sara announced to them that this was no longer their war but the war of a much bigger group. Their interests didn't matter in the big scheme of things.

"So what do we do now?" questioned Mike.

"Do your job," chastised Sara. "You're space truckers. That's all you are—for now." Mike was about to speak, but Sara cut him off. "This isn't Special Forces, and you aren't the lone renegade taking down the Scrat anymore. You work for Sysco Galactic and for Tisch. Get that or get out."

Sara looked around the bridge at each one's face, but no one spoke. She wished them a good day and left. Tisch explained her disappointment with the crew for their actions. "When the going got tough, some of you thought you knew better. You put me in a bad spot." She then left the bridge and went to the galley.

Wilmer suggested they get a good night's sleep and discuss the future of the crew tomorrow. Everyone dispersed, other than Geezer, who still slept.

CHAPTER XVII

BUSINESS AS USUAL

The next morning, Julian boarded the *Blue Eagle* and went down to the galley. Mike sat alone with a glass of juice, pondering his future. Julian pulled up a chair and sat across from him.

"I heard you had quite the experience at the pirate haven," he commented.

Mike looked up and muttered, "It was… not what I expected."

Julian revealed to Mike that the woman he had encountered, Marina, was the leader of the alliance. He also mentioned that better men than Mike had their asses handed to them by her.

"I had no idea," mumbled Mike.

"Nor did any of us until recently," replied Julian. "Everything has changed from when I was part of this crew until now."

Mike nodded again, feeling humbled. "Why are you here, Julian?"

"For one reason. To make sure you don't give up on your friends. Each of you is only as good as the whole crew. Things are different now. Roll with it." Julian patted him on the shoulder and left.

Tisch met with Gemini on the bridge. Gemini informed her that the maintenance group had found a way to temporarily seal the inner gates so they could get the *Blue Eagle* out of the bay. Their new mission was to transport food and medical supplies to a distant colony. This was a trial and, if successful, would mean a contract for delivering supplies to several other colonies and outposts. She emphasized that there was no hidden agenda or secret stashes. Just a boring, long-distance delivery.

Tisch was grateful and assured her that things would go smoothly. She then asked if there were any other stops along the way that they could take on. She hoped to give her crew as much training with the new loading system as possible.

Gemini promised to look into it, considering the increased speed they could travel. She appreciated Tisch's interest and then brought up the subject she dreaded. "What about Mike?"

Tisch lowered her head and replied, "We haven't spoken, but I'll handle it immediately."

Gemini suggested that they use the recent events as a learning experience and grow from it. "If not, scars can be ugly and will haunt a person their entire life," she cautioned. Tisch understood that Gemini was referring to her personal failure with Mike and how it still bothered her. To Tisch's surprise, Gemini hugged her and commented, "We have a lot more in common than either of us ever thought." The two women burst into laughter, and then Gemini departed.

Tisch called the crew together for a meeting on the bridge. She revealed the new schedule and announced that it was time to address some issues. She started with Zenith. "Do you feel you can be a valuable part of this crew and follow orders?" Zenith nodded and apologized for questioning her motives and instructions. "Then you are still an important part of my crew." Zenith was ecstatic and thanked her.

Tisch mentioned that the two new members, Griff and Topa, sought other employment and were no longer with them. Everyone knew they had taken the class four to find their old team. As a result, Mike and Wilmer were expected to handle the onloading and offloading of cargo. Mike suggested that it wasn't a good idea, but before he could announce his resignation, Tisch ordered him to shut up and listen. She informed him that she expected him to consult with her on any actions of significance and to obey her commands, just as everyone else was expected to. She then announced that they were back to business as usual. Everyone but Mike cheered.

Zenith poked him and nodded toward Tisch. She knew he still cared for Tisch and wanted him to be happy. "Something you want to say, Colby?" Tisch prompted.

Mike looked somberly at her for several seconds and then grinned. "I think I'm good with this. You have my loyalty." Tisch was pleased and winked at him.

That evening, Mike stayed alone in his quarters while the others celebrated their upcoming freedom from Taurus on the *Blue Eagle*. Sara's words kept ringing in his head: You are space truckers. That's all you are - for now. The image of Marina kept popping up as well. Her intensity was like nothing he had ever seen, and the way she dealt with him - ruthless. *Who the hell is she that she is that overpowering?* he thought to himself as he tried to figure how she was the leader of an alliance against Kronos. Obviously, she knew a lot more about Kronos than they did. Mike grew weary and slept.

Tisch was encouraged by the camaraderie that had returned to the crew and was confident that Mike would come around. She hoped that peer pressure from the others would encourage him to fall in line.

Shannon and Zenith joked about how Marina had manhandled Mike and left him out cold on the floor. Geezer refused to believe that anyone could do that to Mike until Tisch affirmed his condition when they rescued him from Murgatroyd's Oasis. Geezer remarked that it sounded like his kind of establishment and complained that they hadn't taken him. Tisch excused herself from the table and retired for the night.

On the way back to the ship, she encountered Gemini. Gemini informed her that they had picked up two additional stops and that Julian sent the details to the ship's comm/nav system. Tisch thanked her and promised they'd be successful. Gemini revealed that she was heartbroken over Dax's "accident" and hoped for some quiet time to adjust to his absence. Julian would be in charge for a while if they needed anything. Assuming Dax was deceased, Tisch understood her grief and hugged her.

The next morning, the crew assembled outside the *Blue Eagle* in Bay 11. The new shipping containers with supplies were brought inside the bay to be loaded. Mike and Wilmer took control of the containers from the crawlers and executed the new loading process successfully. Mike enjoyed the ease in operating the system once he had scanned the codes off the containers. On the bridge, Geezer and Zenith discussed the hazards along the route to their first stop. Wilmer and Shannon reviewed the coordinates to each of their stops and the scheduled windows for their arrivals.

Outside the ship, the maintenance technicians installed a bubble-like cover over the inner gates to Bay 11 and pressure-tested it for integrity. When they signed off on it, the transport supervisor notified Geezer that the outer doors were now enabled to permit their departure.

Geezer anxiously announced to the crew that they were cleared to leave immediately. The outer doors opened, and Geezer supervised as Zenith piloted the ship from the bay into space.

Tisch entered the bridge and was pleased to see that they had departed but noticed that Mike wasn't there. She checked with Wilmer to make sure he was on board and was relieved to find that he was. Once they had established some distance from Taurus and there were no abnormal indications from the new engines or the fuel-regeneration system, Tisch left the bridge and went to the galley.

Mike sat alone at a table in the galley and sipped from a container of water. Tisch entered and immediately sensed his sad demeanor. "Mind if I join you?" she asked politely.

Mike nodded to the chair. "Have a seat."

Tisch sat down and studied him for a moment. She still had strong feelings for him but had no idea where they stood in their relationship now or where they would stand in the future. Not knowing what to say, she got up and retrieved two bottles of beer. She returned to the table and offered him one.

Mike glanced at the beer and chuckled to himself. He gulped down the water and took the beer. "Thank you," he said with a brief smile.

Tisch informed him that she had asked Gemini to add two additional deliveries to their schedule. When Mike questioned why she wanted them, Tisch explained that she felt he and Wilmer needed additional work on the onloading system to improve their proficiency.

Mike asked playfully, "Is that the only reason?"

Tisch thought for a moment and then answered, "No." Mike waited for further explanation. Tisch smiled coyly and continued, "You need to work off some of that testosterone that drives you to do crazy things."

Mike burst into laughter and raised his beer for a toast. "Touché," he responded with a smile. Tisch appreciated his reaction, and for a moment, it felt like old times. Mike requested that she allow him to work with Wilmer to install the module in the *Blue Eagle's* power distribution room. He explained how their plans were designed to install it without affecting the ship's equipment.

Tisch was pleased that he discussed it with her and had given her the final say. She felt as though she finally earned his respect. Then Mike mentioned that he had the closing information she sought on her father. Tisch froze and feared the worst. Mike explained how it appeared Marina had instructed John Mallory to obtain the module from the Archaeneans before Antwan's crew arrived. Kronos wasn't happy about being double-crossed and sent Empire to Taurus to retrieve the module and kill her father. He added that they didn't realize he had turned it over to the Scrat, hoping to make an ally of them. "Can we consider this case on your father closed?" he asked and rubbed his bruised jaw. "It's been too painful for both of us."

Tisch burst into laughter, while Mike grinned. "It's closed," she replied. "Thank you for helping me get the closure I needed."

When she finished her beer, she stood and thanked him for supporting her after everything that had happened. Mike raised his bottle to her and then finished it. She smiled and went to the door. Before she could exit, Mike quipped, "Space truckers, huh?"

Tisch looked back at him, grinning at the term. Mike stood, wanting to say something more, but froze. "What is it, Mike?" she asked, curious. She hoped that he wanted to resume their relationship and grew excited over the thought of Mike holding her in his arms again.

Mike blushed and then kidded, "Does cleaning up the table after you leave count as part of my duties?"

Tisch's heart broke. This wasn't what she expected. Then she recalled what Julian had once told her. If you want him, you'd better get him now or else. "No," she replied and returned to the table. "I got these." Tisch took the bottles and the empty water container to the refuse system and deposited them.

Mike then surprised her by asking, "How long are we going to punish ourselves?"

"What?" Tisch was caught off guard, unsure of what he meant.

Mike approached her and placed his arms around her waist. "I need you," he said humbly. "I will do whatever it takes to win you back."

Tisch was stunned. "How about we start with this?" she suggested and pulled him close to her. They kissed passionately for several moments. Finally, Tisch pushed him away. "I have to return to the bridge," she said, disappointed. "After all, we are space truckers, and we have a job to do."

Amused, Mike responded, "Yes, we do."